THE BOAT MAN

A Reed & Billie Novel, Book 1

DUSTIN STEVENS

Prologue

Crystalline spatters of slushy snow hit the windshield, a scattershot pattern spread across the clear glass. Each time they connected the distinct ping of their semi-solid state smacking against the surface could be heard, the only sound inside the car. One by one they accumulated until the outside world was almost completely obscured from view before the wipers rose and shoved them to the side, the rubber letting off a moaning whine as they retreated back into position.

Seated behind the wheel, he waited motionless, his gaze never wavering as the precipitation gathered and was cleared in equal thirty second increments.

Parked in the third row, he knew he was virtually invisible as he sat and stared at the front entrance to the chapel. Slumped low behind the wheel, the windows fogging over around him, there was no way anybody could have seen him. If not for the occasional burst of the wipers there would be no indication at all that someone was seated inside, his car just another anonymous sedan in a lot full of them.

One by one he watched as the other automobiles around him emptied of their passengers, people jogging to the front entrance, using umbrellas or handbills to protect themselves from the falling slush. Once they reached their destination they lingered only a moment, greeted by a solitary man in dark hues before disappearing inside, not to return again.

Sliding his backside forward to the edge of the seat, he sat and let the cold chill inside the car seep into his bones. It passed through his thin suit and brought goose pimples to his skin, the tiny bumps visible on every exposed surface. On the seat beside him rested an unopened bottle of Jim Beam Devil's Cut whiskey and a loaded .38, both of them calling with equal intensity.

Ignoring everything, he remained where he was, watching as the last few stragglers from the parking lot made their way to the door. As they passed inside the guard stood and waited, seeming to look directly at him in the third row, imploring him to come forward. When no movement came a bow of concession was offered before disappearing, the door closing without a sound.

Throughout he remained seated in the third row, watching, waiting, before reaching out and turning over the ignition. Without a second glance he drove away, his tires leaving twin tracks across the pavement behind him.

Chapter One

From his perch in the alley, the Boat Man had a perfect view of his target.

Crouched low on the second floor fire escape, his body pressed against the cool brick of the building, he sat and stared through the iron bars at the small house across the street, waiting. He had been in position since ten minutes after nine, a full four hours earlier, not once moving as he stared at his destination, an exercise in form and discipline.

After an hour, the first bits of cold had started to pass through the flattened cardboard box he was seated on. An hour after that, the jacket he wore gave way to the cool brick behind him, his spine tightening from the chill.

Just before midnight a thin mist had passed through, cloaking the world in dampness, his clothes sticking to his skin. Still he sat and waited, letting the beads of moisture collect atop his head and drip from the front of his hood, paying them no attention as he stared across the street.

As targets went, there was very little to distinguish it from a thousand other identical ones around Columbus. A single story tall, constructed entirely in red brick, it sat on a postage stamp sized lot. Most of the lawn was reduced to nothing more than mud, tufts of dead grass sticking up in the corners. An old pizza box served as a makeshift covering for a broken window, light shining out around it into the night.

It was the fourth night in the preceding few months the Boat Man had sat on his perch observing the house.

There wouldn't be a fifth.

Just shy of one o'clock in the morning a pair of headlights appeared, refracted up from the wet asphalt of the street. Feeling his pulse rise just slightly, the Boat Man drew his feet up beneath him, his knees groaning in protest.

Ignoring the objections of his body, the Boat Man pressed his back hard against the wall and pushed himself upright, watching as the lights drew closer. There was no doubt they contained what he had been waiting on, the only thing that would possibly be out at such an hour.

Without waiting for visual confirmation, the Boat Man swung himself over the wrought iron railing encasing the fire escape and dropped to the ground, his shoes falling silent against the wet earth. Keeping himself tucked into the shadows of the building he jogged forward, his body bent in half, moving as fast as his crouch would allow.

In the dead of the night, the headlights cut a stark beacon through the quiet neighborhood as they drew closer, the pounding of a stereo system growing louder in accompaniment.

The Boat Man made it to the corner just as the car came into sight, confirming what he already knew. He watched as it turned into a driveway and the blinding glare of the front lamps fell away, revealing their source to be a faded burgundy Cadillac Coupe.

A hint of a smile crossed the Boat Man's face as brake lights flared, the car easing its way off the street.

Tonight had been a long time coming. Too long, in fact. The kind of thing slowed first by inability, then by indecision. Only once both were overcome was he able to move forward, this the first step in what would be many.

On the opposite side of the street, no more than twenty yards away, the Cadillac came to a stop. A moment later the dull throbbing of the bass receded to nothing, the silence noticeable in its wake.

From his hiding spot, the Boat Man drew in one final breath. Never before had he been in a situation like this.

Not ever had he felt more certain of anything in his life.

There was no tremble from his hands as he reached back over his head, gripping the braided handle of the sword strapped there. In one movement he slid it from its scabbard, the polished steel coming free without a sound.

An inch at a time the Boat Man rotated it from side to side before him, letting the slightest bit of ambient light from the street outside refract from its surface, his own reflection flashing across it.

Sixty feet away, the driver's side door of the car burst open, a spray of cans and bottles hitting the pavement, released from being pent up inside. A moment later their owner spilled out behind them, his gait uneven, the streetlight above flashing off his exposed arms and clean-shaven head.

The Boat Man watched for a moment as the man kicked at the debris scattered across the driveway, his uneven flailing giving away the fact that he had a few too many on the night. Just as fast he gave up on the venture, muttering a string of obscenities that was audible along the street before slamming the door shut behind him.

Using the sound of the door as cover, the Boat Man sprang from his spot, crossing the roadway in eight long strides, covering the small front yard in half that many.

There was no sound from his feet as he moved, no pause from his body as he covered the distance to his target.

Chapter Two

"On an exceptionally hot evening early in July a young man came out of the garret in which he lodged in S. Place and walked slowly, as though in hesitation, towards K. Bridge."

The narrator's voice was deep and rich, bringing to mind images of James Earl Jones, minus all the heavy breathing used during his stint on *Star Wars*. Without even thinking about it, Reed Mattox reached across the front seat and took up the plastic CD case, flipping it over in search of a picture.

"He had successfully avoided meeting his landlady on the staircase."

Unable to find anything more than a one sentence blurb for each the author and the narrator, the two as far apart as could be, Reed tossed the container away, watching with disinterest as it hit off the seat and landed along the floorboard.

The noise brought a stir of life from the backseat, Reed glancing into the rearview mirror as a pair of pointed ears came into view. Beneath them was a matching set of chestnut colored eyes, two moist discs staring back at him.

"Easy, girl," Reed said, his drawl allowed to slide out in full, one meant to placate. It seemed to work as the creature met his gaze a long moment before dropping back out of sight, her size shifting the car as she moved.

"This was not because he was cowardly and abject, quite the contrary-"

Three paragraphs was as far as Reed made it before reaching out and shutting off the tape, letting silence fill in around him. Once more a whine could be heard from the backseat, though this time no eyes appeared to stare back at him.

Shifting onto his right haunch, Reed twisted his legs beneath the steering wheel, resting his elbow on the middle console. He jammed a thumb into his mouth and gnawed on the nail as he again checked the clock on the dash, watching the minutes crawl by.

Everything about the situation he now found himself in - the car, the dog, the CD's - all of it, was new to him. Even after two months it felt odd, things seeming just a bit left of center, not quite attuned to what he was used to.

Little by little things were improving, but they still had a long way to go.

"Detective Mattox?" the dispatch radio on the dash called, the metallic din of the voice reverberating through the interior of the car. "Detective Mattox?"

Reed waited a long moment before drawing the thumb from his mouth, spitting a bit of nail onto the adjoining seat and reaching out. He took up the mouthpiece hanging on the side of the radio and drew it over to him, his movements slow and deliberate.

"Hey, Jackie."

By day, the procedural protocol for handling the radio was a tightly regimented exercise in tedium. In the preceding months though Reed had become intimately aware with the fact that most such procedures were cast aside in the dead of night.

"How you doing out there this evening, Sugar?" Jackie asked.

A flicker of mirth passed over Reed's face as he imagined Jackie on the other end of the line, her feet propped up on the edge of the desk, a half-eaten box of powdered donuts beside her. On her lap was most likely the latest gossip rag, picked up on the way to work at the local CVS.

As humorous, if not clichéd, as the mental image might have been, Reed was long past commenting on it. Everybody had their own way of passing the hours in the middle of the night.

Jackie preferred pastries and smut mags. He was now trying books on tape.

"Living the dream," Reed replied. "What's going on?"

As much as he didn't mind Jackie, and knew she meant well, he was fast coming to loathe the way she called to check in on him. It grated his nerves in a way he couldn't quite pin down, making him feel defective, like there was a flaw obvious to everybody around him.

"We've got reports of a possible 187 in your neck of the woods," Jackie said, her voice as bored and detached as if she were reading the weather.

187. Police code for homicide.

Reed pulled himself up straight in the seat, his bottom moving flat onto the cushion beneath him. In the backseat, the dog sensed his change of demeanor, rising to full height, just her ears visible behind his head in the rearview mirror.

"Where?" Reed asked, his voice belying a bit more of an edge than intended.

There was a pause long enough to let him know it was heard and wasn't appreciated before Jackie said, "The Bottoms. You want it? Or should I call and wake up Ike?"

The starter whined in protest as Reed cranked on the ignition, the car rumbling to life.

"We're already en route," Reed said. "Just send me the address."

Chapter Three

The flashing lights of his car refracted off the front of the house as Reed pulled to a stop, the fluorescent flickering passing from the left headlight to the right every few seconds. Given the hour and the lack of traffic on the roads he had opted to run without the siren, letting the front lamps clear away what few other drivers there were on the road.

Parked on the curb, Reed let the strobes bathe the front in neon light a long moment, taking everything in.

The house was a simple ranch affair, the kind filling a thousand neighborhoods in the greater Columbus area. He himself had grown up in something similar on the outskirts of Oklahoma City, had seen the same thing in towns ranging from Atlanta to Portland.

Somewhere inside he knew there was a family room with a connected kitchen and dining room. Two or three bedrooms were spaced off a hallway extended away from the main living area, one and a half baths sprinkled throughout.

The front lawn was nothing more than a dustbowl that had been turned to mud by the passing rains, the outward condition of the windows and front door showing the place was in a state far past disrepair.

Flipping the lights off, Reed took a quick glance down the street, confirming what he knew about the area, even if he had never been at this particular location before.

The house was one in a line of single family dwellings, all equally spaced, all having the same basic design. On the opposite side of the road were a handful of multi-story buildings that looked to have at one time been apartment complexes but now appeared deserted.

Like the houses they stood facing, everything was done in red brick, splashed liberally with aging graffiti.

"Stay here," Reed said, leaving the keys in the ignition and stepping out of the car. A thin mist enveloped him as he did so, clinging to his hooded sweatshirt, beading up on the badge hanging from his neck.

A single blue-and-white patrol car was parked at the edge of the driveway a dozen feet in front of Reed's sedan. Halfway down the asphalt drive sat a burgundy Cadillac, make and model appearing to be from the mid-80's.

Everything he'd seen of the block so far, it seemed to fit in perfectly.

Huddled together in front of the patrol car was a pair of officers, both turning to stare as Reed approached. Neither one seemed enthused to be standing there, neither making a move forward as Reed drew near.

"You guys call in about a possible 187?" Reed opened, closing the gap between them, letting a hint of annoyance show in his voice.

"Called in a definite 187," the man on the right said, taking a half step forward and meeting Reed just past the front bumper of their patrol car. He thrust out a hand and said, "I'm Officer McMichaels, my partner Jacobs."

Neither man appeared to be older than their mid-twenties, most likely paired together once their training years with a senior officer were complete. McMichaels was tall and lean, his face clean shaven. Behind him his partner was shorter and a bit fleshier, a thin goatee encasing his mouth.

Reed accepted the shake, noticing it cold and wet from the weather, and nodded to Jacobs. "Detective Mattox."

"No partner?" Jacobs asked.

It wasn't the first time Reed had been asked the question, each time drawing the same clench in his stomach, though he had learned to mask any outward display. "In the car."

A moment later came the second part that always grated him, the two exchanging a glance.

"K-9," Reed said, answering before they had a chance to ask. "So what makes you say this is a definite 187?"

The two officers exchanged another glance, both of them drawing their mouths into tight lines. They stood that way a long moment, Reed looking from one to the other, before both turned back to face him.

"Just walk a little ways up the drive," McMichaels said. "You'll see."

Agitation continued to grow within Reed as he looked at them. He opened his mouth, prepared to offer a lecture on proper police procedure, but decided against it.

Almost certain was the fact that there was a body lying nearby, quite possibly their first. Not that long ago he was in their position, unsure how to handle it, staring at death for the first time. The last thing he would have wanted then was a senior officer acting like a prick about it, and he'd be damned if he did the same to them.

Not that he gave a shit what anybody on the force thought of him anymore.

"Scene secure?"

"Yes, sir," McMichaels said. "Nobody is around."

Rotating on the ball of his foot, Reed unsnapped the flashlight from his waist and drew it up to shoulder height. He clicked the rubber stopper on the end and a cone of white light shot forth, spraying the driveway in a bright hue. Halfway down he paused a moment, listening for the sound of footsteps.

None came with him, both men content to let him proceed alone.

Whatever was lying in wait for him clearly had them both spooked.

Slowing his pace to a half step at a time, Reed came up alongside the Cadillac and aimed his flashlight inside. The interior of the car was in even worse shape than the outside, the seats cracked and peeling, the floorboards covered in garbage. An ashtray sat in the middle of the dash, cigarette butts overflowing.

No body.

Shifting the light back to face forward, Reed walked to the front of the car and stopped, his breath catching in his chest. After twelve years working for the Columbus Police Department, he had seen just about all there was to see. Every possible form that evil could take he had encountered at one time or another, ranging the full spectrum of deeds and far exceeding anything he thought human beings capable of.

Even at that, this was a first.

Rooted in place, Reed raised the light, letting it splash over the remainder of the driveway, six feet of cement in either direction rimmed by more muddy yard. In the center of the space, lying flat on his back, was a single male victim. He wore pants and a white ribbed tank top, his head shaved bare.

That was about the sum total that Reed could confidently ascertain, unable to move any further, the combination of blood and rainwater having painted the entire slab of asphalt red.

A bit of warmth rose along Reed's back as he moved the flashlight over everything once more before retreating a step. After another he clicked off the light and turned back towards the curb, both officers waiting with arms folded across their stomachs, looking at him expectantly.

"How'd you guys find him?" Reed asked, his voice carrying through the silent night.

The two exchanged a quick glance.

"Anonymous call came in," McMichaels said. "We were on patrol in the area and fielded it."

"Said it was a DD," Jacobs added. "We got here and found this."

DD. Domestic disturbance.

More than once Reed had seen the excuse come in. Somebody out for a run or taking their dog for a walk stumbled across something and made an anonymous call, not wanting to be near the crime scene any longer than necessary, thinking they didn't know anything that would be of use anyway.

"Any ID yet?"

McMichaels looked down at his feet as Jacobs shifted his weight from side to side. "Not yet. We'd only been here about a minute when we called for you. Didn't want to disturb the scene."

It was obvious from his tone that the last sentence was added as an explanation and an apology of sorts. Reed let it go with a nod, conceding that in instances such as these it was better they did less than more.

If the victim did have an ID on him, the techs could pull it in half an hour. If the patrol guys had gone on ahead to check for themselves, they could have destroyed evidence beyond repair.

"What do you need us to do?" McMichaels asked, looking up from his shoes, a bit of color having returned to his cheeks.

Reed turned and glanced over his shoulder, again picturing the scene behind him in his mind. "Cordon off the whole place, yard and all. I'll call in the crime scene crew. Sit on it until they get here and at first light start canvassing the neighborhood. I want to know everything we can about this guy and if anybody saw anything here last night."

Both men nodded at the directive, each appearing thankful to have some heading, even more glad it wouldn't put them anywhere near the body.

"187?" Jacobs asked.

Turning towards his car, Reed was already moving to call in support. "Definitely."

Chapter Four

The rear door wrenched open with an ugly screech of metal scraping against metal. Reed was careful to stand back as he held it wide, positioning his body to avoid the solid black bolt that shot out. Once she was gone, he shoved the door closed, turning to watch his partner sprint across the park, covering enormous swaths of ground in long strides.

After two months together, both knew the routine. Reed turned and rested his back against the side of the car, waiting as she pounded out a few revolutions of the park. At ten minutes after six it was still too early for anybody to be using it, nothing to stand in her way as she sprinted in an oblong loop, a solitary black streak tearing across the field.

Most nights the weather was nice enough that Reed had her out a fair bit, working patrols, checking in wherever was necessary. On evenings like the one before, the city blanketed in mist, him caught up in a crime scene, she was forced into the back seat for almost ten solid hours.

Shaking his head at her insatiable energy, Reed brought his palms to his eyes and pressed down hard. He held the pose long enough for stars to begin dancing behind his eyelids, the odors of the crime scene lingering on his clothes. The familiar scents of blood and garbage flitted across his nostrils as the sound of a car approaching crept into his consciousness, the slight squeal of wet brakes being applied.

Dropping his hands away from his eyes a shudder passed through Reed, the wet fabric of his hooded sweatshirt clinging to his body, his skin clammy to the touch. For a moment he considered stripping the garment away before thinking better of it, opting to wrap his arms across his chest, drawing himself in as tight as possible to maintain a bit of warmth.

He did not bother to look over as the driver of the car exited the vehicle, her presence announced by the sound of square heels clicking against the pavement.

One of the more ironclad rules in the Columbus Police Department was mandatory psychiatric meetings following the loss of a partner. It was something Reed had fought and begged and pleaded to be set free from, requests that had all been summarily dismissed. The best he had been able to finagle was an agreement with his attending doctor to meet him at the park a couple of mornings each week, blaming his schedule for not wanting to go to her office.

"Good morning," Pia Mehdi said as she approached, her hands thrust into the calf length brown coat swirling around her.

"Morning," Reed said, not making any movement away from the side of his car. "How are you, doc?"

"I am well," Mehdi replied. "And yourself?"

Reed turned away from the question, watching as his partner went about her business, paying them no mind.

After two months, she had learned not to take the doctor for a threat.

"Last night was a big one for us," Reed said, motioning towards the field. "First homicide together."

He could sense a shift in the woman by his side, her body moving but coming no closer to him.

"Yeah? And how was it?" she asked.

On the whole, Reed had no problems with Mehdi. In her early forties, she was a stylish woman with light brown skin and glossy black hair, the kind of look that could have made her a lot of money in Bollywood. She had a direct manner that he appreciated and had been accommodating in meeting him so early in the morning.

Still, it was the requirement that they meet that he resented so much, the insinuation that he needed some sort of evaluation to ensure he was still a capable lawman.

"Fine," Reed said, shrugging his shoulders.

It was the first body he'd come across in nearly four months. The sight of it had done nothing to his system, his heart rate remaining even, his breath never once picking up as he'd helped to process it.

As he did so though, he couldn't help but feel a small twinge in the pit of his stomach, the slightest hint of something he hadn't felt in a long time. It was clear there was something missing, his former partner Riley's absence an enormous void that made the entire thing feel incomplete.

Just as apparent though was a tiny jolt deep within him. Whether or not that was a good thing he had not yet decided.

"Same old thing," he said, looking over at Mehdi.

She met the gaze a long moment before giving him a look that relayed she didn't believe him, though she wasn't about to press it.

"And how did your new partner react?"

A bit of a smile pulled at Reed's lips as he turned back towards the field, *his new partner* still sprinting circles around it. Her name was Billie, a four year old Belgian Malinois that was solid black, her dark brown eyes the only exceptions. In a previous life she had been a military dog, a bomb sniffing machine employed by the Marines on two tours in Afghanistan.

Six months prior her handler had been killed trying to diffuse a roadside IAD. After his passing the Corps had tried to keep her on, working with different disposal experts, but the situation never stuck. She was cycled back stateside and soon thereafter turned over to law enforcement, finding her way to Columbus through a combination of dumb luck and timing.

"Unfortunately the scene was pretty messy," Reed said, "so she had to be kept back. That's why she looks like Steve Prefontaine out here this morning."

The comment drew a bit of a smile from Mehdi, though the mirth was located in her mouth only.

"Are you sure that was it?" she asked, a cautious tone in her voice. "Or did you just prefer to go it alone again?"

When Reed first moved over to the K-9 Unit he himself had gone through a couple of new partners, never once finding the right fit. For his first month on the job he went solo, a dog patrol detective without a dog, waffling between waiting for the right animal to come his way and debating calling it quits altogether.

Whether or not the two were actually a good pairing or if both just knew they were down to their final option Reed wasn't sure, but he was willing to take a chance on finding out.

Thus far, Billie seemed to be up for the same.

"Not at all," Reed said. "This was legit. Lot of blood, lot of mud. Not the kind of thing we could risk footprints through just yet."

Once more Mehdi nodded, Reed again getting the impression she didn't quite believe him. It had been the same situation for the better part of two months now, both settling into their respective roles. Reed, stonewalling as much as possible, giving just enough to offer the illusion he was trying. Mehdi pushing where she could, backing away whenever it became apparent he was blocking her out.

"I see," Mehdi said, lifting her foot and nudging a rock with the toe of her shoe, her tone betraying just the smallest bit of frustration.

Chapter Five

The day had yet to even start and already Captain Wallace Grimes looked ready for a drink. Dark circles underscored his eyes and his tie was loosened a half inch from his neck, the black fabric twisted to the side, hanging at an odd angle down his chest.

He was on the phone as Reed appeared at his door, tapping with the back of his knuckles, notebook in hand. Without verbal acknowledgment Grimes waved him inside, a scowl across his features.

More than a decade Reed's senior, Grimes had been a sergeant in nearby Precinct 19 when Reed signed on. In the intervening years he had risen to the post of captain and shifted over to Precinct 8, a job that nobody was quite sure he wanted but all seemed to agree he was well suited for.

When making the switch to the K-9 Unit Reed came over as well, Grimes the only familiar face in a house that always seemed to be staring his way.

"Yeah, I got it," Grimes said into the mouthpiece, dropping the phone into place without signing off. He made a face at the plastic implement, followed by waving his middle finger at it, his face contorted with anger.

"That good, huh?" Reed said, taking a step into the room.

"You have no idea," Grimes muttered, passing a hand over his scalp before motioning it to the threadbare chair opposite him. "Sit."

Approaching his fiftieth year in age, the captain was beginning to wear the time spent behind the desk. The bottom buttons of his shirt were starting to strain and the thinning hair atop his head was fast transitioning from black to gray.

"I'll keep this brief then," Reed said, sliding down onto the chair, not bothering to ask about whatever was on the phone.

In his experience asking could only lead to bad things, namely his being forced to take part in something.

Getting right to it, Reed dropped his focus to the notebook in his lap and said, "Last night at approximately one a.m. I was called to a house in The Bottoms about a possible homicide. Line came in from an anonymous citizen claiming DD, patrol officers called on us."

Reed kept his voice neutral as he read off the information, rattling it out in rapid-fire sequence. "Upon arrival, confirmed as a homicide, called for crime scene crew and a full workup. No ID on the victim, had to run the plates on the car to get a name."

Using his finger as a pointer, Reed scanned down the sheet and continued, "Edwin Mentor, in the system for some small time stuff a while back. Possession, assault. Nothing heavy, nothing after 2009."

On the opposite side of the desk, Grimes laced his fingers across his stomach, his fingers lined up like thick brown sausages. He pulled his chin back into his throat as he listened, his frown and the ensuing folds of skin around his jaw giving him the appearance of a human bullfrog.

"I put the patrol officers on duty canvassing the area this morning to confirm the identity and to see if they could figure out who made the call. Given the neighborhood, I'm not holding my breath on either."

The Franklinton area of Columbus was fast becoming notorious, the highest concentrated rate of crime and poverty in the metro area, behind only parts of Cleveland on a statewide scale. After the success of the Short North gentrification downtown there were some rumblings from local businesspeople that the same could be done in the west side, though momentum seemed slow in materializing for the project.

The area was technically dubbed The Bottoms because it was below the water levels for the nearby Scioto and Olentangy Rivers, though many in the area believed the moniker to have a far more dubious origin.

Whether that was true Reed wasn't certain, though he wouldn't be surprised if it was. Since moving over no less than half of his time had been spent covering the same turf, though he was still far from an expert on what went on there.

Especially given that he was assigned to night patrol.

Grimes nodded at the information and assessment, his gaze unwavering. "What made you certain it was a homicide?"

Again recalling the scene from the night before, Reed forced himself not to wince. "The victim was found face up on the ground, his stomach slashed, an oversized puncture wound through his heart, his right arm removed just below the elbow."

The left eyebrow tracked higher on Grime's forehead as he stared across at Reed. "Removed? As in taken?"

"As in, dismembered," Reed said, answering without consulting his notes, recalling the horrific sight of the limb sprawled across the concrete.

"Damn," Grimes muttered, letting his own face register the wince Reed had just bitten back.

"Mhmm," Reed agreed, nodding for emphasis. "Lot of blood. Mixed with all the rainwater, whole damn place was painted red. Looked like some kind of art demonstration or something."

On the desk the phone rang again, the sound shrill inside the office. The same look crossed Grimes's face as he reached out and lifted the receiver, smashing it down just as fast.

"I'm not on the clock for another forty-five minutes. They can call back then," he said by way of explanation. "Anything unusual found at the scene?"

"No," Reed said, again ignoring his notes. He had spent almost five full hours scouring everything with the techs. More than once he had gone over what little evidence there was, coming up with a lengthy list of questions, ready to be handed off to the duty detectives that would investigate.

As a night patrol detective, his job was more about containment than apprehension. He and Billie were on constant call, ready to assist with whatever should arise, whether it be a possible homicide or the detection of an unusual package.

Once the night ended, they handed it off to the daytime crew to solve.

"Just the usual assortment of things. Wrappers and trash. Some coins and stuff scattered about. Nothing to give us a good idea about anything."

Again the scowl formed on Grimes's face as he pursed his lips, twisting his head at the neck to peer outside. Following his gaze, Reed looked over to see his unmarked patrol car sitting in front of the building, Billie's head visible in the backseat.

"How's it going with you two?" Grimes asked, jutting his chin at the car, motioning towards the dog.

The question caught Reed off guard for a moment, his mouth dropping and closing before he found his voice. "It's getting there. We're both adjusting to working with a new partner, but I think we'll be alright."

"How's her training going?"

Unable to stop himself, Reed let out a smirk, his head rocking back an inch. "She's a pro. The Marines taught her well. The training is more for me, showing me how to properly employ her skills."

An indecipherable sound rolled out of Grimes as he nodded in agreement.

"Still meeting with the doc?"

This time the reaction Reed failed to hide was an eye roll, the gesture tilting his head to the side. "Just left there, actually. Scintillating stuff, let me tell you."

"I bet," Grimes answered, his face still completely impassive.

It was obvious from the questions and the lack of outward reaction that the captain was building to something.

"Why do I get the impression these questions are leading somewhere?" Reed asked, keeping his voice clear of any accusation.

"I want you two to handle this," Grimes said, thrusting the words out, not the slightest bit of hesitation in his tone.

For the second time in as many minutes a statement took Reed by surprise, his mouth again dropping open. "Captain, I mean..."

"I think it will be good for you," Grimes pushed on, not waiting for an explanation, "both of you."

He nodded as he spoke, motioning towards Reed and the window in turn. "But more importantly, that call you just walked in on was from the Chief downtown. She's pulling two of our detective teams to work a drug case in the Near East Side and I'm short staffed. You have eyes on the scene and are the only available man I have with detective experience."

A thousand thoughts, objections, passed through Reed's mind. He forced his face to remain impassive, knowing there was more coming, waiting for it all to hit before he said a word.

"And like I said," Grimes added, "I think it will be good for you."

He didn't further elaborate on the comment, but he didn't have to. Reed knew exactly what he was alluding to.

Whether the entire thing was a ruse, a form of baptism by fire to force Reed back into the fray, or not, there was no way of being certain. It was clear from the captain's tone that it was a directive and not a request, meaning it didn't really matter either way.

Again the various thoughts welled within Reed, a bit of apprehension pooling in the pit of his stomach.

"We'll have to keep different hours," he said. "I can't run an investigation on the graveyard shift."

A long moment passed as Grimes stared across at him, making no effort to hide the fact that he was measuring him. Despite being thirty-four years old with a dozen years on the force Reed couldn't help but feel like a child in the principal's office as he met the gaze.

The two held the pose a long moment, Grimes eventually deciding whatever internal debate was being waged.

"I'll have some uniforms cover your patrol. You have seventy-two hours of complete freedom to do whatever is necessary on this."

"Seventy-two hours?" Reed asked, his eyes narrowing. "Is there something special about the next three days?"

Leaning back in his chair Grimes broke the gaze, rotating himself towards the window, his fingers still piled across his stomach. "Yeah, right now nobody knows about it. If that scene was really as bad as you say though, it's only a matter of time before somebody finds out."

Chapter Six

The soft, sweet smell of cloves wafted up at the Boat Man as he squeezed a thin line of *choji* oil along the blade of his sword. For a moment he sat motionless, his eyes fluttering shut, inhaling deeply of the scent. He allowed the breath to fill his lungs, lifting his shoulders towards the ceiling, enjoying one brief bit of contentment.

Just as fast, the moment dissipated. The Boat Man opened his eyes and took up the roll of cotton cloth from the ground beside him. Starting at the base of the blade, right where the polished steel and the handle came together, he pulled the cloth the length of the instrument. Moving in long, even strokes, he spread the oil over the surface of the blade, the dried blood from the previous night striping away as he went, staining the cloth pink.

The sword was known as a *ken*, a Japanese fighting sword similar to the much more famous *katana*. While quite close in appearance, the Boat Man had carefully selected the piece for two distinct reasons, both lending themselves towards his mission.

The first was the length of the blade, coming in right at two *shaku*, the traditional unit of measurement for such weapons. By modern American standards it was just shy of two feet in length, easy to maneuver and even easier to conceal.

The second was that the blade was straight, unlike most other swords coming from the island nation. Such a design allowed for both edges of the weapon to be honed to a razor's edge, providing for maximum destruction when wielded by the right person.

The Boat Man was more than such a person.

Traditional Japanese swords were created for a single purpose, to be used on the field of battle. Their blades were never intended to be used to prepare food or chop wood, instead designed for the sole purpose of carving through flesh.

Just ten hours before was the first time the weapon or the Boat Man had ever done so, though he couldn't help but smile at the performance of both. The sword had worked admirably, swiping through its target without opposition, ending the confrontation before it ever truly began.

Ten long strokes on the top side was all it took to wipe the blade clean, the polished steel buffed to a mirrored shine, a thin coat of oil remaining behind, gleaming in the overhead light.

Rotating it over to the opposite side, the Boat Man balanced the blade across his folded knees. He squeezed another thin trail of *choji* oil out over the blade, allowing the aroma to hit him in a second wave as he refolded the cotton material, the dark blotches disappearing from sight.

Again he began at the handle, moving in slow strokes the entire length of the implement.

The sword had performed beautifully in its first outing, though his own effort still left something to be desired. So fearful had he been of being discovered, his planning had become too meticulous. His prey never knew he was there until it was over, his death coming much too fast.

It was a mistake the Boat Man would not make again.

The goal of his mission was not just the elimination of his targets. The intent was for them to feel the same fear they had inflicted. They must know the horror they were once the source of, looking over their shoulder as they walked the streets, fearful of every sound in the night.

Such was the vow he had made, one that he would not let go unfulfilled.

Cleaning the weapon took just five minutes, the blade gleaming in the half-light of the morning. Staring down, the Boat Man could feel it beckoning him forward, urging him to continue, letting him know that it too was ready for their next test.

Once more the Boat Man closed his eyes and drew the rich scent in through his nose, rolling his head back, his face aimed towards the ceiling.

With the cleaning of the sword, last night was now behind them.

It was time to prepare for the next one.

Chapter Seven

Billie wasn't especially fond of being left in the car again, the second time in less than twelve hours. The sound of her whining droned out from the backseat as Reed walked away from it, filling his ears, drawing the stares of a pair of employees standing out in front of the Medical Examiner's office. Between drags on their cigarettes they glanced from Reed to the car, letting the accusation they felt show on their faces without voicing as much.

After just a few months, the rules on when and if Reed should leave Billie in the car were still a bit blurry. While nowhere near as imposing as the traditional German Shepherd, she was still a large animal, tipping the scales at sixty-two pounds, her head coming almost to his waist. An inky black coat lent itself to the appearance of a wolf, matching rows of sharpened teeth only adding to the ensemble.

While classified as a police officer Reed had no doubt that few would protest her presence, though he still was far from wanting to test it.

Besides, the odds of something lurking in the bowels of the ME's office that would need her assistance weren't good.

Less than four hours after lying down, Reed had remained flat on his back, staring at the ceiling, his fingers laced behind his head. There was no way of telling how much sleep he had managed to attain over the course of the morning, though it couldn't have been more than a few minutes, his mind working too fast to allow his body to shut down.

Just before noon he gave up on the notion, tossing the covers aside and stomping through his house into the living room. In short order he went straight to the back door and opened it wide, brisk air pouring into the kitchen, covering his body in goose pimples.

"We roll in fifteen."

The words were no more than past his lips when Billie shot past him, a flash of black bolting from her bed beneath the dining room table and out into the backyard.

At the time, Reed had hoped that the time outside would give her the chance to burn away a bit of excess energy, preparing her for the day ahead.

The sounds being emitted behind him now proved how naïve that hope had been.

The pair of employees, both middle aged women with bright lipstick and too-tight blouses, continued to watch him as he trudged past, offering a small nod as he went.

"Doesn't like being left in the car," Reed said, adding a half smile for effect.

"Who does?" the woman on the left asked, her mouth twisted up, a look of disdain on her face.

Ignoring any further attempt at conversation Reed walked on past them, the rubber soles of his running shoes slapping against the sidewalk.

The Franklinton office of the Franklin County Coroner was a recent addition to the government roll, a satellite division of the main site downtown. Built as a direct response to the escalating rates of violent deaths in the city in recent years, it was one of three outposts that had popped up since the turn of the century.

A far cry from what Reed expected the first time he pulled up in front of it, the place was constructed entirely of steel and glass, resembling a health club more than a coroner's office. Standing two stories tall, it had a fountain spraying recycled water in a fan before it, an even hedge lining the front walk.

The ground underfoot changed from concrete to white tile as Reed stepped inside, the surface swallowing the sound of his shoes as he walked across the front atrium and found a young woman seated behind a desk. A bank of elevators stood off to the left and a small cafeteria behind her seemed to be serving most of the staff.

Government spending at its finest.

"Good afternoon," the young woman said as Reed approached, a half-eaten salad on the desk, an iPad beside it with a television show Reed couldn't place frozen on the screen.

"Afternoon," Reed said, reminding himself that it wasn't still morning, no matter how early it felt. Sliding a hand through his half-zipped hoodie, he slid his badge out and said, "Detective Reed Mattox, 8th Precinct. We sent a body over here this morning from The Bottoms, Captain Grimes was told it would be fast tracked first thing today."

"Let me check," the young woman replied, turning her chair to face the computer on the corner of her desk, the glow of the monitor reflected off her glasses. She maintained the pose a long moment, the sound of her clicking with the mouse audible over the dull throb of dining room chatter nearby.

"Yes," she replied, shifting her body towards him, but keeping her face aimed at the screen. "That was handled by Dr. Solomon downstairs. Would you like me to call her up?"

It was only third time Reed had ever been in the new coroner's office, both times having dealt with a miserable old man named Wilbern. Never before had he encountered Solomon, but she had to be a welcomed change.

"Just let her know I'm on my way down?" Reed asked, phrasing it as a question, but already drifting towards the elevator.

"Certainly," she replied, an oversized smile crossing her features. She reached for the phone in front of her as the gap between them widened, adding, "Room oh-one-six," just as Reed stepped into the elevator.

Thirty seconds later he was deposited in the basement, the scene before him much closer to what he expected from government operations. Gone were the bright lights and open floor plans, replaced instead by polished black tile and pale fluorescent bulbs. The smell of formaldehyde hung heavy as he walked forward, a chill in the air as he counted off door numbers.

Halfway down the hall he found his destination, stopping outside a wooden door with the top half etched in wired glass. On it was stenciled Dr. Patricia Solomon, Medical Examiner, the dark letters distinct against the window shade pulled down behind it.

More pale light peeked out from the edges of the shade, the only signs of life on an otherwise deserted floor.

Curling his hand into a fist, Reed knocked three times, the door rattling against its frame, the combined sounds echoing like gunfire through the hall.

On instinct Reed felt a small kick in the pit of his stomach, glancing in either direction. His hand slid to his waist, touching at the base of his weapon, as a voice called from within, "Open!"

Reed stepped inside to find a closet-sized office, most of the free space filled with white paper boxes. Each one was labeled with a name and date in blue marker, stacked from floor to ceiling. Wedged in tight between their towering columns was a small metal desk, a serial number tag visible on the front edge of it. Atop the table was an aging computer that resembled something Reed had used as a school child.

"Dr. Solomon?" Reed asked, moving a step forward and sticking his hand out.

Across from him a woman in her mid-to-late forties stood, the top of her red curls stopping just below Reed's chin. A pair of glasses hung from a string around her neck, resting atop a thick wool sweater. She was chewing as she stood, meeting his shake with one hand, covering her mouth with the other.

"Sorry," she began, her voice muffled through the bite of half-eaten food. "You caught me between cases."

"No, I apologize," Reed said. "Didn't mean to interrupt."

She finished the bite with a heavy swallow, the lump it formed visible as it traveled down her throat. "Please, call me Patricia."

"Okay, Patricia," Reed said, releasing her hand and stepping back. "I'm Detective Reed Mattox. Captain Grimes called ahead this morning and said I would be by sometime this afternoon to speak with you folks about the homicide that came in last night."

A look somewhere between sorrow and repulsion passed over Solomon's face as she stepped past Reed and slid a pair of case files from the only other chair in the room, stacking them on the edge of her desk.

"Please, have a seat," she said, motioning towards it as she lowered herself down. At her elbow on the desk was a half-eaten Subway sandwich, the scent of mustard finding its way to Reed, reminding him that despite living with a canine garbage disposal, he himself was now going on fourteen hours without eating a thing.

"I'm guessing by the look on your face you know which case I'm referring to," Reed said, leaving his voice free of inflection, not wanting to affect her report in any way.

Again the look passed over her features. "Yes," she replied, "as much for the fact that we don't often get rush requests as for what it turned out to be."

For the previous ten hours, Reed had been unable to shake the image of what he found the night before from his head. In his years he had seen a few murders that surpassed its grisly nature, but the number could easily be counted on just a single hand.

The reaction of the patrol officers that first found it wasn't without merit.

"Yeah, when I arrived last night it resembled something from a bad horror movie," Reed said, a stab at professional collegiality.

What it had actually resembled was a snapshot from Hell itself.

"I can't even imagine," Solomon replied, reaching to the edge of her desk and sliding the top file towards her. She pulled it over onto her lap and flipped it open, a few typed pages and a handful of pictures visible as Reed glanced down at it.

Pausing just a moment, Solomon raised her glasses and slid them onto the end of her nose.

"High level overview," she said, her voice taking on a detached tone, "COD: Stab wound to the chest. TOD: Approximately one a.m."

Reed aimed his gaze at the file on Solomon's lap, his eyes blurring over as he listened to what she said, superimposing it onto his memories from the night before.

"Stab wound to the chest," he muttered, his voice just barely audible, letting the information sink in. "So it wasn't the slash across his abdomen?"

"No," Solomon said, shaking her head from side to side. "The laceration to his torso and the removal of his right arm both occurred before death, but were not the cause."

Once more the image of the previous night flashed into Reed's mind, of the ground painted with the victim's blood. "Any defensive wounds?"

"Nothing," Solomon said, twisting her head. "Low levels of adrenaline in the bloodstream seem to indicate the attack was by surprise, the victim never even had time to react."

Reed's head bobbed up and down as he chewed on the information, adding to what he already knew. "That or he was familiar with his killer, didn't have reason to be alarmed."

"Possible," Solomon said, raising her eyebrows in concession. "The level of excessive mutilation would indicate a personal connection."

The words *excessive mutilation* were the same ones Reed would choose to describe the scene. It seemed to indicate that the goal wasn't robbery, or even death, but to make a statement.

"Any ideas on murder weapon?" Reed asked, blinking himself into focus, his attention still aimed at the folder on Solomon's lap.

Flipping the top page on her report, she held it perpendicular to the file and read aloud. "All three wounds seem to be made from the same weapon, a large blade with a minimum eighth inch thickness, maximum of a quarter inch."

A low, shrill whistle slid out of Reed, though he refrained from speaking.

"Also, each of the wounds looked to be made at a downward angle, indicating the attacker was taller than the victim."

Lowering the sheet back into place, Solomon closed the file and extended it to Reed.

"Anything else?" he asked, accepting it and turning it to face him, though not bothering to open it.

"Yes," Solomon said, dropping the glasses back from her nose, letting them bounce against the front of her sweater. "All three wounds were single slashes, clean cuts that showed no sign of remorse or hesitation.

"Whoever attacked this man wanted him dead."

Chapter Eight

"Come on out, girl," Reed said, pulling the back door open and standing aside as Billie bounded down, stopping just a few feet past the car and waiting, her entire body rigid. She held her nose to the wind, sniffing at it, her ears lowered on her head as she recorded the scent.

"Search," Reed said, a bit of bass in his tone, the voice reserved for issuing a command. At the sound of it Billie dropped her nose to the ground, drawing in deep inhalations, her tail and ears all three tucked low as she worked.

Remaining by the car, Reed watched as she went, leaning against the driver's side door, his arms folded across his chest. He stayed fixed in that position as the same blue-and-white he'd seen sixteen hours before pulled up beside him, the brakes emitting a low whine as it came to a stop.

Jacobs was the first one out, climbing from the passenger seat, followed a moment later by McMichaels. Both were already in uniform, agreeing to meet before their shift started. As a sign of appreciation Reed had let them choose the location, requesting only that it be far from any prying ears until they knew more about the victim and the murder.

Why they had chosen an abandoned gas station he wasn't sure, but he didn't press it.

Across the parking lot, Billie raised her head as the two officers approached, a low growl rolling from her. Drawing her head out straight from her shoulders she bared her top teeth, staring as they moved forward.

"No!" Reed said, the word drawing a visible slackening from the dog. "Search."

On cue, she lowered her head, her gaze remaining on the pair of men a moment longer before shifting back to the ground before her.

"What's it looking for?" Jacobs asked, watching Billie work, coming to a stop by the rear bumper.

"She," Reed corrected, seeing Jacobs raise an eyebrow in question. "She's a girl."

Both men nodded at the explanation, though if it was a move of understanding or to placate him he couldn't be sure.

Either way, it was the right response.

"She's getting a blueprint for this place," Reed said. "In the Marines they trained her to alert on dozens of different compounds and agents. If anything is here, she'll pick it up."

The two partners exchanged a glance.

"You really think somebody's been making a bomb here?" McMichaels asked. "We just picked this place because it's close to where we start patrol."

"I figured," Reed said, nodding for emphasis, "and no, I don't expect her to find anything. If we come across something in the future though that is here, she'll recognize it.

"We still haven't spent a lot of time in The Bottoms. Never know when it might come in handy."

Both men again nodded in unison, their mouths easing open as they raised their faces towards the sky.

"So, what were you guys able to find out?" Reed asked, bypassing any further discussion of his partner.

While both had been civil, even respectful of her, he was fast finding that others on the force didn't share the same feelings. Once upon a time he had trended in that direction, so he understood the resentment, even if he didn't like it.

The fact was, he still wasn't entirely sure about how he felt having Billie for a partner. He'd grown up with dogs, had always liked them, but had never considered one to be something he could trust his life to if necessary. The only reason he had considered the notion was because force regulations mandated he work with somebody.

Billie seemed a lot better than the alternative.

"Exactly like you pegged it last night," Jacobs said, no small amount of acrimony in his voice. "We got basically nothing."

"I wouldn't say that," McMichaels corrected, "we caught a lot of hell from various folks."

The left corner of Reed's mouth turned upward as he shifted to gaze at Billie, still working her way across the open expanse of concrete. The sound of her sniffing could be heard carrying towards them, one long breath after another.

"Let me guess," he said, "called you pigs? Told you to stop hassling innocent people?"

"Isn't there a donut somewhere that's missing us?" Jacobs added.

"Don't we have anything better to do than interrupt people trying to have their morning coffee," McMichaels finished, the same tone of voice as the other two.

Every officer to ever work patrol had heard the lines before, the same rhetoric spouted by citizens that were angry about something they couldn't quite articulate.

"So nobody saw a thing?" Reed asked.

"If they did, they aren't talking about it," Jacobs replied.

"Not one of them heard anything either, right?"

A smirk pulled at Jacobs's face, revealing just the slightest bit of teeth. "Most of them acted like we were crazy for even asking. Took it as some mortal offense that we would even insinuate they had been out at that time of night."

"Shit," Reed muttered, dropping his gaze to the ground. He nudged a rock into position with the toe of his shoe before swinging his foot at it, sending it skittering across the concrete.

"There was one woman you might be able to circle back to in a day or two," McMichaels said, drawing a small slip of paper from his shirt pocket. Folded in half, blue ruled lines were visible on it and one edge was frayed, consistent with a sheet ripped from a handheld notebook.

"Her name and address is here," he continued. "I got the impression she might know a little bit, but by the time we made it to her there were a lot of sideways glances going around. Know what I mean?"

Reed nodded, taking the sheet of paper and opening it up. He knew exactly what McMichaels meant, had seen many similar witnesses over the years. People that wanted to help, but had to balance that with the fact that once the investigation was over, they still needed to coexist with the neighborhood around them.

It was no secret what citizens in most communities thought about cops.

That feeling was heightened tenfold in a place such as The Bottoms.

"Thanks," Reed said, stuffing the paper into the front pocket of his jeans. "I'll run her down tomorrow or the next day, once things cool down a bit."

"Sorry we couldn't be more help," Jacobs said, taking a step back towards the car.

"You did everything you could," Reed said, stepping forward and thrusting a hand out. "Appreciate it."

One at a time the officers shook his hand before retreating to their car, both offering a wave as they climbed inside. A moment later they backed out and circled east around the block, neither looking his way as they disappeared down the street.

Checking his watch, Reed resumed his position against the side of the car, waiting as Billie continued to work the lot over. He closed his eyes and raised his face towards the sky, the cool late afternoon air settling over him. A breeze pushed in from the nearby river, carrying with it the smells of garbage and the remnants of gas from the station he stood before.

Despite it, he remained in place, content to let Billie take as long as she wanted in canvassing the lot.

Their next destination was definitely not one he wanted to arrive to early.

Chapter Nine

Under the cover of early morning darkness, there was nothing imposing about the 8th Precinct. Made entirely of brick that had faded from decades of exposure to the elements, it resembled an old school house, replete with a roundabout out front and a flag pole standing dead center of it. At three stories tall, triplicate rows of windows lined all four sides.

More importantly, at that hour most of the windows were dark, the majority of the stalls in the parking lot empty.

Just twelve hours later, the scene was markedly different.

Parked in the rear of the lot, Reed drew in a deep breath and stared up at the building, watching as a handful of employees filed out. Lumped into groups of two and three, they carried their lunch sacks and purses with them, smiling, lost in conversation. Nobody noticed him in the back row or heard the sound of Billie whining at the sight of them.

Reed waited a full five minutes after the end-of-day crowd filed out before climbing from the car. For a moment he considered leaving Billie behind before opting to bring her along, clipping her to the short leash and marching her towards the front door.

Few things in the world discouraged conversation as much as an all-black Belgian Malinois, Reed was fast discovering. While she was far from vicious, gentle even when the time required it, her appearance alone seemed to insight some sort of internal mechanism for most people approaching. Even without realizing it they would recoil or shift their trajectory just enough, making sure the respective paths didn't cross.

It was that exact response that Reed was hoping to evoke here.

The short leash afforded Billie just two feet of length, designed so Reed could keep a strong hold on her. Far more cumbersome than the eight foot lead he could clip to his jeans, or the complete freedom they both preferred, it kept her body pressed close to his side. As they walked he could feel her thick fur rubbing against him, the striated muscle of her abdomen flexing along his thigh.

Side by side they walked towards the front door, crossing inside, the sound of Billie's nails on the floor sounding out on contact, drawing a few stares their way.

The interior of the first floor was designed in an office format, large open spaces to either side. Strewn throughout both were handfuls of desks, arranged in haphazard patterns, stacks of papers piled high.

A few lamps still blazed bright, though most of the occupants had vacated for the day.

Behind them a wall bisected the first floor, the back half of the building sectioned off into individual offices. A set of double doors with frosted glass separated them from the front bullpen areas, reserved for the captain and senior level staff.

Ignoring the offices, Reed aimed his focus at the stairwell rising before him. He didn't bother to issue a command to Billie as he went, letting her follow his lead in silence. Together they ascended the stairs two at a time, the wood beneath them groaning in protest, before coming out on the second floor.

Following the same design as the first story, the space was cut in two, the back half used for the evidence room. The left side was reserved desk space for detectives, most of them standing empty, left untouched as much as possible.

On the right was the dispatch desk, behind it the only pair of holding cells in the precinct.

At the moment, the cells were both empty.

The desk was not.

Seated at it was Jackie, her wreath of white-blonde hair standing in a halo around her head. Bright pink lipstick framed gleaming teeth, a smile stretched across most of her face.

The sources of her mirth stood on either side of her, both leaning on the opposite side of the counter. Even with their backs to him Reed recognized them on sight, feeling a bit of dread well within him.

Beside him Billie seemed to sense his trepidation, her body going tense to the touch.

Turning on a heel, Reed headed for the opposite side, moving fast in an effort to make it to his desk before being spotted. Tugging on Billie's lead they made it less than four steps before Jackie's voice echoed through the room, a mix of maternal scolding and mock disappointment.

"Reed Mattox, I know you aren't trying to sneak in here without stopping to say hello!"

The words stopped Reed mid-step, his foot hanging suspended in the air as he twisted around to face forward.

The exclamation had turned Jackie's visitors around to look at him, any mirth the previous conversation had brought them long since evaporated. Both wore matching scowls as they stared back at him, contempt obvious on their faces.

To the right was Pete Iaconelli, a senior detective that had pointed out three times in their first meeting that he was less than a year from retirement. The unspoken message in there was that he was biding his time until the day his walking papers were issued, meaning Reed should neither do anything to provide him with more work or that might jeopardize his pension.

Reed couldn't think of two things he would rather do less.

At first glance, Iaconelli was a slovenly mess, someone that liked to refer to himself as a throwback to mask the fact that his lifestyle and his wardrobe were both stuck in the seventies. Weighing somewhere north of two hundred and fifty pounds, a hefty paunch hung down over his belt, a polyester shirt tucked in tight accentuating the bulge. Over it he wore a brown faux leather jacket, the material just a shade lighter than his bottle-tanned face.

Opposite him was his partner, Martin Bishop, the quiet one of the pairing that closely resembled the skeleton yard decorations Reed's parents still put out every Halloween. His skin was pale to the point of translucency, his hair buzzed to just an eighth inch all around.

Standing a full half foot taller than his partner he weighed at least a hundred pounds less, his cheeks sunken and hollow.

"Well, if it's not Ace Ventura," Iaconelli opened with, a sneer masked as a half smile on his face.

Reed felt his grip on the leash grow tighter, glancing down to see his knuckles show white beneath the skin. The name was one the man had come up with some time before, a dated allusion to the old pet detective movies of the nineties. At the time nobody in house seemed to find it humorous except Bishop, which was more than enough for it to take hold.

On cue, the oversized man let out a chortle, ensuring that it would continue further.

Again he sensed Billie grow stiff, lowering herself an inch in height, her legs coiling to act if necessary.

"Detectives," Reed said, forcing his voice to remain neutral. He walked forward until a half dozen feet from the desk before stopping, raising his head upwards in a nod. "Hey, Jackie."

"Hey, Sugar," she cooed, her mouth curled up in a smile as she stared at the odd couple before her. "How you two doing this evening?"

At the mention of two, Reed glanced down at Billie, her attention still trained on the pair of detectives. "Excellent. You?"

"I'm good," she said, raising a hand and fluffing out her plume of hair. "But you know me, I'm always good."

"Yeah," Reed agreed, his voice low, already wanting the conversation to be over, feeling the accusatory glares of the men on his skin. "I hope you don't mind, but we'll be over on the desk for a while tonight."

The smile grew wider on Jackie's face as she lowered her hand from her hair. "You know I don't mind one bit. Be nice to have some company around here in the evening for a change."

The comment only served to deepen the scowls of Iaconelli and Bishop, the two exchanging a glance.

"On the desk, huh?" Iaconelli said, his nose curling up in a snort. "Actually going to do some detective work today, are you?"

Again Reed could feel his grip tighten on the leash, a dozen comments springing to mind. His nostrils flared as he pushed out a long breath, forcing himself not to lash out, not to succumb to the prodding.

At every precinct there was always one pairing, one group that could be counted on to give the new guys a hard time.

In the 8th, it was Iaconelli and Bishop, a grown-up bully and his lackey. For whatever reason they had decided to make Reed their target, regardless how hard he tried to stay out of their way.

"Something like that," Reed said, dismissing the man and his comment, fixing his attention on Jackie. "We'll be down there if anything comes in tonight, alright?"

She seemed to sense his impending anger and accepted the statement with a nod, watching as he retreated.

"Yeah, you and your *partner* have a good evening, ya hear?" Iaconelli called as he went.

Reed didn't bother to respond.

Chapter Ten

Two distinct voices drifted out into the night, one male, one female. Their tone indicated the pair was definitely at odds, their respective volumes just shy of shouting. Every few moments the sound of something being thrown or glass breaking punctuated the argument, echoing through the small home and carrying out into the cold evening air.

Tucked away behind the free standing garage next to the house, the Boat Man sat and listened to every word, waiting for the opportune moment. With each sound of dissension that floated out, the feeling of satisfaction welled within him.

The joy that came with the elimination of this target wouldn't only be felt by him.

Cloaked in black, the Boat Man sat with one shoulder leaning against the rear of the garage, the rotting wood splintering beneath his weight. Every few moments a few flakes wrenched themselves free and drifted to the ground, spotting his clothing.

Each time he brushed them away, careful not to let anything touch his bare skin.

Concealed between a pair of ragged box hedges, there was no concern of detection. After the events of the previous night though, and all that was about to unfold, it would only be a matter of time before the police made a connection between the two.

Now, more than ever, it was vital that he not become sloppy and leave something behind for them to work with.

Not with so much still left to do.

"I told you, we were just talking!" the male inside bellowed, rage creeping in to his voice.

"It sure as hell didn't look like talking to me!" the woman replied, vehemence plain, her din just shy of a shriek. "What would have happened if I hadn't gotten there when I did?"

The question brought a hint of a smile to the Boat Man's face, the right corner of his mouth tracking upward. The woman's absence was what had allowed him to get into position so easily, finding the spot just after dusk, unnoticed by the darkened homes nearby.

The target was the second in as many nights, chosen for his place in the hierarchy.

Unlike his previous target, the scouting had been easy for this one. There was no need to watch for patterns or determine a time when he could find the man alone.

Everything the Boat Man needed was curled up less than ten feet away, pacing back and forth in the yard, the sound of his chain dragging across the ground audible between outbursts from the home.

Drawing his legs up beneath him, the Boat Man climbed onto his feet, peering out from around the edge of the garage. Branches of the hedges scratched at his body as he rose, the ragged plants rattling just slightly with his movement.

"Dammit, I told you, nothing!" the man called again.

Twisting his body at the waist, the Boat Man slid his head around the side of the building to peer up at the house.

Built to match the garage, it was a one-story home with a porch and wooden siding. Much like the structure he now leaned against, it appeared to be aging badly, in dire need of paint.

Framed in the kitchen window, the Boat Man saw as a pair of silhouettes moved back and forth, both with arms flailing. He waited, watching as the two grew closer together, one lashing out at the other, the darkened shape of a hand connecting with the head of the other.

All sound fell away as the Boat Man watched the scene play out, his resolve growing stronger as his heart rate picked up just slightly.

It was time.

Extricating himself from behind the garage, he crept heel-to-toe towards the small wooden doghouse filling the bulk of the space between the home and garage. Just beyond the scope of the overhead street lamp, it remained shrouded in darkness, its occupant moving back and forth in silence.

Inch by inch the Boat Man made his way forward, the smell of wet fur and feces reaching his nostrils. A sheen of moisture coated his eyes as he proceeded, extending one hand and knocking against the back of the structure.

The move delivered the intended effect.

The moment the sound reached the dog's ears, it exploded in a frenzy of angry fervor, the barking starting loud outside, becoming muffled as the animal ran to the back of the structure. It reverberated off the walls as the Boat Man knelt low, waiting for the hysterics to serve their purpose.

Ignoring the howling of the dog separated from him by just a single piece of wood, he focused his attention on the house, anticipation roiling through him as the sound of arguing died away.

In its place was only the angry baying of the dog thundering out over the neighborhood.

After a moment the sound began to fade away, the animal losing interest, the barks becoming a bit softer, some space appearing between them.

Once more the Boat Man tapped at the back of the structure, sending the dog into a second burst of concentrated venom, the sound now distorted by a heavy dose of saliva, a tongue starting to wag from exertion.

Poised in his hiding spot, the Boat Man reached back over a shoulder and extracted his sword, the freshly oiled blade sliding from its scabbard without a sound. Gripping it tight he waited, listening as the springs on the rear door to the house wheezed in exertion, followed a moment later by boots hitting steps.

"What the hell are you out here barking at?"

The voice was male, a trace of familiarity present. The sound of it enforced the Boat Man's hold on his weapon, his breath picking up just a bit.

Seconds passed as the footsteps drew closer, passing over from the back walk to the dirt.

"Hey," the man snapped, "get your ass out here. What's going on?"

Three long, torturous seconds passed as the Boat Man allowed his prey to draw closer before he sprang.

Chapter Eleven

The face of Edwin Mentor stared back at Reed, filling over half of the computer screen.

At first glance he appeared Latino, though his records indicated he was half-Caucasian, half-Filipino. The mug shot had been taken almost a decade before when Mentor still had hair, the top of his head framed with short, dark spikes that were gelled into place. A thin beard and goatee encased his face and a thick gold chain hung from his neck.

All in all, a look that screamed 2004.

The folder Solomon had given him sat open on Reed's lap as he glanced down at the photos she had taken and the image on the screen. Somewhere in the bottom of the crime scene report lying across his keyboard were the photos taken the night before, though Reed preferred to work off of the sanitized ones sent over by the ME.

Before touching any of the paper Reed had started in the electronic databases, intent to learn everything he could about Mentor before going back over what he already knew.

The first step for any homicide investigation was the crime scene. Having spent six hours there within the last day, Reed felt reasonably comfortable with everything that was found.

A whole lot of gore, and not much else.

After, the second place to look was at victimology, trying to work backwards from the person that was killed to determine who might have done it. Often there was no clear throughway that connected one with the other, but if digging around long enough an investigator could at least determine the why, which generally led to the who.

Beginning with the large national databases, Reed entered Mentor into ViCAP – the Violent Criminal Apprehension Program – and NCIC, the National Crime Information Center. Both were run by the FBI, meant to warehouse data on violent or egregious offenders, running the gamut of criminals from identity thieves to foreign fugitives.

Once both came back negative, he shifted his attention to the local files, finding only a pair of arrests six months apart in the fall of 2004 and the spring of 2005.

The first offense occurred after being picked up for driving with a busted taillight, the officer on the scene smelling marijuana and asking Mentor to step out. A search of the car found three-eighths of an ounce inside, enough to warrant a possession charge but not approach the line for being considered a dealer.

Half a year later Mentor was arrested along with eight others after a bar fight in Grove City. The narrative read that two groups of young men, one of which Mentor was a member of, had gotten into an argument over a basketball game on television. The disagreement had turned violent and all nine had entered into an altercation.

None of the participants had pressed charges, but the bar owner had been forced to for insurance purposes.

After that, the trail went cold. He owned his car, paid his rent on time. For the past six years he had been employed as a mechanic at a shop in Franklinton, a quick call over revealing the shop was closed until morning.

Parents passed when he was seventeen, no spouse or children.

Once the low hanging fruit was stripped clean, Reed fell to the files. Thus far they had revealed little beyond the fact that the years had not been especially kind to him.

"You got anything?" Reed asked, the question aimed at Billie as she laid flat on the tile floor near his feet. The upper half of her eyelids opened at the sound of his voice, her ears rising on her head.

"Yeah, me neither," Reed muttered, shifting his attention back to the files. "Tomorrow we'll see if we can track down this woman the uniforms found, maybe swing by the scene and let that nose of yours have a look around. Sound good?"

"You always talk to her that way?" a voice asked, snapping Reed and Billie's attention both to face forward, the latter's chin rising from the floor.

Across from them Jackie approached, her wide figure barely squeezing along the narrow pathway between the desks. In her hand she carried a paper cup of coffee, a lid fastened in place, a red plastic straw extended above it.

A wan smile crossed Reed's face as he leaned back in his chair, folding the file closed on his lap. "The hard part is getting her to talk back."

A wistful expression fell over Jackie's face as she looked at the dog, her eyes glossing for a moment. "If only."

She held the pose a moment before extending the coffee out in front of her, setting it down on the only square of clear space on the desk. "Here, honey, I brought you this."

The smile fell from Reed's face as he looked at the cup and then up at the expression on Jackie's face. The familiar feeling of nervousness settled into his stomach as he read the situation, knowing that her act wasn't entirely one of propriety.

"What happened?" he asked, letting the thought show in his voice.

"We just got another call. Sounds a lot like the one you're looking at right now."

Chapter Twelve

Unlike the night before, the scene was alive with activity as Reed pulled up. A squad car was parked across the end of the driveway, an ambulance behind it. A third truck with an insignia on the door Reed didn't recognize came next in line, orange flashing lights atop the cab striping the neighborhood with their tangerine hue.

"What the hell?" Reed muttered, easing to a stop on the opposite side of the street. In the back seat he could hear Billie moving around, straining to look, her paws squeaking against plastic.

"You better stay here," Reed said, glancing over his shoulder as he pulled the keys from the ignition and stepped out, his partner again whining from the back seat to join him.

Ignoring the sound of her, Reed slid his badge out from beneath his sweatshirt, letting it swing free around his neck, bouncing off his chest. It glinted under the bright lights of the truck, reflecting the light every two seconds as it rotated in a circle atop the hood.

Halfway across the street, one of the responding officers spotted him and stepped out in front of his car. The same height and a few pounds heavier than Reed, he looked to be approaching forty. Bits of grey striped his temples, framing a face of mocha colored skin pockmarked from previous acne.

"Detective Reed?" he asked, standing perpendicular to Reed, his body angled towards the house.

Reed nodded, stepping forward and introducing himself, a hand outstretched.

The officer met the shake and the nod, shifting to face forward. "Derek Greene."

He pointed over towards the ambulance, the back doors standing open, bright light from within splashing out. Seated on the edge of it was a young woman with dark hair, a blanket draped over her shoulders. Beside her stood a second officer in uniform, much younger than Greene, holding a pad and pencil out in front of him, motioning for the woman to calm down.

He didn't appear to be making much headway placating her, or getting her statement.

"My partner, Adam Gilchrist," Greene said.

Reed's glance lingered on the scene behind the ambulance a long moment before shifting forward. It was something he had seen many times over the years, something he had done on more than one occasion.

"Rook?" Reed asked.

"Less than a year in," Greene confirmed, his features impassive as he stared straight ahead. His voice was free of inflection, meant merely to relay information, not scorn.

In his experience, Reed had found that was usually the best that could be said about rookies. Even those that came in with military training seemed to be like a newborn colt their first year, all knees and elbows, barely able to stand on their own.

"Is he talking to her because she has pertinent information or because you want him far from the crime scene?"

"Yes," Greene replied, glancing over at Reed, no sign of mirth anywhere on his features.

Reed had figured as much.

"Alright, what do we know?"

A long, slow breath passed from Greene as he folded his arms across his chest, shifting his weight from side to side. "Call came in twenty minutes ago from the girlfriend, said that she and her boyfriend were home this evening when something outside caused their dog to go crazy. The boyfriend stepped out to see what was going on, never came back."

So far, nothing Greene had said seemed consistent with the night before, from the amount of activity surrounding the area to the presence of another person on site.

"Was reported as another 187," Reed said. "Can you confirm?"

"Yes," Greene said without pause, not the slightest hint of hesitation in his voice.

A nod pulled Reed's head upward. "Last night I got one that had been hacked up pretty bad, looked like someone took a damn broadsword to the body. Dispatch said it might be connected."

Reed left the statement open-ended, allowing Greene to match it against what he had already seen, free from any leading at all.

A long moment passed in silence before Greene arched an eyebrow, rotating at the waist to look Reed's way. "I heard some chatter about that on the line this afternoon, wasn't sure if it was true or not."

"It was," Reed said, drawing his mouth into a tight line. While it was generally not his policy to share the gruesome details of cases, there was no reason to withhold information from Greene. If the two were in fact connected, he would need every relevant detail he could get.

That only happened if he played ball with the responding officers.

"What's with the laser light show?" Reed asked, motioning towards the flashing orange lamps illuminating the neighborhood, drawing gawkers to their windows like moths to a flame.

"Animal control," Greene said, again twisting to look over at Reed.

Once more a feeling welled within Reed, a combination of dread and adrenaline, his body's natural response to what was bound to be an ugly situation. A handful of questions passed through his mind as he tried to make sense of why animal control was on site, but he let them go.

So far, Greene seemed to be pretty in control, handling things much better than the young crew the night before. His lack of impairment hinted that it wasn't the first body he'd seen, the police tape and relocation of the witness displaying the scene was secure.

"How bad?" Reed asked, again leaving his voice flat, letting his colleague draw from it what he would.

"Top...two," Greene said, pausing in the middle to consider his answer.

The feeling within Reed intensified a tiny bit. Two didn't leave a lot of wiggle room. Two meant that this was going to be ugly, potentially even worse than what he'd seen the night before.

"If it's alright by you Officer, I'm going to go ahead and declare it a homicide, call in the tech crew so they can start making their way over here."

Greene remained motionless a long moment, his arms still folded across his chest. "That's what I would do, too."

Chapter Thirteen

Top two might have been a stretch, but Reed was not above ranking the crime scene in his top three.

Never did he want to call something the very worst, fearing angering karmic forces enough to view the statement as a challenge, sending him something straight from a Stephen King novel. Instead he tended to group things in terms of round numbers, usually multiples of five.

The previous night was a top ten scene, maybe cracking the top five if he really tried to force it. The shock value of the blood and the severed limb had made it seem much worse at first, his senses not expecting to respond to such a visceral visual.

The facts were though, there was only a single victim, and the kill was fresh. There was no mass grave, no gang shootout that had ended with bodies strewn through the street. Nobody had been left in the summer heat, their tissues bloating and desiccating under the hot sun.

Top ten, possibly top five.

This scene was top three, no questions asked.

The victim's name was A.J. Wright, the girlfriend saying he always went by his initials, short for Alex Jason. Thus far that was the only useful information they had gotten out of her, though standing over the scene, Reed didn't begrudge her a bit for it.

Walking out to find a loved one in that position would have shaken him too.

Wright was sprawled face up on a dirt patch between the house and a detached garage, the area clearly beaten free of grass by a dog. Its house and chain were both a few feet from the victim's head, standing silent and empty.

Dressed in jeans and a t-shirt with a flannel open over it, his torso was carved with two intersecting slashes, both consistent with what Reed had seen the night before. The depth and ferocity of the cuts were such that bits of bowel and intestine were distended up from the wounds, bodily fluid staining the front of his clothes. A single gaping stab wound was present in the man's chest.

In addition, unlike the previous victim, both of his arms had been removed mid-forearm. The left one remained on the ground by his body, the right one having been drug through the dirt, a trail of blood congealing in the dust behind it.

Some of the flesh from the open end of it had been gnawed away, the work of Wright's own pit bull, the reason for animal control having been called to the scene. For the briefest instant Reed imagined what it must have looked like for the control workers that arrived, finding a fresh corpse, the victim's dog gnawing on part of it.

The thought turned his stomach as he fought the urge to look over his shoulder and nod to Greene. When he'd first heard that animal control was on the scene before him, a pang of something resembling professional jealousy had struck him. Now he understood it was for the preservation of the crime scene, making sure no evidence was disturbed, no more of the deceased consumed.

At some point soon Reed would have to track down the animal control specialist and examine the dog to determine what, if anything, could be learned.

The odds were overwhelming that it would result in nothing but a heavy bout of nausea, but he still had to do it.

Keeping his distance, Reed made two loops around the scene, careful not to disturb anything. He drew his cell phone from his waist and dialed dispatch, waiting as the metallic scent of blood wafted up at him. Thick stripes of it painted the ground mere feet away, beginning to harden in the cold night air.

"Hey, Sugar," Jackie's voice cooed over the line, skipping all formality.

"Hey, can you patch me through to McMichaels?" Reed asked, bypassing any greeting and getting straight to his request. Despite standing over the scene he wasn't sure he could accurately describe it to her if asked, certain that he wouldn't want to even if he could.

Jackie seemed to sense the strain in his voice and did as requested without further comment, a moment of static coming over the line before a gruff male voice answered.

"McMichaels."

"Officer McMichaels, Reed Mattox." He knew from their earlier meeting that they were on patrol, couldn't be more than a few miles away. "Any chance I can ruin your night for the second time in a row?"

There was a long pause, followed by a deep breath. "Aw hell, you've got another one?"

How that could have been ascertained from a single question Reed wasn't sure, but he let it go without comment. Instead, he pushed forward with his request, shoving it out in one quick burst.

"I do, and I need you guys to start working the streets again if you can. This is two in as many nights, and this is more gruesome than the last."

Again there was a brief pause, Reed imagining the two officers exchanging a look.

"I don't care who we wake up or piss off this time," Reed said. "We might have a serial killer on our hands here."

Chapter Fourteen

Just twenty minutes after leaving the scene Reed stood on the opposite side of the one-way glass, looking through it at Lucinda Barr. She was seated on a black plastic chair before a solid wooden table, the wool blanket given to her by the paramedics still wrapped around her shoulders.

Within the confines of the makeshift garment she looked even smaller than Reed remembered, her upper body swallowed by the plain grey material. All that was visible from the waist up was her neck and face, both wearing the telltale signs of the night she endured.

"Thanks for bringing her in and staying with her," Reed said without glancing over to Officer Gilchrist beside him. "Couldn't have been easy."

"Actually, it was," Gilchrist replied, a hint of surprise in his voice. "She's been almost catatonic since it all went down. I hope you're able to get something useful out of her."

Reed shifted his focus from the room to their reflection in the glass, seeing Gilchrist standing beside him, his thumbs looped into his front pockets. Still in his twenties, he had a boyish face and thick dark hair, his height a couple inches more than Reed.

"Still, I appreciate it," Reed said, skipping over the fact that he and Greene had agreed to keep the younger man far away from the scene.

"I'll talk to the captain, make sure you guys get your OT for sticking around this morning."

Gilchrist raised a hand to wave off the comment as Reed stepped past him, Barr not even looking up as he moved into the room and closed the door behind him. In slow steps he walked over and drew out the chair across from her, lowering himself down and lacing his fingers on the table between them.

Had she been more responsive, or if he had any hope at all of actually coaxing much of use from her, Reed might have brought the early version of the case file in with him. He may have referenced his hand-written notes from the scene, using them to ensure accuracy, jog his memory to ask pertinent follow-ups.

Given her state though, he arrived empty handed, knowing any physical reminder of what had happened might be enough to push her over the edge, causing her to clam up for good. More than once he had seen similar things happen, a person's response being so strong that their minds more or less erased it, a natural form of self-protection.

"Ms. Barr," Reed opened, his tone gentle. He waited a long moment for a response, or any sign of recognition, and when none came he lowered his head a few inches, changing the angle to look up into her face. "Ms. Barr?"

Across from him, she kept her attention aimed down at the table, her face framed by lank dark brown hair. Matching eyes were red and puffy, tear stains streaking her dirty features.

Along her left cheekbone looked to be the beginning of a bruise, though given the overall state of her appearance, Reed couldn't be certain.

Once more Reed waited, watching as the tiniest flicker caught behind Barr's eyes, her attention rising to meet his gaze.

"Lucy," she whispered.

"Okay," Reed said, lowering his voice so it almost matched hers. "Lucy, can you tell me what happened last night?"

Having spent most of the night on the scene, Reed had a reasonable sequence of events worked out in his head. Even at that though, he wanted to hear if there was anything he might be missing.

At the sound of the question, Barr pressed her lips together, again lowering her attention back to the table. Her bottom lip quivered a bit before she drew in a deep breath through her nose.

"A.J. and I were in the kitchen, having a discussion about some things," she began.

The condition of the house, combined with a statement from a neighbor and the possible bruise on Barr's cheek, seemed to indicate that it had been more than a discussion. At the same time, the details of their dispute were far from relevant at the moment.

If that's how she had to handle things, that was fine by Reed. He just needed her talking.

"Outside, Bruno started to barking," she said, flicking her gaze up at him. "Bruno is A.J.'s pit bull."

The sign above the dog house door had said as much, but Reed nodded as if it were an important detail, wanting her to keep going.

"He didn't usually bark a lot, so when he started going crazy, A.J. went outside to see what was going on," she said, her voice cracking on the last words. She drew in a loud sniff and managed, "That was-"

She never finished the sentence, her voice fading as her face contorted. She drew her arms up on the table in front of her and thrust her head down into the blanket, her entire body racked with sobs. The sound of them echoed off the walls, filling Reed's ears as he sat and waited.

Dozens of questions floated to the front of Reed's mind, things that he desperately wanted to ask, things that would at the very least narrow his investigation down a bit. As he sat and watched her cry though, he let them every one of them pass.

Maybe there would be a time to ask them eventually, this just wasn't it.

He stood and walked from the room without another word, leaving Barr in solitude behind him.

Chapter Fifteen

A droplet of sweat hit the polished wood floor beneath the Boat Man, landing with a tiny splash, completely contained within the misshapen circle. It remained there, alone, for a long moment before a second one joined it, a third hanging from the tip of his nose, threatening to complete the trio.

The Boat Man aimed his focus on them as he lowered his face towards the floor, lactic acid coursing through his deltoid and trapezium muscles. The concerted force of it caused his entire shoulder yoke to feel like it was on fire, pulling the breath from his lungs.

Slow and controlled, he finished the repetition, raising his feet towards the ceiling. His core ached as he pushed himself upward in a vertical pushup, his vision blurring from exertion, unable to focus on the drops on the floor any longer.

There he stayed as long as his body would allow, until his side throbbed and his arms shook from exertion, before dropping his feet to the ground.

There the Boat Man remained, fighting to catch his breath, his body poised on all fours, like an oversized cat ready to pounce.

"Getting better," he whispered, drawing his feet beneath him and standing, his breath still coming in ragged pants. Walking to the low-slung table beside him he took up a sweat towel and ran it over his face and torso, cutting a matte swipe through his shiny body.

Towel in hand, the Boat Man walked across the open floor, his shoulders rising and falling with heavy breaths. He fixed his attention on the wall before him, a series of photos arranged on it, all pinned into place.

The wall had taken him months to put together, made through painstaking research and a patience he didn't know he possessed. On it was every last thing he had uncovered since that night, every person and place, every time and occurrence that was even remotely pertinent.

Dropping the towel to the floor, the Boat Man took up a red marker from the table. With long even strokes he drew a circle around the face of A.J. Wright followed by two heavy slashes. Together the lines formed an X, coming together just above the tip of the man's nose.

"That's two," he said aloud, the sound swallowed up by the empty space around him.

By now, people would be starting to notice. A single occurrence could be written off. Sometimes even a second could as well, but rarely for something as unique, as salacious as what he had set out to do.

After last night, word would be circulating. People would be talking, knowing he was out there. If they hadn't already, soon they would start to realize what was happening, would start to look over their shoulder, begin to feel the anxiety he had lived with for so long.

At the same time, they wouldn't be the only ones that were able to piece things out. For a long time the cops had been a non-entity in The Bottoms, but even they wouldn't be able to stay away from something as attention grabbing as what he was doing.

Soon, people would be talking, loud enough to convey their fear, loud enough that somebody would have to listen.

The thought brought a smile to the Boat Man's face.

That's all any of this was about, to make people listen.

Capping off the marker, the Boat Man tossed it aside, the writing utensil hitting the top of the table and rolling to the floor. He let it go, the sound receding as he stood and stared at the wall.

After a long moment he took a step back from it, and then another. Once he was far enough removed he again dropped his hands down to the floor and hoisted his heels towards the ceiling, ready to begin anew.

Chapter Sixteen

The top on the canned double shot of espresso let out a wheeze of pressurized air as Reed popped it open, waiting for the hissing to stop before upending it. He held it there a long moment, letting half of the can's contents slide down his throat before pausing, taking a deep breath, and going back for more.

Just eight seconds after opening it, the can was empty.

Reed made a face as he worked his tongue around the inside of his mouth, trying to force the rancid taste down, and dropped the can into the wastebasket beside Grimes's desk. It landed with an audible thud, the metal hitting against the bottom of the empty container.

"Am I going to be smelling whatever that was for the rest of the day?" a voice asked from behind Reed, turning him around in his seat. Leaning forward he raised his backside off the chair, waiting until the captain was past until dropping back down into position.

"No," Reed said, his voice even, a bit of exhaustion audible. "Just espresso. Given that it was completely tasteless, there shouldn't be an odor."

Under different circumstances the comment might have earned at least a smirk, though this time Grimes kept his face even, a look just short of a scowl on his features. He settled into his seat and resumed his position of leaning back, his fingers laced across his stomach.

"Tell me last night wasn't as bad as it sounded."

Reed glanced away for a moment, envisioning the scene in his mind, before shifting his attention back to Grimes. "I could give you the clichéd answer and say it was worse, or I could give you the real answer and say it was a hell of a lot worse."

It took a moment for Grimes to process the response, blinking several times before fully registering what he'd been told. "Christ."

"Yep," Reed agreed, his chin rising and falling just a bit.

"Where are you at with it?" Grimes asked, rocking his head forward and peering across at Reed.

The question had passed through Reed's mind a half a dozen times on the drive in, trying to balance what he knew and where he could go next.

What he knew was that somebody was pissed, and wasn't shy about taking it out on the residents of Franklinton. Where he could go next was a veritable spider's web, scads of different directions that may or may not be connected.

"I tried speaking to Lucy Barr this morning," Reed said, "the girl-friend of last night's victim. As of five hours ago she was a wreck, so I'm guessing she's still out of play for the next day or two, minimum."

"That leaves only a single possible breathing witness, a woman that the uniforms came across yesterday while canvassing."

Grimes arched an eyebrow, his chin again having been pulled back against his chest. "Anything promising?"

"Not sure," Reed said, his shoulders rising a bit in a shrug. "They said she didn't say much at the time, felt like maybe she was being watched, but they got the impression she might be willing to talk."

"Hmm," Grimes said, considering the information. "Try to get her somewhere else and ask a few questions?"

"That's what I'm thinking," Reed said. "After that, now that all indi-cations are that these two crime scenes are connected, I can start looking for commonalities, try to link the victims."

"And there are two bodies," Grimes offered.

"And there are two bodies," Reed said. "Dr. Solomon over at the coroner's is set to take a look at Wright this afternoon. I'll meet with her in there somewhere, too."

Grimes nodded, pursing his lips in front of him. "Do you foresee anything new coming from the autopsy?"

"No," Reed said, "just a confirmation that the same weapon was used."

Silence fell between the two as they sat, staring across at one another. For the first time since arriving Reed got the impression the meeting had nothing to do with giving a rundown of where the case stood. He couldn't quite put his finger on it, but sensed there was something that wasn't being shared.

He gave it a long moment, waiting for Grimes to share, before prompting him.

Time wasn't something he seemed to have much of these days.

"You going to tell me or do I have to ask?"

The question sounded a bit harsher than Reed intended, though that didn't change the purpose. He made no attempt to retract or even soften the delivery, instead staring across at his captain, waiting for a response.

"I asked you to stop by this morning to let you know this is your case," Grimes said.

If any offense was taken to Reed's question, he didn't let it show.

"Right," Reed said, unsure how to interpret the statement. "I know."

A pair of doleful eyes stared back at him. "No," Grimes said, "I mean, this is *your* case."

Reed opened his mouth to respond before closing it, his eyes narrowing. Upon hearing it a second time he understood what the captain was getting at, the words falling into place in his mind.

This meeting was a warning shot, a first and most likely last chance to let Reed know that pressure was being applied. If not by the higher-ups, by the clock that was momentarily keeping them at bay.

"Is somebody calling for me to be removed?"

A flicker of something resembling approval crossed Grimes's face, signaling that Reed had been correct in his assessment. He glanced out to the parking lot, watching as a pair of uniforms headed for their patrol car, before shifting his attention back to face forward.

"No," Grimes said. "Luckily, right now that mess I mentioned yesterday about the Near East Side is still dominating the headlines and the Chief's attention."

Once more Reed thought of the crime scenes he'd been called to the previous two nights. If either of those were to hit the air waves they would fast become prime time viewing, played on a loop during all major news cycles.

"But if this got out..." Reed said, his voice falling away.

"I'd say that's a safe assumption, wouldn't you?" Grimes asked, staring hard at him.

There was no pause in Reed's response, no need to take a moment for debate.

The captain was absolutely right, and everything that fact brought with it meant the pressure now on Reed was higher than ever.

"Yes," Reed agreed, his voice soft. "Yes, I would."

Chapter Seventeen

The woman on the other end of the line had sounded uncertain when Reed called and asked her to meet. No matter how insistent he was that she was in no trouble herself, and that anything she said would be kept confidential, she was resistant to speaking with him.

Three times she claimed to know nothing, having given her complete statement to the officers the day before. Not until Reed asked if she liked coffee did her stance relax even a little, a small tell in her voice indicating he had her attention, if not yet her acquiescence.

Once he landed on barbecue though, any trepidation fell by the wayside.

Reed was the first to arrive at Old Smoque Barbecue, a west side institution that had been turning out brisket and ribs for decades. Located a mile outside of the freeway encircling Columbus, it was just a twelve minute drive from The Bottoms, but might as well have been in a different country given how far apart the two seemed.

Made from rough hewn wood painted to resemble a barn, Old Smoque was a single story structure that stood twice that in height to accommodate the steepled roof. White board fencing surrounded the grounds and an even hedge ran the perimeter of the place, mulched flower beds around it waiting for spring to officially arrive.

Half of the lot was already full despite the odd afternoon hour, most of the vehicles ranging from SUVs to luxury cars, indicative both of the neighborhood and the clientele coming in for an early dinner.

The scent of hickory smoke and barbecue sauce passed through the vents of the car as Reed pulled the sedan to a stop, his stomach rumbling in response. Behind him Billie seemed to have the same reaction, a low whine drawing his attention to the rearview mirror before a pink tongue shot out over her muzzle.

"Yeah, I know," Reed said, keenly aware of how far off both of their body cycles were at the moment. Neither one had slept more than a few hours at odd times, both grabbing small meals at random hours, Billie shifting her patterns to match his.

Six minutes after arriving, a faded mint green Chrysler pulled into the lot, instantly recognizable. Pockets of rust dotted the sides and Reed noticed a hubcap missing as it rolled into a spot on the front row and stopped, emitting a vicious hiss from the brakes.

Leaving Billie in the backseat, Reed tucked his badge away beneath his sweatshirt and stepped out, already halfway to the car before the driver's side door opened.

From the description given by McMichaels and the voice on the phone, a pretty close match to what Reed was expecting climbed from the car, moving slow and with great care. He waited until she was completely out and the door shut behind her before stepping forward, his hand outstretched.

"Mrs. Pearlman? Detective Reed Mattox."

The woman waved a hand at him as she shuffled forward, shaking her head. "Aw, phooey with that Mrs. Pearlman stuff. My name is Gale."

At some point Reed guessed she had stood close to 5'9", though those days were long past. Hunched forward at the waist she just barely came to his shoulder, her breath coming in small bursts as she moved forward. Silver curls were bunched tightly around her head, her chocolate colored skin lined with age.

Without regard for Reed's attempted handshake, she grabbed hold of the inside of his arm, her grip surprisingly strong. With her other hand she motioned towards the door and said, "Help an old woman inside?"

Reed did as asked, maintaining the position until they were seated and waiting patiently as she stared over the menu. After ten full minutes of intent study and confirming that Reed was buying, she ordered a full rack of ribs with fries and a Coke, frowning in disapproval as Reed opted for a pulled pork sandwich for himself, some link sausage for Billie.

Only then were they left to themselves, Reed having a few free minutes before the food arrived to determine all he could.

"So, Gale," he opened, his voice low. Even tucked away in the corner he wanted to be sure he wasn't overheard, the case itself still very much a secret. "My officers tell me you might have seen something two nights ago."

"Never said anything of the sort," Gale said, snaking a hand into the tin bucket of peanuts on the table between them and removing a loose cluster.

Reed waited for her to clarify her statement but she remained silent, shelling the peanuts and tossing them back into her mouth with surprising gusto.

"You didn't tell them you might have seen something?" Reed asked, shifting his head an inch to the side, his brows coming together.

Bits of peanut shell fell from her mouth as she chomped down, already reaching for more. "Well now, that's not what you said the first time. You asked if I saw something that night, which I did not."

Reed felt his eyes widen a bit in surprise, leaning back in his chair. "Oh, I see," he paused a moment, pushing a breath out through his nose, willing himself to remain calm.

It was not the first time a witness had chosen to be a touch difficult, using the temporary position of power to extract some small modicum of pleasure. In most instances they did end up providing something useful, a fact Reed reminded himself of as he leaned back in.

"Okay, then, please tell me what you might have seen at any time that would aid us in this investigation."

Placing a hand on the smooth tabletop between them, Gale swept her hand from left to right in front of her, sending the small pile of loose shells she'd amassed onto the floor. "Definitely never said I *might* have seen anything."

Reed could feel a rush of blood come to his cheeks, the warmth of impending sweat along with it. He pressed his lips into a tight line and rocked forward another inch, glancing out into the restaurant.

Nearby, a pair of servers stood in idle chatter with a bartender, all three in their mid-twenties, appearing to flirt with each other regardless of gender. Around the outside of the room most of the tables were filled, singles and couples in conversation or working their way through an early dinner.

"Gale," Reed said, careful to keep his voice neutral, "I'm very sorry if I've offended you in any way. I have spent the last two nights at crime scenes involving some of the most horrific things you can imagine and therefore seem to have forgotten my manners a bit.

"Please, if there is any way you might be able to help us catch whoever is doing these unspeakable things, I would greatly appreciate it."

From across the table Gale stopped her work on the peanuts, her gaze boring into him, seemingly sizing him up. She remained that way a long moment, the folds of skin around her eyes creased tight, before nodding once in response to whatever she was trying to decide.

"Thank you," she said, her fingers going back to work while she continued to maintain eye contact. "When you first called me, and even started offering me bribes to meet, I couldn't tell how serious you were taking this."

"I assure you, this is my top priority," Reed inserted.

"I don't just mean the case," Gale said. "Of you caring about that I have no doubt. I meant about you coming out here to meet with an old woman and hear what she had to say."

The confusion that splayed across Reed's face was far more pronounced than any contrived response he could have come up. He genuinely had no idea what she was speaking about, letting her see the reaction on his face, hoping it would induce her to explain.

"It didn't always used to be this way you know," Gale began, her gaze still meeting his. "When my husband, God rest his soul, and I first moved into The Bottoms, it was a respectable place. Poor, for sure, but it didn't have all the stuff you see around there nowadays, the drugs and violence and whatnot."

As she spoke a look of disgust passed over her features, her voice rising to match it.

"Began in the late eighties, early nineties, things slowly starting to decline. Gangs showing up, businesses getting robbed, closing their doors and never looking back."

She paused a moment, moving her attention out the window behind Reed, her eyes glassing over. For a long moment she fought to keep her face from crinkling into a sob.

When she spoke again her voice was clear, though her eyes remained rimmed with moisture.

"I'm telling you this so you know, that place used to mean something, and it still does to a lot of us old timers. I don't know who is the one doing this right now, but I tell you, I'm not so certain it's a bad thing."

Of everything she could have said, Reed was reasonably certain nothing would have surprised him more. His cheeks puffed out as he pushed the air from them, his eyes widening.

"Mrs. Pearlman, Gale, are you telling me the people of The Bottoms are supporting vigilante justice?"

There were a handful of additional things Reed could have said, giving her the full litany of standard police statements about letting them handle things, but decided to let it pass. Any concerns he had had an hour before about her cooperating with law enforcement were only now heightened, raised by her latest statement.

"No," Gale said, twisting her head at the neck in a shake of disagreement, "I'm saying we support justice. That's the reason I'm sitting here with you now, and it's the reason I don't feel real bad about what happened to that boy the other night. Or the one last night."

Over the course of no more than a minute, Reed felt his reaction traverse the full circle from shock to realization. As salacious as the statements were, they weren't an insight into the greater community or even a sweeping condemnation of the CPD, they were the thoughts of a woman that was longing for the old days, someone that had romanticized the past to a point of golden nostalgia in her mind.

With that realization came a bit of peace, letting his shock and hostility bleed away, though maintaining his pose across from her, careful not to offend.

"Gale," he repeated again. "What did you see outside that house?"

Chapter Eighteen

Half a dozen homemade pork links sat on the passenger seat of the car, filling every nook and cranny of the space with the smoky aroma of meat. It permeated upward through the thin paper sack they were wrapped in, steaming up the window, driving Billie mad.

Reed could see her stomping back and forth in the rearview mirror, her tongue flicking out, one long unending whine spurting from her. The sound of her paws rubbing against the plastic on the seat reverberated in his ears, the sedan rocking with her perpetual movement.

"Not yet," Reed said, sliding the car to a stop two doors down from the home of Edwin Mentor. Leaving the sausages in place he took up the long lead from the well of the passenger seat and exited, clipping it onto Billie's collar and pulling her out.

"Come."

Just a single word spoken in the correct tone and all thoughts of the sausage were gone. Billie dropped any pretense of even knowing they existed, bolting from the car and standing beside Reed, awaiting instruction.

Attaching the opposite end of the leash to his belt, Reed said, "Search."

On his first day of training he had made the mistake of attempting to hold the lead, wrapping it through his palm. The instructor had seen the error right off but refrained from saying anything, letting Billie almost break his hand as a manner of teaching a lesson.

Reed had not repeated the misstep again.

Attaching the lead to his waist gave him enough weight to anchor against her, though the real purpose of the long lead was to allow her the freedom to roam. For the sake of the crime scene, and anybody that may be passing by, he couldn't allow her complete autonomy, though in truth that would be best.

This was a decent enough second though.

The moment the command passed his lips Billie dropped her nose to the ground, drawing in deep breaths, the sound passing out into the brisk afternoon air.

While she worked Reed scanned the neighborhood around him, seeing it for the first time under the light of day. Somehow it appeared even shabbier than he remembered, the illumination serving to make visible many of the inconsistencies that were masked by darkness.

Mentor's home was one of a string of seven exactly like it, low-slung structures meant for single families. All followed the same basic design and appeared to have the same sort of tenants, each losing battles with time and disrepair.

On the opposite side of the street a trio of multi-story brick buildings appeared to be empty, many of them with broken glass for windows, jagged shards hanging down. Graffiti of various colors covered the bottom floor of the brick, tapering off as the buildings grew out of reach overhead.

A tug on the line drew Reed forward as Billie continued to work, her ears and tail all lying flat, her nose propelling her forward.

The move to Billie was one Reed hadn't been crazy about upon returning to active duty, but it was the only way he could come back to work under the requirements of the department. Regulations mandated that all active investigators work with a partner, whether it be human or canine.

Faced with the options of a dog or a new recruit fresh off the beat,

Reed had chosen Billie, preferring to work with a dog over having to train someone from the ground up.

At least that's what he tried to tell himself.

In the time since, he had come around on the unique skill set the animal brought to him, gaining a new appreciation for her ability to track. Unlike humans, born with five million scent receptors, Billie was blessed with more than two hundred twenty five million individuals synapses in her nose that could detect and differentiate an odor.

It allowed her to paint an internal image of something using smells the way a human with perfect vision might with their eyes. She could not only tell if someone had passed through, but tell the previous people that had been through and how many times their pets had relieved themselves as well.

Having worked with the Marines in a prior life, Billie had far superior training to many others in the precinct, able to alert on over two dozen possible explosives.

For the purposes of this crime scene though, Reed only needed her to do something much simpler.

Confirm Gale Pearlman's story.

Giving Billie a fair bit of lead, Reed steered her past the standing crime scene tape to where the murder took place, watching as she covered every inch of it.

The Cadillac was still parked in the same place it had been, the stretch of concrete in front of it stained red in places with dried blood. The presence of so much water the night before had washed much of it away, though residue still covered the entire ten foot square swath between the yard and house save a few large blotches in the center, where Mentor's body had once been.

At scenes in the past, when blood was pooled into a small location, Reed had seen it grow sticky and form mildew, attracting flies by the thousands. Here it did neither, the wide spread and cool temperatures allowing Billie to work her way over it without disturbing a thing.

With his hands deep in the pockets of his sweatshirt Reed stood and watched, waiting as Billie made a complete inventory of the scene, content that should she ever come across anything again that had been present there she would alert him.

It took almost ten minutes for her to find what Reed was hoping she might, picking up the scent just shy of the blotches in the center of the space and following it back towards the road. Reed felt his pulse increase as she picked up speed and traveled down the length of the driveway and out across the street, heading fast for the alley.

"I saw someone watching, from across the street," Gale had said. "Maybe a week or more before it happened. At the time I thought it odd, but a lot of vagrants hang out over there."

"So what made this particular one stand out?" Reed had asked.

"Because this one," Gale explained, leaning forward, dropping her voice into a conspiratorial tone, "was sitting on the fire escape."

Reed could feel his belt pulled taut as Billie drug him forward, gaining momentum, her own senses accelerating as she bore down on the target. She increased her pace to just shy of a jog before sliding to a stop.

Glancing up at Reed, she moved in a quick circle, almost puzzled as she sat back on her haunches.

The search was over. The scent was gone.

"Good girl," Reed said, reaching out and rubbing Billie behind the ears, his attention aimed at the wrought iron landing on the fire escape above. Standing ten feet off the ground and back eight feet from the corner of the building, it would be the perfect place for someone to conduct surveillance, masked from the world outside.

The fact that Gale Pearlman had even noticed was nothing but dumb luck, a woman out walking her dachshund that just happened to be at the optimal angle and look up at the right time.

For Reed, the tip was an enormous score, well worth the cost of a barbecue dinner. It told him that someone had in fact stalked Edwin Mentor with the intention of putting him down, and had probably done the same with A.J. Wright. It provided the possibility that DNA evidence might be up on the landing somewhere, perhaps attached to the cardboard he could see piled in the corner.

It also meant that whoever was behind this was meticulous and had a significant head start.

"Come on," Reed said, tugging Billie back towards the car. "Let's get the criminologists out here to take a look at that balcony."

Billie balked a moment, remaining on her haunches. Reed pulled once more on her to no avail, the dog remaining rigid. She stayed like that a long moment, meeting his gaze, before sliding her tongue out over her nose.

A smile pulled up the left side of Reed's mouth as he read her directive, nodding in agreement. "Yeah, let's go see if we can't get you some of those sausages, too."

Chapter Nineteen

Any lingering effects of the canned espresso were now long gone. Reed could feel his eyelids starting to droop, his body fighting back against the odd schedule that had been forced upon it in the preceding days.

The abnormal hours themselves weren't the sole source of his exhaustion, more the proverbial final straw that was breaking the camel's back. For three months now he had lived a vampire's lifestyle, interacting with the world almost exclusively during nighttime hours, having as little human contact as possible.

Mixed in was a healthy avoidance of sleep for fear of what might be lying in wait for him, a bout of self-imposed guilt that would make any Catholic mother proud preying on his subconscious.

The combined effects caused him to do something he hadn't in over five years, not since his early days of pulling double shifts on patrol. Unable to summon the requisite strength on his own to keep moving forward with any degree of clarity, he went past the occasional canned espresso and called on the coffee dispenser in the basement of the coroner's office, watching as the muddy brown liquid filtered down into the paper cup held beneath it, a healthy swath of steam rising from it. The oversized machine rumbled as it dispensed the liquid, the entire thing shaking in place, before the stream stopped, a low hiss emitted in its wake.

Making a face, Reed pulled the cup from the bottom rack and wrapped both hands around it, carrying it out in front of him towards Solomon's office at the end of the hall. Halfway there he raised it enough to blow across the top of the coffee before taking a drink, an involuntary wince crossing his features.

"What the hell is that smell?" Solomon asked as he entered, peering up at him over the glasses perched on the end of her nose. She was still dressed in her lab coat and apron, right out of the examination room.

Reed held the cup up for her by way of an explanation, dropping himself into the same chair he'd used just a day before.

"So that's what that rumbling was a little bit ago," Solomon said, disapproval on her face as she looked at the drink in his hand. "That's the first time I've ever known anybody to be brave enough to give that thing a try."

Chancing one more drink, Reed let the caustic beverage slide down his throat, the burn reminding him more of high-proof whiskey than coffee. Under any other circumstances he would have poured it out and flushed it away to ensure no other living creature stumbled across it, but at the moment the need for caffeine overpowered any lingering qualms about taste.

"Tastes like it, too," Reed said, placing the cup on the floor beneath his chair, sliding it back out of range from his heels. "What were you able to find today?"

Reed realized after asking that the question sounded pointier than intended, though Solomon seemed to brush by it without noticing.

Busy people tended to be less caught up in such things. As Riley used to say, manners were a creation of the bored.

Pushing the glasses up a bit higher on her nose, Solomon spread the file across both thighs. She flipped through two pages fastened at the top with steel pins before dropping them back into place.

"Two requests for rush jobs in as many days, Detective," Solomon said as she scanned the top page. "When I got here this morning and was told another was en route for the 8th, I admit I was a little peeved. Once I got in there though, I understood why."

The words, serving as an opening, did more to jolt Reed's system than any amount of coffee could have. He leaned forward and rested his elbows on his knees, waiting for her to continue.

In the chair opposite him, Solomon looked up from the file and said, "Don't take this the wrong way, because I don't imagine you appreciate someone telling you how to do your job any more than I do, but all signs point to you having a serial killer on your hands."

Reed felt his jaw drop open an inch as he stared back, not sure how to respond to the statement.

"And from what I saw in there this afternoon, he's escalating."

The only thing that could have possibly hit Reed harder than the first sentence was the second, smacking him in the solar plexus. He remained still a long moment to mask any reaction as the shock fell away, his mind taking back over, processing what he'd heard.

"Start at the beginning."

Pausing a moment, Solomon nodded in approval at his response and said, "COD: again a stab wound that pierced the aorta, TOD: best guess would be twelve to sixteen hours before I opened him. ME on the scene marked it at eleven last night, which I would agree with."

She rattled off the information without glancing down at her notes. "That's where the similarities to the previous night stop. On this victim there are two lacerations across the abdomen, not enough to disembowel but pretty close. Had the attacker wanted to, he easily could have."

Reed thought about the final statement, fitting it in with the report from the night before. "So he was playing with him?"

"Seems that way," Solomon said. "I didn't have time to run a full tox screen, but took a look at his blood and found adrenaline levels to be through the roof. This guy was in serious pain when he finally passed."

The familiar sense of dread heightened with Reed. The killer was evolving, improving on his craft.

"Defensive?" Reed asked.

"No," Solomon said. "Though I did find dirt under the fingernails of both hands, as if he'd been trying to crawl back away."

Focusing his attention on the opposite wall, Reed pinched his brow in tight and remembered the scene from the night before. He had extensive photographs that were by now waiting on his desk, images covering every angle of the scene.

From what he remembered, footprints from the dog were the predominant thing visible in the dirt.

He made a mental note to check for signs of flight.

"What about the arms?"

"What a mess," Solomon muttered, shaking her head. "I'm sure you noticed on site that bleeding was heavier on the right side than the left?"

Again Reed furrowed his brow, thinking back. "Yes," he said. "And that's the one the dog had gotten hold of. There was a trail of blood from the body out through the dirt."

"That's because the right one was removed while the victim was still alive," Solomon said. "The veins and capillaries were still open, blood loss in the tissue surrounding the area almost complete."

"And the other was more window dressing than anything else," Reed finished, working the sequence out in his mind. Once more he put himself back at the scene, thinking of what he saw.

"Dog did a number on the arm, too," Solomon said. "Tore away a pretty good chunk of meat, scratched the hell out of the skin."

"Damn," Reed muttered, his eyes pulling tight in a wince. "Man's best friend, huh?"

He had caught a glimpse of the dog under the guard of animal control, the pit bull no more than half the size of Billie. Before finishing the thought he pushed it away, shuddering even at the idea of her jaws going to work on a victim.

"So one arm before death, one after," Reed said, fixing things into place in his mind. "Same murder weapon?"

"That I don't know," Solomon said, "but I put some side-by-side photos in there for you comparing the two victims. It's impossible to tell one knife wound from another with a complete degree of certainty, but I can tell you they are very consistent.

"Almost identical, in fact."

Again Reed nodded. He had expected that to be the case, the other similarities too pronounced to be coincidence.

"Okay," he said, running his hands down the front of his pants. "Anything else?"

"Yes, actually," Solomon responded, turning in her chair and taking up a small evidence bag from the desk behind her. It was made of clear plastic, an ID tag filled in with ink along the top. She held it between her index and middle finger, extending it towards him.

"I dug this from the victim's trachea, so far down I'm not surprised the ME missed it on the scene. I didn't even notice it until I saw some scraping along the inside of the throat."

Reed accepted the item and held it up towards the light, the overhead bulb shining through the plastic. At the bottom of it was a small metal disc, the diameter of a nickel, though much thicker and non-uniform in shape.

"Scraping?" Reed asked. "Meaning it was forced there?"

"That would be my guess," Solomon replied. "Looked to be inserted post-mortem, meaning it wasn't swallowed, and there was no way the victim did it to himself."

Chapter Twenty

"Hey, buddy, can you hold that a second?"

The Boat Man put a friendly smile on his face as he said the words, jogging forward to the gate. In one hand he carried an oversized lunch cooler with nothing inside, the other a gym bag filled with just enough crumpled newspaper to give the item some shape. Both bounced by his side as he shuffled forward, his boots dragging against the concrete underfoot.

The man holding the door did so without a word, a look of exasperation on his face as he watched the Boat Man grow close. When he was just a few feet away he shoved it out wide, the Boat Man catching it with his shoulder and stepping through.

"Thanks."

The man already had his back turned, moving on into the building.

Three times a day the Midwestern Paper factory made a shift change, once at seven in the morning, again at three in the afternoon, a final time an hour before midnight. Operating in three even groupings, the place stayed fully operational regardless of hour, the only difference being reduced manpower at night.

Under optimal conditions, the Boat Man would have preferred that this target went first, but he had to wait until he cycled onto the night shift for it to happen. The man's living situation was too crowded to ensure invisibility and as far as could be ascertained, he very rarely went anywhere that wasn't home or work.

If only that had always been the case.

Peeling himself away from the foot traffic flowing in, the Boat Man hooked a right into the restroom and locked himself in the back stall. There he remained while the last few stragglers of the afternoon shift filtered out, shedding both the bag and the cooler, stowing them along the wall behind the toilet.

Every moment he had been in possession of the items he had worn gloves, ensuring that no physical evidence of any kind could tie him to them.

Considering what he was about to leave behind, he highly doubted anybody would care about a duffel bag and a miniature Igloo.

Stepping out from the stall, he stopped and peered at himself in the mirror. The look he had put together would blend well, a far cry from his actual appearance in the off chance there was a camera anywhere on the grounds.

Raising his hands to the brim of the Browns cap he wore on his head, he adjusted it a half inch lower on his forehead, bringing it down to touch the top of his yellow safety glasses. Thick black curls spilled out between the two, the wig hot and itchy, though a necessary precaution.

Reaching down to his side he tapped the fingernails of his right hand against his hip, the hollow sound of the scabbard tucked beneath his clothes echoing out.

It was time.

Exiting from the restroom, the Boat Man crossed the yellow safety line on the edge of the factory floor, headed for the rear of the building. Beside him, three large conveyor systems fed finished cardboard boxes into stacks, a machine wrapping them tight in green plastic strips for hauling. Moving amongst them were a dozen employees, all dressed in the same jeans and flannel look he now sported, nobody glancing his way as they got to work for the night.

Keeping his right leg extended straight, the Boat Man walked with a bit of a limp as he moved through the main hull of the building, past the inking stations and the baler where two kids fresh out of high school fed scraps to be repurposed for use again.

It was the third time the Boat Man had been inside Midwestern, using the same ruse each time before to gain entry. In a place as large as the factory, with over a hundred people coming in and out at every shift, it wasn't difficult for him to gain entry, blending seamlessly with the masses.

Spread out over the last couple of months, the Boat Man had gotten a clear idea of where everything was located inside, of the best place to find his target.

Throwing a wave to one of the young guys working the baler, the Boat Man walked through the oversized doorways leading from the main factory floor into the storage room in the back. The whining call of machinery fell away as he passed through, absorbed by the concrete block separating the two sides.

What was just a few feet earlier noise and heat fell away to cool silence, the room half the size of the factory floor, stacked floor to ceiling with enormous rolls of raw paper. Stripes of black rubber crisscrossed the floor from the modified forklifts used to transport the product, a series of railroad cars positioned along the back wall, ready to move out as soon as they were loaded.

A smile crossed over the Boat Man's face as he made one pass through the room, making sure everything was in order, before settling himself into position.

All he had to do now was wait.

The Boat Man was good at waiting.

Chapter Twenty-One

Through some sort of merciful twist in karmic logic, Reed was unable to dream, or rather, unable to remember them. He was fully aware of the fact that he had a subconscious that was far more active than the common person, for almost without fail when he awoke he found himself in a worse state than when he'd fallen asleep.

This evening was no different.

The sky outside his window was still dark as his eyes opened. The sheets beneath him were wet, the thin fabric sticking to his skin, beads of sweat streaming down the side of his face. Most of the blankets had been balled into a tangle at the foot of the bed, twisted into a heap that looked like he had been thrashing just moments before.

From the doorway, a soft whine met his ears, pulling his attention from the world outside to a pair of moist circles standing three feet off the floor. There they remained, unblinking, as he ran a hand back over his forehead, pulling sweat away and wiping it against the bed beneath him.

"Hey, girl," he said, his voice betraying the exhaustion he felt.

At the sound of his voice Billie took the initiative, stepping forward into the room, her toenails clicking against the hardwood floors of the house. She walked up alongside the bed and rested her chin on the mattress, her nose cool and wet against his skin.

Curling his arm at the elbow, Reed buried his fingers into the thick black hair behind her ears, low moans escaping her as he kneaded the skin back and forth.

"Care to tell me what the hell had me sweating like a pig in here?" Reed asked, not expecting an answer, appreciating the effort as Billie forced her eyes back open to look at him.

"No? How about how many times a week you stand there watching over me?"

Reed waited a full moment for a response he knew wasn't coming before raising himself to a seated position. Sleep was now gone, any chance at returning to it futile. His right hand he kept on Billie's head, the left he used to rub the crust from his eyes as he turned and focused on the glowing red clock face beside the bed.

Half past two in the morning.

Less than three hours since he had lain down to sleep.

Kicking away the last bits of blanket around his feet, Reed rose and pulled on a pair of gym shorts, the floorboards of his farmhouse creaking as he made his way through it. Behind him he could hear Billie following him into the kitchen, her feet beating out a steady beat.

Starting in the pantry, Reed filled the silver bowls on the floor by the sink with kibble and water, watching for a moment as Billie fell to her breakfast. He watched her attack the food with vigor, feeling his own hunger rise within.

Most nights they would be in the middle of a shift, the both of them breaking for food, their internal clocks telling them this evening should be no different.

Putting on a pan of water to boil eggs, Reed extracted a Gatorade from the fridge and sat down at the kitchen table, resuming the same position he'd been in just a few hours before. Splashed across the polished surface were the conglomerated effects of two case files, the photos nothing short of horrific as they stared back up at him.

He was making progress, though it seemed to have a clear ceiling on it that Reed was fast approaching.

Both murders had been committed in the same fashion, with only moderate variation on the MO. The fact that the second one seemed far more vicious than the first concerned him, though he had tried to reason with himself that the escalation could have been caused by anything, ranging from a personal connection to somebody walking by before he could finish with Mentor.

The only way to know for sure would be the appearance of a third body, something he desperately hoped didn't happen, no matter how much harder it made his investigation.

It was the agreed opinion of both he and the coroner that the same weapon had been used twice, which if nothing else indicated it was only a single person. He hoped that the criminologists were able to pull something from the balcony perch that could be useful, or at the very least confirm that supposition, though he wouldn't know until morning and wasn't holding his breath.

Thus far the guy had been spotless. There was no reason to believe that would suddenly change.

The water on the stove started to boil as Reed drew himself up and dropped a trio of eggs into it, pulling it from the heat and covering the pot. On the floor beside him Billie finished up the last of her meal, shoving the empty dish along the ground, her muzzle buried deep into the corner of it, trying to get out every last morsel.

Remaining standing, Reed folded his arms and put his back against the counter, waiting for his eggs to finish as he stared at the mountain of paperwork across from him. So far the scenes had given him little to work with, almost everything he knew originating with the bodies themselves, which practically begged to be noticed.

Otherwise there was nothing, meaning the connection had to be with the victims themselves.

The sound of his landline blasted Reed from his thoughts just as he was putting together an agenda for the morning, jerking his head towards the wall where it hung. As far as he could tell it was the first time the object had been used in years, the sound so foreign a growl rolled from deep within Billie as she tensed, trying to place it.

"Down," Reed said, the familiar feeling of anxiety bubbling up within him. He patted Billie atop the head to calm her nerves and stepped around her, lifting the white plastic receiver from its cradle and holding it to his ear.

"Detective Reed."

There was no way the call wasn't work related. There was no point in answering as such.

"Hey, Sugar," Jackie said, concern plain in her tone. "Everything alright over there?"

"Yeah, why?" Reed asked, deciding not to comment on the question or the hour at which it was being asked.

"Oh," Jackie replied. "I called your cell a half dozen times but wasn't getting a response. Not like you."

Again Reed contemplated reminding Jackie he wasn't on the night shift for the time being, but decided against it. "Yeah, sorry. It was in the bedroom, Billie and I were working in the kitchen."

The line fell silent for a moment, a sure signal to Reed there was a reason Jackie was calling that had nothing to do with concern for where his cell phone was currently parked.

"What is it?"

"You've got another one," Jackie said, her voice just north of a whisper. "Midwestern Paper. Call just came in a few minutes ago."

Chapter Twenty-Two

A halo of light rose above the Midwestern Paper factory as Reed pulled up, a mixture of multiple hues, each refracting off the trees and the front of the building, rising into the night.

"Oh, shit," he muttered, easing the sedan into the back of the lot and taking up the short lead from the passenger seat.

"You ready to clear a path for me?" he asked over his shoulder, Billie moving back and forth in answer to his question.

Opening the back door just halfway, Reed reached in and attached the clip to Billie's collar, holding her tight as she jumped to the ground, head already aimed at the commotion by the front gate. Letting his badge swing free against his chest, Reed fell in beside her.

The Midwestern Paper factory was something Reed had driven by a hundred times in his life but had never been inside of. Located on the edge of Franklinton and neighboring Hilltop, it employed a fair number of people from both, making and distributing boxes to various frozen food corporations around the state.

Normally the place looked the part of a factory from the road, an oversized warehouse stretching several blocks long, a parking lot out front to accommodate employees. A chain link fence ran the length of the property separating the two, a single strand of barbed wire visible along the top.

Tonight it was lit up like a Christmas tree, a small handful of cruisers parked out front, their overhead lights flashing red and blue. Beyond them was the source of Reed's trepidation, presenting a new angle to the case that had not yet been a concern.

Media.

At first glance, Reed felt almost a bit of relief pass through him. Everything about the scene was wrong, from the public site to the presence of so much fanfare. It was a far cry from the previous killings, ones that felt meticulous in their bid for privacy.

There was no way this could be the same perpetrator.

A moment later a second thought came to mind, forcing him to wonder if this was the next step in the escalation. No longer was the killer content to commit such atrocious acts, now feeling he needed an audience.

The front gate stood open as Reed approached, allowing his badge and the oversized black dog by his side to peel the crowd away. At the sight of them the scads of employees and media that were grouped up cleared a path, casting sideways glances as they walked through.

Just once a brave media member tried lobbing a question his way, but he pressed on as if he hadn't heard it.

On the opposite side of the cage were a half dozen uniforms, among them Gilchrist. He nodded in response to Reed as he came near, moving away from the pack and lowering his voice.

"Fair warning, the captain is looking for you," Gilchrist opened.

Reed felt his eyebrows rise. "Grimes is here?"

"Just stepped away," Gilchrist said, "should be back out any second."

"Hmm," Reed replied, absorbing the news. There were only a couple of reasons that a captain would be on the scene at such a late hour, all of them bad. "What have we got?"

"I don't know exactly," Gilchrist said, again checking the crowd for anybody that might be listening in. "Greene and a couple other senior patrol guys are back there to secure the scene. He sent me a text message a few minutes ago that said it's ugly, and it's definitely another one."

"Great," Reed said, lifting his chin towards Grimes making his way forward. "Here he comes, you might want to disappear."

Gilchrist gave a quick glance over his shoulder and seeing Grimes approach nodded his farewell, heading off into the crowd a moment before the captain arrived.

"You just get here?" Grimes said, glancing down at Billie as he came to a stop near Reed, folding his arms over his chest.

"Yeah," Reed said. "Jackie called twenty minutes ago, we rolled right up."

Again Grimes glanced between them, bags drooping beneath his eyes, a frown set on the lower half of his face. "I think she called you at the same time the chief called me."

The questions of how the chief had known and why she called Grimes both popped into Reed's mind, but he let them pass. He had more pressing matters at hand, things that more directly concerned him.

"How bad is it?"

The frown on Grimes face moved a bit deeper as he took another step or two away from the gate, motioning for Reed to do the same. "Bad," he confirmed. "I obviously didn't see the other two scenes, but I'm guessing it has to be on par, if not worse."

Everything about the area, from the people clumped outside to the state of Grimes, had already told Reed as much. After two consecutive nights of seeing the horrors, he liked to believe he was as steeled as he could be to it.

A wave of raised voices drew both their attentions out towards the parking lot, Billie giving a single tug on the leash, leaning that direction as well. It took a moment to locate the source of them, another rash of media having arrived, boom mics and lights visible overhead.

"I'm guessing they're the reason you're here?" Reed asked without looking away from the spectacle.

"They are," Grimes said, a mix of exhaustion and disdain in his voice. "This many employees on site, no way to issue a gag order to everyone. Somebody over at KCBS gave the chief a call, she in turn called me."

"Hmm," Reed said, nodding, not the least bit surprised. "She tell you how to handle the media?"

"Not exactly," Grimes replied, "but she let it be known that diplomacy would benefit everyone involved."

The corner of Reed's mouth drew back a fraction of an inch before returning to place, a natural reaction to the captain's insinuation that anything coming from the chief had been handled in such a hands-off manner.

"So she told you how to handle the case."

"Not exactly," Grimes repeated, giving one long look before taking a step forward towards the crowd ahead, "but she let it be known that this better get solved fast."

"I guess that means our seventy-two hour window of solace is gone?"

Grimes left Reed standing with Billie, moving on to make a statement without answering the question.

He didn't have to.

Chapter Twenty-Three

The smell of wood pulp and dye filled Reed's nostrils as he walked through the hub of the factory. Beside him, the oversized lines used for producing boxes stood silent, resembling extras from a *Transformers* movie set, all steel and rollers assembled in odd patterns. The place had an almost eerie vibe to it as he stepped forward, following the directions the officer at the front door had given him.

Reed imagined it was the first time in ages that the place had been so quiet, the buzz of overhead lights replacing the usual pandemonium of machinery.

Flood lights poured from the enormous opening separating the main floor from the storage warehouse in the back, beckoning him forward. In the distance he could see a few silhouettes moving back and forth, a larger crowd having already gathered than the previous two scenes combined.

Pushing a heavy breath out through his nose, Reed stepped through the gateway demarcating the two halves of the building, the bright light and silent mechanical structures replaced with dim hues and floor-to-ceiling stacks of brown rough stock.

The new scent of paper came to him, intertwined with the familiar coppery odor of blood.

The room stretched almost eighty yards in length and half that in width, though all of the activity within was concentrated into a twenty foot square in the middle of the space. Around it were a handful of uniforms, a perimeter already established. Within the yellow police tape were three crime scene techs, each clothed in white paper suits.

Somebody had been quick to bring in the criminologists, no doubt the same person that had called on Grimes. Any hope Reed had had of trying to figure this out before it went out over the airwaves was gone, a classic case of trickle down law enforcement.

The media had leaned on the brass, who would now be leaning on him.

Opting against joining the circus going on nearby just yet Reed switched out the leads on Billie's collar, attaching the end of the longer one to his waist. He left one hand gripped tight on the nylon cord for extra support and said, "Search."

The order seemed to come as a welcome surprise to the Belgian, her body jumping from a low-energy state into a poised crouch, her nose dropping towards the floor. Starting just inside the corner of the room, she swung her nose over the polished concrete floor, great deep breaths that echoed inside the warehouse.

Given the surface she was working with, Reed hadn't expected it to take long for a confirmation. Even without having seen the victim yet, he knew from the presence of Grimes and the extreme exposure already being granted that his killer had been there.

Just the same, he wanted Billie to verify his supposition.

His canine unit trainer had said that while she would never lose a scent once she had encountered it, the more it could be reinforced the better. It took just over three minutes for Billie to hit something familiar, her entire posture changing the moment it met her muzzle. Her pose switched from searching to tracking, leaning forward, tugging Reed onward.

Toenails scraped against the floor as she moved in a serpentine pattern up the back of the room, winding her way through stacks of paper. Several of the officers standing by turned and openly stared as she moved past the scene without ever glancing over, her entire purpose focused on the trail laid out on the ground.

At the far end of the room, she led Reed in a sweeping loop that brought them back towards the center of the warehouse. The trail popped in and out of every tight nook in the room before moving on, Billie never slowing her pace as she followed it.

"He was casing the place," Reed said, staring up at the towers of paper waiting to be processed. From each corner he looked out over the room, checking the view it afforded, the angle of approaching foot traffic.

The trail took ten minutes to follow, the killer having made a loop and a half over the space before settling down to wait. A significant amount of time must have passed as the scent appeared strong there, Billie taking a long time to decipher the pattern.

Once she did, she angled her body towards the crime scene, again pulling forward with urgency.

"Heel," Reed snapped, cutting her off halfway there, extra bass in his voice for emphasis. The sound of it drew over the stares of all seven people, Billie drawing to a halt and lowering her backside by his feet.

"Good girl," Reed said, reaching down and rubbing her ears, ignoring most of the stares.

He walked forward to the closest officer and nodded, Billie remaining on her haunches behind him, the long lead pulling taught. "Officer Greene."

"Detective," Greene replied, glancing at him and back to Billie before turning to face forward, his arms folded across his chest.

"What have we got so far?" Reed asked, finally seeing the crime scene for the first time.

Standing silent fifteen feet away was what looked like a forklift, the tongues on the front having been swapping out for a pair of elongated paddles. Reed guessed from the size and shape they were used for clamping and moving the rolls stacked nearby.

On the floor beside it was the victim, first appearances seeming to fit exactly with the established MO.

The man appeared to be in his early thirties, dressed in jeans and what had once been a grey t-shirt, judging by the sleeves. A pair of work boots covered his feet, their toes aimed at the ceiling.

Across his torso was a trio of wicked slashes, almost a complete disembowelment as bits of intestine rose forth, resting atop the t-shirt. In his chest was a single puncture wound, a deep gouge that painted his entire upper quadrant in blood so thick it was almost black.

As with Mentor, his right arm was severed mid-forearm, though the left one appeared to be intact.

"Victim's name is Mason Durell, friends call him Mace. He operates a roll truck here."

"Same shift every night?" Reed asked.

"No," Greene said, adding a shake of his head. "Warehouse foreman said the whole place runs on a swing shift, week on each of the three, rotating through."

Reed nodded, glancing down at Billie. The information fit with what she had just found, the killer having to do some reconnaissance on the spot, unable to survey the place for days on end.

"Who found him?" Reed asked.

"This time of day, there's only a single driver on," Greene said, reciting the information from memory, his attention still aimed forward. "He was found by a janitor pushing an industrial vacuum through the place."

The information brought a scowl to Reed's face, the realization that evidence could have been sucked up without even knowing it. "What time was that?"

"Discovery was made less than an hour ago, though it's unclear exactly how long he'd been here before being found."

Another look around the place confirmed that. At this time of day, the likelihood of there being anybody passing by would be slim. The perpetrator had likely known that, accommodating for it in planning both the action and the getaway.

"Any cameras?"

"Just out front, on the mechanical stuff," Greene said. "Used for quality control, that kind of thing."

It too was in line with what Reed was expecting, though the news did nothing to soften the scowl on his face.

"Let me guess, nobody saw anything unusual?" Reed asked, letting a bit of sarcasm seep into his voice.

If it had been heard there was no acknowledgement from Greene, his face remaining impassive. "Some uniforms from the 16th have everybody that was on shift up front in the cafeteria. They're sifting through them now, trying to see if anything useful can be gleaned out."

Instinctively, Reed turned at the waist and glanced over his shoulder, nothing visible but stacks of paper.

Without cameras, he didn't expect a lot of information to come out one way or another. There was no doubt the killer had been inside, having gained entry without drawing attention at some point before making his way to the warehouse and committing the crime.

Taking a step back, Reed again shifted his focus over the room, his gaze settling on the row of railroad cars along the back wall. He took in the stripes of rubber on the floor and the pattern they seemed to lay out, covering every facet of the room, always ending along the far wall, makeshift ramps leading up into the enclosed spaces.

A thought occurred to him, sparking in the back of his mind, his hand tugging on the lead, drawing Billie to her feet.

"Excuse us, Officer."

Chapter Twenty-Four

Reed could feel the stares on his back as he led Billie towards the towering roll-top in the back corner standing closed. The combined weight of them seemed to burn between his shoulder blades as he went for the single door beside it and pushed through, the metal release bar on it squealing in protest, echoing through the room.

A moment later the dim light from within was extinguished, cool night air washing over his skin.

A concrete ramp descended away from the roll-top, a loading dock beside it with room for two semi trailers backed in. Behind them the front engine of a rail car sat silent, waiting to pull away the loaded freight behind it.

"Search."

On cue, Billie once more dropped down into a crouch, canvassing the concrete ramp, using her nose to guide her back and forth over the area.

It wasn't until he had seen the layout of the crime scene that Reed had thought much about the exit strategy. Up until that point he had been focused on the point of entry and the act itself, hoping that the killer might have made a mistake, left some trail back to himself.

Once it appeared that that was not the case, he shifted to the aftermath, the moments once the deed was committed, trying to determine how the man might have gotten away.

As best he could tell, there existed only two ways in and out of the factory. The first was back out through the front entrance, which would have required him to walk back the length of the building without drawing suspicion.

Given the amount of blood present, the odds of him not having at least some small bit on him weren't good. Compounding that would have been the weapon he was carrying, much harder to stow after the fact.

That left the other option, which was to disappear out through the loading dock.

Three minutes after being given the order, Billie came across the scent, the same jolt of electricity flashing through her, propelling them both forward. Reed gave her more length on the lead, allow her to increase her pace, the trail strong in her nose.

Deep within Reed felt the same sense of excitement roil, hopeful that they might be on to something.

The path cut across the concrete expanse at the back of the building in a diagonal pattern, linking up with the railroad tracks running straight away and passing through the fence encircling the property. It followed the metal trail for over two hundred yards before cutting to the left, just at the point where the tracks began to curve towards the river.

Reed knew from years in the area that the line would link up with the major railway running alongside the Olentangy River, the waterway bisecting the city through the middle.

Leaving the evenly spaced ties of the tracks behind, Billie led him through thick weeds, the footing rocky as he stumbled to keep up. Chunks of concrete and garbage did little to faze Billie as she went, her pace never once wavering.

Any bit of hope Reed had once felt fell away as Billie pressed forward, continuing to loop away from the tracks. Out to the side he could see the lights from the cruisers and camera crews rising into the sky, hear the din of voices carrying through the night.

The path was taking them back to the parking lot.

The killer had parked right out front, walked in the building, killed Mason Durell, and then walked back to his car and drove away.

Reed fought the urge to swear as he pulled his phone from his pocket and dialed. A moment later it was answered, the voice low, the sound of muffled voices in the background.

"Gilchrist."

"Officer, this is Reed Mattox. How long are you guys on here tonight?"

There was no delay as Gilchrist processed who was calling him, no questions about the seemingly odd request. "We're on until seven. Judging by this zoo out front, maybe even longer."

The path they were on leveled out, drawing parallel with the building and continuing in a straight line. Billie continued to move fast through the low-level brush, every step confirming Reed's theory.

"I might be able to help get you away from that for a while," Reed said. "This time of year, twilight should hit around six. As soon as it does, can you check the loading dock out back, follow the railroad tracks until they bank, then loop around to the front through the weeds?"

"My partner and I are walking it now, you should be able to see the path pretty clear."

"Okay," Gilchrist replied, just the slightest hint of confusion in his voice. "And what am I looking for? You think the killer just walked out?"

Towards the back of the parking lot their path veered again, this time headed for the corner of the blacktop expanse currently half full of automobiles.

"No," Reed said, shaking his head from side to side, "I know he did."

Chapter Twenty-Five

It took every bit of self control the Boat Man possessed not to fly over the counter at the diminutive Japanese man standing across from him. One frame at a time he let the scenario play out in his mind, watching as he vaulted the glass case separating them in a single bound and drove the man's skull into it.

The man had done nothing to the Boat Man, it was only the second time he had ever seen him. The problem was that he needed some place, any place, to aim his anger, the source of it now balanced across the case between them.

Resting on a pale green cloth was the *ken* sword the Boat Man had purchased over a year before. The handle of it was wrapped tight and completely clean, the blade polished to a mirrored shine, the sheen of oil catching tiny bits of overhead light.

Three-quarters down the length of the blade on the side closest to the shopkeeper, a v-shaped notch was missing from the razor's edge, a single hairline fracture running away from it. Compared to the rest of the weapon it was an ugly blemish, the only mar on a perfect creation.

The marring had occurred as the Boat Man went to remove the right arm from his most recent victim. The man was already gone, his arm propped up for removal. At the moment just before dismemberment his body had convulsed, a final spastic tic of a dying nervous system.

The move had caught the Boat Man by surprise, throwing off his aim, missing his target and driving the end of his blade into the ground. The sound of breaking metal had entered his ears just a moment before his own cry of despair, the sound resonating with him as he finished the job and collected the chips of metal before disappearing into the night.

"How did this happen?" the man asked, his height rising no more than half a foot above the counter. His grey hair was still thick and his eyes clear, defying the sagging skin on his features.

"My dog," the Boat Man said, reciting the story he'd concocted that morning. "He ran into the table it was resting on and knocked it from its stand."

The man nodded once, looking again down at the sword. "I can't imagine a wooden floor would take a notch this large out of such a blade. What did it hit?"

Again the overwhelming urge to grab the man by the nape of his neck and smash his forehead into the glass came to mind, but the Boat Man shoved it down, forcing in long breaths.

"It caught the corner of the fireplace nearby," he replied. "The blade was no match for masonry stone."

A flicker of something behind the old man's eyes told the Boat Man he knew he was being lied to, but to his credit he chose not to press it.

Doing so would have led to a most unfortunate situation.

"I can pay you," the Boat Man said, throwing the statement out there before any more questions could be asked. "Whatever it takes to make it like new."

The old man once more looked up at him, arching an eyebrow.

"It has extreme sentimental value to me."

At that, the old man nodded, seeming to for the first time believe what he was being told. He returned his attention downward and slid his hands beneath the blade, lifting it as carefully as a parent holding a newborn. Raising it to eye level, he rotated it under the light, examining it from every angle.

"Normally I would suggest getting a new sword," the old man said, pushing on, seeming to ignore the Boat Man as he opened his mouth, about to offer rebuttal. "But since I can see you are quite attached to this implement, I might be able to patch it for you."

"Oh, thank you," the Boat Man, the words thick with exhalation, a heavy sigh passing from him.

"It will take some time though," the old man said. "I have a few in front of you, and will need to obtain some things before I can work on a blade such as this."

The Boat Man felt his jaw drop open as he heard the words. In his mind he could picture the wall at his home, the three red X's already scrawled out, the others yet to come.

The entire situation was predicated on speed and precision. There was no time for him to wait.

"Please, I can pay you whatever it takes to get it back home fast."

The old man seemed to sense the desperation coming across the counter, one eyebrow again rising. "Money isn't the issue. I told you, this is very special steel. I'll have to obtain a few things."

Heat rushed to the Boat Man's cheeks, a veneer of sweat coating his feature. His tongue felt thick in his mouth as he stared across, his heart rate rising more now than it had eight hours before.

"Please, it is very important."

A long moment passed as the old man stared unblinking back at him before nodding, returning the blade back down onto the cloth. "Tomorrow afternoon. That's the best I can do."

Chapter Twenty-Six

For the second time in as many days, Reed met Gilchrist outside the interrogation room of the precinct. Unlike their previous encounter, the look of enthusiasm was gone from his visage, replaced by a deep rooted exhaustion. His eyes appeared puffy, the skin on his face loose and drooping.

There was no need to comment on the young man's appearance, Reed quite certain his own looked much the same. Both were used to working the overnight shift, though the things they were now encountering was enough to wear down anybody.

Instead, he decided to go straight for it, looking through the glass at the large man seated behind the table. He was African-American, though his skin tone was light, like he might be of mixed race. His head was shaved clean, reflecting the lamp above, and a couple days of growth outlined his jaw bone.

Dressed in work clothes, he sat with his hands resting on the table, one knee bobbing up and down at a frenetic pace.

"Looks nervous," Reed said, seizing on the movement, motioning towards the window with his chin.

"Just anxious," Gilchrist said, weariness present in his tone. "Must have mentioned five times on the way in that he was usually the one to get his kids on the school bus."

"We think he was involved at all?" Reed asked.

"No," Gilchrist replied. "Name is Hank Winters, sheet's completely clean. Been at the factory fifteen years, married, two children."

Reed nodded, not expecting to come across anything that easy. So far the guy they were chasing had been very careful, to the point of paranoia.

Partnering with somebody didn't seem to fit.

"Were you able to get out behind the factory this morning?" Reed asked, having spent the time since at his kitchen table, scouring through the case files he had, trying to jot down as much as he could before the third one joined the mix.

So far, nothing had jumped out at him.

"We were," Gilchrist said, nodding. "Greene was still on the scene itself, so I grabbed a guy named O'Shea from the one-six I went through the academy with.

"Spent over an hour out there, couldn't find anything. A lot of junk, trash, stuff that should have been hauled off years ago, but nothing at all resembling evidence."

It too jived with what Reed had thought ahead of time. He nodded, patting Gilchrist on the shoulder. "Thanks for taking a look. Appreciate it."

Gilchrist mumbled an indecipherable response as Reed passed through the door, Winters sitting up straight in his chair as he entered.

"Mr. Winters, my name is Detective Reed Mattox. I'm sorry you had to come down here like this this morning."

In his experience when speaking with witnesses, opening with an apology seemed to work best, helping assuage any hostility they had about being pulled in. Reed paused, hoping it would have the same effect on Winters, as he slid back a chair and lowered himself into it.

"Is there any chance we can make this fast?" Winters asked, the look on his face and the tone of his voice not quite matching up. "The school bus comes for my girls at a quarter after eight and I'm always the one to walk them down to the stop."

Gilchrist hadn't mentioned an address on Winters, though if it was anywhere nearby Reed could understand his wanting to be there. By any measure he was an imposing man, the kind of person that would send a message to anybody that might be lurking, especially in rougher neighborhoods where physical encounters were more commonplace.

Without glancing at his watch, Reed nodded. "I understand, and I promise to be brief. I'm sure by now you heard what happened to your co-worker last night, so we're trying to be as thorough as possible in our search.

"Anything you know, anything at all, would be appreciated."

Winters pressed his lips together, looking over Reed's shoulder at his own reflection in the mirror, as if trying to let whoever was on the other side know he was aware of their presence. He held the pose a moment before looking back, Reed expecting to be read the riot act about having not seen anything.

It wouldn't be the first time.

"Like I told the guy last night," Winters said, "somebody tailed me inside. A lot of people work there, it might be nothing."

The last sentence confirmed Reed's prior thought, a hint that he was already wishing he had never mentioned it.

"But you seemed to think it was worth remembering," Reed said. "Why?"

A loud breath came from Winters's nose as he looked across at Reed. "Fifteen years, and I'd never once seen the guy. Even the ones I don't work with, like Durell, I know by sight."

Reed nodded, agreeing with the assessment. He'd never seen the other three cops working the scene with Greene the night before, but he would now recognize them moving forward. That was only a single meeting, fifteen years would give somebody quite a mental bank to work from.

"You didn't think he might be new, though?" Reed pressed, just to flush out the thought a little further.

"No," Winters said, the right said of his face crunching up in a squint. "A new guy would have introduced himself after I let him in, at least mentioned what line he worked on. This guy just said thanks."

"So you let him in?" Reed asked, careful not to make the question sound like an accusation.

"I did," Winters said, the slightest hint of guilt crossing his features. "He came jogging up as I approached, lunch box in one hand, bag in the other, asked me to hold the gate.

"I've been there myself, so I helped him out."

Reed felt his pulse quicken a bit. The early report had mentioned a lunch box and gym bag found in the front men's restroom, both empty, most likely props.

"What did the guy look like?" Reed asked, fighting to hide any internal enthusiasm.

For a moment Winters leaned back, fixing his gaze on the window again. He pressed his lips together and thought on it, shaking his head.

"I don't know, pretty standard. White guy, curly black hair. Had a hat pulled down low, couldn't see a lot of detail."

"Tall?" Reed asked, scribbling the information down.

"Shorter than me," Winters replied. "Maybe six foot?"

Reed nodded, continuing to write. "I know you have to get out of here, but I'd like to send a sketch artist by this afternoon if that's alright. So far you're the only person we know to have gotten a look at the guy's face."

Even if the guy had in some way altered his looks, the black curls jumping right out to Reed as a wig, he couldn't change his facial structure on the fly.

Another sigh came from Winters as he seemed to contemplate the request. "Okay," he said after several long moments, "but have them come by before three. I don't want my babies seeing them and asking questions."

Reed nodded in affirmation that the request would be met, writing it down at the bottom of the page. He hadn't thought of it before asking, but if in Winters' place he would most likely do the same.

"Just one last question," Reed asked, "and then I'll let you go. You said you only knew Durell by sight. Was there any talk around the place? Anything at all that might point out why he was targeted?"

Both of Winters' thumbs twisted up towards the ceiling as he raised his palms, a half-shrug using only his lower arms. "Like I said, he was in the back, so I didn't really know him. Never heard anything bad about him, but can't say I heard anything good either."

Chapter Twenty-Seven

From his second floor desk Reed watched Winters jog out to his truck, waiting with a cell phone pressed to his ear. Elevator music played through the line, a terrible brass rendition of *Love is a Many Splendored Thing*. He continued to stare as Winters started his truck and drove away, a plume of exhaust streaming from the tailpipe.

"Man's got a bus to catch," Reed said, drawing Billie's attention up at him, her eyes blinking in response.

"Hello? Detective Mattox?" Dr. Solomon asked over the phone, the music falling away, snapping Reed's attention towards it.

"Yeah, still here," Reed said, leaning forward and resting his left elbow on his knee, his ear pressed down atop it.

"Sorry about that," Solomon said, not a trace of apology in her voice. "I wanted to check something quickly, make sure I wasn't giving you bad information."

"Not a problem," Reed said. "To what do I owe a call this morning?"

The body of Mason Durell had been sent over less than two hours before. There was no way there had been time for a thorough examination yet, Reed willing to bet the doctor hadn't been on for more than thirty minutes at most.

"On a hunch," Solomon said, "that I will admit was no small part curiosity, I took a look inside the young man's throat when he arrived."

Reed's eyes opened wide and he raised his gaze to the opposite wall. In the commotion of the night's events he had forgotten that piece of evidence, the bag still sitting at home on his table, an oddity he wasn't sure how to handle so he had chosen not to just yet.

"Yeah?"

"It was there on this one too," Solomon said.

Pushing out a breath, Reed fell back in his chair. "Same thing as last time?"

"I don't know," Solomon said, "I gave that one to you. I'd have to see them side by side to know for sure. What I can tell you is there was definitely a coin, certainly not American, placed deep in the victim's mouth."

"Thank you," Reed said. "That is very helpful."

"I'll get to the rest of the autopsy later today," Solomon said, "another rush job request from your higher-ups downtown."

Reed didn't bother to point out the pressure levied was only about to get worse now that the media had caught the scent of the story. Thus far he had made a point of avoiding the television, but it was only a matter of time before somebody slapped a newspaper down on his desk.

Both sides disconnected the call without comment, Reed sliding the phone down on the desk.

This now made two consecutive scenes where the coin had been present, both placed there deliberately. Solomon hadn't mentioned anything from Mentor, though he guessed she would have already gone back to check, mentioning it if anything had surfaced.

"Coins," Reed muttered, his voice just audible, barely enough to raise Billie's eyebrows, her chin remaining rested on her paws. Swiveling his chair towards the aging Acer perched on the corner of his desk, he called the computer to life and opened a search engine.

His first search was simply "Rare Coins," a broad topic that brought back over two hundred million responses in less than three seconds. Reed scrolled down through the list and clicked on the first Wikipedia article, scanning it quickly, picking out a few key words before backing out to the search engine again.

The second search was for the study of rare coins, bringing up half as many responses, many of them as scattered as the previous inquiry. Once more he clicked on a single link, hoping something would jump out at him before retreating back out.

Staring at the blinking cursor inside the search engine box, Reed took a deep breath. He sat with his elbows resting on the desk, body hunched forward, his fingers drumming the wood.

It was fast apparent there was no way he could educate himself on everything he needed to know about rare coins in the span of a few minutes at the computer. His first couple of stabs had proven he was clueless on the topic, barely able to formulate proper queries, let alone decipher usable information.

The third entry he attempted was for "Someone Who Studies Coins," the first response coming back as an entry from an online dictionary with the listing for numismatist.

"What the hell is a numismatist?" Reed whispered, clicking on the hyperlink.

Numismatist. A person that collects or studies coins, medals, tokens, or paper currency.

"Nice," Reed said aloud, backing out a final time to enter "Numismatic Columbus Ohio."

His hope was for a professor at one of the universities in the greater Columbus area, perhaps a national expert that happened to reside nearby. In a crunch he could speak to someone over the phone, but his hope was to take the coins by and have someone examine them, giving him a better heading on what they meant and how he could use them to track the killer.

What he found was a close second.

Chapter Twenty-Eight

A wooden sign was affixed to the front fence running along the building, a solid metal affair with two bars stretched parallel to the ground. Four silver bolts were visible in each corner of the sign, fastening it to the bars. Made of a dark-shaded wood, the sign gleamed under the midday sun, deep-set letters welcoming visitors to the Greater Columbus Numismatic Association.

While hoping for a college professor of some sort, Reed had reasoned that the field was extremely narrow, the likelihood of any local universities having a specialist on staff being quite low. If he knew anything at all about the coins or the images found on them he might have been able to narrow his search and find a subject matter expert to help, but as it were his needs were too broad.

And it's not like he had the time or the patience to spend dealing with the traffic and congestion of making his way onto a campus.

Instead he had settled on the member association for the central Ohio region, speaking with a man that practically jumped at the opportunity to meet with him. Together they had set an appointment for early afternoon, giving Reed time to swing by the coroner's office and grab the second coin.

A quick look through the evidence locker revealed a similar object tucked away in a mass of coins pulled by the criminologists at the Mentor scene, the misshapen disk recognizable at a glance beside basic nickels and pennies.

All three were on the passenger seat beside him as he pulled into the small lot on the side of the building and parked in the closest stall. Only one other car sat in the available spaces outside, presumably from the man he had spoken to a few hours earlier.

"Stay," Reed said, taking up a note pad and the coins from the seat beside him, a low whine rolling from Billie as he climbed out. It grew louder as he walked away from the car, not once looking back.

The building was small and squat, made entirely of dark red brick with black shutters and black handrails leading along the walk towards the door. A sign matching the one out front hung by the door announcing the shop hours, just four hours a day, three days a week.

A bell rang overhead as Reed stepped inside, the smell of pungent cleaning solution hitting him full in the face. Bright lights beamed down from the ceiling spotlighting a room lined with glass cases. Atop each of them sat desk lamps and magnifying glasses, the entire space void of human life.

"Hello, there!" a voice called from the back, its owner appearing a moment later through the doorway on the opposite side of the room. "You must be the detective, come on back."

Reed passed through the room into a second one of equal size, the lights reduced to normal halogens, the cases replaced with bookshelves, the combined effect making the room seem much darker than the one before it.

"Reed Mattox," Reed said, thrusting his hand out as he stepped through, his foot sinking into a thick woven rug on the floor.

"Jim Shatley," the man replied, returning the shake, his hand weathered and dry to the touch.

On first impression, Reed guessed Shatley to be in his mid-sixties, the shop most likely a retirement hobby venture. He was dressed in jeans, a turtleneck, and a tweed jacket, a grey beard matching the hair on his head.

Combined with the handshake Reed would have ventured him a former physician of some sort.

"Thank you for meeting with me on short notice," Reed said. "I know it was an unusual request to make this morning."

"Bah!" Shatley said, waving a hand for effect. "You saw the sign on the way in. I would have been here anyway this afternoon. Talking to you for a while gives me a nice break from going through the new recruits."

Reed glanced around the room once, seeing nobody.

"New recruits are what we call coins left to us when a member passes on," Shatley said, offering the expected amount of solemnity in his face and tone. "Often times the family has no real interest in them, and they know we'll take good care of them, find them a proper home."

It was a curious choice of words, the explanation sounding more the way someone would discuss a pet than a coin collection.

Still, Reed let it pass without comment. He was there to obtain information, something that would become much more difficult if he offended his host.

"Ah," Reed said, nodding as if he understood. "So, you run the association here in Columbus?"

"That's right," Shatley said, nodding. "Been in charge here since retiring four years ago. There's not a whole lot to it, but it gets me out of the house some, keeps the wife from getting sick of me."

The last sentence was offered with a grin, an aging man's attempt at levity. Reed humored him with a matching smile, nodding as if he knew exactly what Shatley was referring to.

"So, Mr. Shatley, I apologize in advance if I seem abrupt, but as I mentioned before we are working under the clock on this. I'm sure you saw on the news last night what happened over at Midwestern Paper."

The lead-in was meant to protect them both, giving Reed an excuse for avoiding any idle chatter and allowing Shatley not to be offended by it.

"I understand," Shatley said, "and it's actually Doctor, but please call me Jim."

Reed twisted his head just a bit to hide the half smile curling up on the left side of his face, his original supposition confirmed.

"Okay, Jim," Reed said, his face falling flat, pushing right ahead. He reached into the front pocket of his hooded sweatshirt and extracted the evidence bags, extending them towards Shatley. "I was hoping you might be able to tell me what these are."

Shatley reached into the inside pocket of his jacket before accepting them, removing a pair of reading glasses and placing them on the tip of his nose. He took the bags from Reed and held them in either hand, lifting them up to the light and glancing at each in turn.

"Oh, my," he said, a bit of reverence in his voice, the tone no louder than a whisper. "Oh, my."

A long moment passed as Reed waited, allowing the man to continue looking, an expression of awe on his face.

"You've seen these coins before?" Reed asked, leaning forward, resting his elbows on his knees.

Another moment of silence passed before Shatley pulled them down from the light, resting them on either thigh. "Detective, these aren't coins at all. They're obols."

Confusion passed over Reed's features as he tried to place the word. It rang vaguely familiar in the back of his mind though he couldn't place exactly why or from where.

"Obols?" he asked, drawing a smile from the man across from him.

"Please," Shatley said, standing and leading him into the adjacent room, placing each of the bags on the closest counter. He pulled a desk lamp across the glass and turned it on, a bright white hue hitting the objects flush.

With his opposite hand he drug the closest magnifying glass over, positioning it so both men could see the enlarged detail on the items before them.

"Obols are a coin of sorts," Shatley began, his demeanor taking on the tenor of a teacher at work. "They come from ancient Greece and Sparta and were used as currency thousands of years ago."

The look of confusion grew on Reed's face as Shatley extracted a pen from the same pocket as his glasses, using the end of it as a pointer.

"See how they are of a non-uniform measure? That's because in those time they were made individually, not like the presses we have today. Every single obol ever created was unique, the same generally, but just different enough to stand apart."

Reed nodded along with the explanation, not at all sure how it related to his work, but content to let Shatley keep going until something came out he could use.

"These in particular came from Greece, part of a matching set depicting King Demetrius. I'd guess them to be from somewhere around 180 BC, right towards the end of his reign."

"What makes you say that?" Reed asked, leaning forward onto his toes to better view the obols.

Shatley arranged two of them so a different side of each coin was showing, the third left off to the side. Starting on the right he said, "See here how the head of Demetrius looks to have an elephant atop it, with tusks and trunk extended? This was late in his time as ruler, after he had brought Buddhism into the land."

He moved to the opposite edge and said, "On this side is a caduceus, the sign of reconciliation between two fighting serpents, meant to portray the peace achieved between the Greeks and Sungas."

Once more Reed nodded as if the information was directly pertinent to his case, casting his gaze upon the obols. As objects alone they were quite exquisite, small in size but detailed to a great degree. Given that they had been constructed thousands of years before, they were a testament both to design and craftsmanship.

Still, they did nothing to help his case.

"But I'm guessing this little history lesson isn't why you're here," Shatley said matter-of-factly, pushing back from the magnifying glass and disappearing into the other room.

Reed wasn't sure how to respond to the statement so he said nothing, waiting, listening as the floor in the opposite half of the building echoed with movement.

A moment later Shatley reappeared beside him, an oversized leather volume in hand. He slid the evidence bags to the side and lowered the book in their place, the light and magnifying glass both positioned above it.

"Let me guess," Shatley said, looking up from the book and turning to face Reed. "You found these inside someone's mouth, didn't you?"

There was no stopping Reed's jaw as it fell, a tremor of excitement passing through him. "How did you...?"

A knowing smile curled the corners of Shatley's mouth as he returned his attention back to the book before him. On the page open in front of them was a depiction of a painting, the image stretching across the entirety of two pages.

Reed forced his features back to neutral as he bent forward and took in the picture, the magnifying glass expanding most of the middle of it. The part it encompassed looked like a scene from a riverbank, people piling from the shore onto a ferry. At the back end of the makeshift raft was a muscled man with a pole, herding them forward.

"Have you ever heard of Charon?" Shatley asked without looking over.

"Karen?" Reed asked, his eyebrows coming together as he tried to place the name.

"No, Detective," Shatley corrected, "not Karen the woman's name, Charon the ancient Greek deity."

Even using the new frame of reference Reed drew a blank, trying in vain to grasp where the information was going.

"Greek mythology believed that the river Acheron separated the world of the living from the world of the dead. In order for those souls to get across, they had to pay a toll to Charon, the boat man that ferried them there.

"Ancient burial practices dictated that proper fare, the obol, was placed into the mouth of the deceased to ensure they made it across."

For the first time, bits of what Reed knew began to line up. It still did nothing just yet to help him track the killer, but it gave a key piece of insight into the motivation behind the crimes. From there, he might be able to work backwards to where he needed to be.

"And if they didn't?" Reed asked.

"Legend dictated that the souls must wander the shores of Acheron for one hundred years, their own form of purgatory, before being granted a ride across."

Images from movies such as *Boondock Saints* and *Troy* came to Reed's mind as he processed the information. The practice wasn't common in modern society, but it wasn't completely without precedent either.

"Tell me," Reed asked, "in your opinion, why would somebody be placing these in the mouth of their victims?"

It was generally bad form to divulge more to someone not affiliated with law enforcement than necessary, though after three bodies in as many nights, Reed wasn't entirely concerned with protocol. He now had a subject matter expert in front of him, free of any outside pressures, and wanted an unbiased opinion before leaving.

Shatley stood back a moment, crossing his arms over his chest. He curled his right hand to his chin and rested it there, his lips pursed in thought.

"As a numismatic, I can't think of a one," Shatley said. "What you're looking at there are some of the most sought after goods from antiquity."

He paused there, long enough that Reed got the hint that he would like first crack at them if they ever became available.

"After that? My guess would be whoever did this wanted to make sure his victims made their way straight to Hell the moment he was done with them."

Chapter Twenty-Nine

The final declaration from Shatley reverberated through Reed's mind as he reversed course and headed back towards the coroner's office. It bounced from one side to the next, fitting with one mental image after another, each twisting his stomach a little tighter.

Since seeing the first crime scene, Reed had been certain that the killer was out for some sort of vengeance. The crimes were too well planned, too graphic in nature, for there not to be a personal angle to them.

Hearing that the end goal though was to ensure the victims ended up on the right side of the river, residents of Hell itself, made things much worse though. It told him the end was the ultimate goal and while thus far the means had been limited to only the targets, there was nothing to say that that wouldn't change if necessary.

Reed was looking at a vendetta killer, and in his limited experience with them he had found that never did they just stop. They had to be stopped.

The parking lot of the coroner's office was half full as Reed pulled into it, remaining in the back row and letting Billie out for a few minutes. Once she was done and resumed her place in the backseat he headed inside, fast becoming a familiar face, needing only to toss a wave to the girl working the front desk before passing into the elevator.

Halfway down the basement hall a flash of white caught his attention, a sheet of paper affixed to the door of Solomon's office, a single thumbtack holding it in place. It hung flat against the closed door, no light extending out from beneath the jamb.

Detective Reed – Please meet me in the lab.

There was no closing to the note, just the single line. Reed left it in place and made his way to the end of the hall, hanging a left before pushing his way through the metal double doors that demarcated the lab.

The faint smell of formaldehyde touched Reed's nose as he stepped in, the ambient temperature dropping fifteen degrees compared to the hall outside. The sound of classical music was in the air, low, coming from a speaker system in the corner of the room.

"Afternoon, Detective," Solomon said from her post, smack in the center of the space. She wore a full examination gown and apron as she looked up at him, a plastic shield pulled down over her face. Bits of bone dust and blood spatter dotted her outfit, strewn across in a haphazard pattern.

Beside her was an older woman, her entire torso splayed open in the standard Y-cut, the flaps pulled back. Most of her internal organs had been removed, her rib cage resembling an empty cavern.

"Afternoon, Doctor," Reed replied, stopping a few feet away from the macabre scene, his hands thrust into his pockets. "Thank you for giving me the heads up this morning about the obol. It helped."

An eyebrow arched behind the mask as Solomon looked up at him. "Obol?"

"Sorry," Reed said, his mouth turning up in a half smile. "That's what the guy I met with this afternoon kept calling it, kind of stuck."

"Ahh," Solomon said, nodding as if in acceptance of his explanation. "By obol I'm guessing you mean fare for the ferry man?"

A spark of surprise passed through Reed as his eyebrows rose higher.

Until a few hours ago he had never heard the word obol, had no idea that they were placed inside of mouths.

Now, the last two people he had spoken with seemed to be experts in ancient Greek rituals.

"Very same," Reed confirmed. "Seems whoever is doing this wants to be sure these guys stay gone."

On the opposite side of the stainless steel examination table, Solomon flipped off her headlamp, the loss of luminosity doing little beside the enormous spotlight aimed down from the ceiling. She peeled the lamp from her head and laid it on the utensil tray beside her, removing the mask and doing the same.

"Sorry about asking you to meet me in here today," she said, snapping off her gloves and depositing them in the wastebasket by the head of the table.

"Not a problem," Reed said, shaking his head. Compared to what he'd seen the last few nights, the lab seemed downright tame. "I imagine you're getting behind with all these rush jobs we keep sending your way."

"True," Solomon said, the statement coming out flat and direct, "but that's not why I asked you to meet me here. I think there's something else you should see."

She motioned with a finger for him to follow her, walking across the room to a row of tables matching the one being used for the autopsy nearby. The first three in the line sat empty, nothing but bare polished steel.

On the third was an oversized surgical towel, the lower half of three different arms laid out in a line.

The trio ranged in size and shape, each one starting a couple inches below the elbow. They were positioned palm down on the towel, their chalky skin seeming extra pale beneath the overhead glare.

It took only a moment for Reed to identify all three, moving backwards in chronological order.

"All the general stuff is in the file," Solomon said. "A copy is in my office for you when you go."

She said it in a manner that indicated it was more of the same, the cause of death and weapon consistent with the previous nights.

"But this I thought you might want to see. It may be nothing more than a complete fluke, but it might not be," Solomon said, starting with the arm of Durell.

She turned it over, pointing at the pale underbelly. "Anything jump out at you there?"

The lower part of the arm had been cut clean from the upper half with a single slice, as with the prior victims, the nub ends of the ulna and radius bones visible in the center of the pink flesh.

Unlike the others though, a second cut had been inserted in the flesh just before the severed end, a diagonal slash that removed most of the skin and meat clear to the bone.

"Huh," Reed managed, looking at the wound, trying to make sense of it. "Did the first one not go clear through?"

"Oh, no," Solomon said. "It more than finished the job. This one was for pure cosmetics."

"Cosmetics?" Reed heard himself ask before even realizing it, a look of confusion on his face.

"Yes," Solomon said, her voice betraying nothing. "Like the others, this limb was removed posthumously. However, I think something happened that made him miss his target."

There was a slight trace of satisfaction that crossed Solomon's face, the tiniest indication that she was enjoying having the upper hand, drawing out her find. For a moment Reed contemplated prompting her to jump ahead to the end but decided against it, choosing to let her have it.

She was too professional to prolong things forever. She also worked underground and needed the chance at recognition whenever it presented itself.

Reed knew the feeling.

Leaving the arm of Durell palm up, Solomon moved on, turning over the arm of Wright.

"We didn't pick it up yesterday because Wright's pit bull chewed away so much of the meat around the lower arm that there was nothing left to see."

The three inches beneath the severed end had been chewed away to almost nothing, the tissue left behind a gelatinous mess that resembled the last bit of meat on a ham bone. Dirt and dried saliva coated everything, the end result of a meal interrupted.

"But when I took a look at Mr. Mentor's arm, it made sense," Solomon said. She flipped the third hand over with a bit of a flourish and stepped aside, allowing Reed to move forward and take a closer look.

The cut had been made at a diagonal angle, the weapon sheering the skin in a clean line.

Sticking out the bottom of it was a tattoo, the lower half of it visible.

"Is that...?" Reed asked, feeling his pulse tick upward, sweat flushing his back despite the cool temperatures in the room. He moved forward and twisted his body for a better view, the black ink plain against the pale skin.

"I don't know what it is," Solomon said, "but I think it might be the link between your victims. The killer seems to be making a point of crossing out that image, whatever it may be."

For three days the victims had been coming in so fast, Reed had not had the time to work proper victimology on them. Now, he might not need to, the killer finally tipping his hand.

All moisture was gone from Reed's mouth as he stared at the image, quite certain he couldn't remember seeing it before, though with only half of it present there was no way to be sure.

"We have the other half on ice in here, right?" Reed asked without looking over at Solomon.

"Already took pictures," Solomon said, her voice back to normal, her moment of triumph gone. "They're in the file on my desk. Door is unlocked."

Chapter Thirty

The Boat Man felt naked.

Despite having spent the previous months observing from afar, unarmed in his pursuits, since tasting the pleasure of carrying the sword with him he had grown attached to having it on hand. It served both as a sense of power, feeding off the fear of those who saw him with it, and as a reminder for why he was out here.

There were only a few left to go, and he needed that reminder now more than ever. He craved that connection, both to the power and to the past.

"Get you anything else?" the waitress asked as she stopped at his table, one hand pressed into her hip, the other holding a pitcher of coffee at shoulder level. Her gaze bore into him as she asked, almost daring him to say yes, her body language already leaning towards the next table in line.

"No, thanks," the Boat Man said, forcing a nervous smile into place. He looked down at the last smears of a slice of cherry cheesecake on his plate, the final dregs of coffee in his mug.

Both had been dreadful, the mere thought of forcing any more down repulsive.

"Just the check, please."

The waitress nodded, seeming to approve of his choice, turning on the ball of her foot, stringy blonde hair spinning around behind her. The Boat Man waited until she was gone before leaning back in the booth, his attention fixed on the vacant gas station across the street.

The few other cars that had congregated there for the evening left about a half hour before, leaving the same two as the last to leave, just as they were every night. A bulge of bile rose in the back of the Boat Man's throat as he sat and stared at them, their respective owners leaning against the front hoods, self-assuredness rolling off of them.

After everything that had occurred, the destruction that he had wrought, these two should be concerned at the least, scared shitless at worst. They had to have figured out what was happening, that it was only a matter of time before their turn came due.

The fact that they must have known and still didn't seem to care galled the Boat Man, his knuckles showing white as he clenched his fist. The way they were behaving meant they either didn't respect him or were trying to bait him, both of which would be grave errors on their part.

"I'll be your cashier whenever you're ready," the waitress said, slapping the check down on his table without breaking stride.

The Boat Man looked over as she passed, catching nothing more than the clicking of heels and the whiff of Aqua Net.

He glanced down once at the total circled at the bottom without moving to pull it close or extract his wallet. Instead he shifted his attention back to the window, watching the pair as they lounged, both taking the occasional pull from bottles wrapped in brown paper.

Had Mason Durell's body not given one last gasp of life, had his corpse not contorted itself at the most inopportune moment, he would now be crouched low in the shadows across the street. The young men, both of them, would be such easy targets he would be on them and gone before either even knew what happened.

Nothing more than a pair of chalk outlines on the sidewalk, two more chapters in a vow fulfilled.

The thought brought a smile to the Boat Man's face as he stared, every detail about them both, the scene, the cars they drove, already committed to memory. For the first time all night he almost appreciated what had happened to his sword, forcing him to slow down, to enjoy what he had accomplished.

For three nights in a row he had terrorized the streets of The Bottoms and nobody, from the cops to his targets, had the slightest idea who or what they were looking for. He had done such a masterful job that even now many believed he didn't exist, the next pair on his list leaving themselves exposed in the open.

Doing the math in his head, the Boat Man counted out the money for the bill, adding exactly twenty percent to it. The food and the service had both been abysmal, but it was imperative that nobody remember a single thing about him, even something as innocuous as a tip too far one direction or the other. It had been his first and last trip into the diner, there being no reason to make it memorable for a soul inside.

The Boat Man slid from the booth and stepped into the cold night air, giving one last look at the vacant station before turning away and walking off into the night. The smile returned to his face as he went, his body tingling with the sensation of impending action.

Enjoyment was never the goal, far from it in fact. Now that it was here though, it felt wrong to turn away.

She would have wanted it that way.

Chapter Thirty-One

"You back on the night shift already, Honey?" Jackie asked, looking up from her magazine, her pink lips pursed in front of her.

Reed paused a moment at the top of the stairs, his body turned to keep her from seeing his eyes pressed closed. The last thing he wanted was a lengthy conversation, the very reason he waited until after the third shift went on to come in.

"Naw," Reed said, "just following up on a few leads. Easier to use the computers at night when the place is empty."

Billie stood beside him, looking between him and Jackie, unsure if she should approach the desk on the far end of the room or remain in place. She seemed to sense from Reed's body language he had no interest in moving forward, her rib cage pressed against his calf.

"That's true," Jackie said, nodding in agreement. "You just missed Ike and Bishop. Should have the place to yourself until morning."

"Great, thanks," Reed said, glad he hadn't crossed paths with Iaconelli and his Marfan-afflicted sidekick. He paused long enough to see her raise the magazine back up, the image of Brangelina splashed across the cover, before turning and heading to his desk in the corner.

Lying flat on the seat of his chair was a single brown folder, so thin no more than a couple of sheets of paper could be inside. Without unloading anything he picked it up and thumbed through, the top sheet a rendered pencil drawing of the man Hank Winters had seen the night before.

Caucasian, with a small nose and curly hair, the person looked in no way remarkable, the same visage Reed had seen a hundred times before.

An explicative rolled out under his breath as he moved to the next pages in the file, the report from the criminologists. They had gone back to Mentor's and took a look at the balcony, finding several fibers from a coat and gloves, though nothing with any usable DNA information.

Cursing once more Reed removed the lead from Billie, allowing her to roam free as he shook the mouse to life, dropping the files he'd carried in. Extracting a single photo from the top of the stack he made his way to the copier, scanning the image and emailing it to himself.

A moment later it was up on his screen.

Placed on the green background of a surgical towel was the entirety of Edwin Mentor's arm, the two severed parts positioned as close together as possible. At a glance, the image looked as if someone had drawn a line through the middle of it in black magic marker, a clear gap separating the two halves.

Despite the splice through the middle, the image tattooed onto the skin was clear, a script letter K standing two and a half inches tall, the letters OTB stretched between the two bottom legs.

After thirteen years with the force, Reed had seen a fair bit of ink before. He had watched up close as it was applied to Riley's skin in a high-end shop in Worthington, the lines clean and the colors bright. On an almost daily basis he had seen shoddy homemade efforts, made using little more than a needle and a ballpoint pen.

More times than he could count he'd seen prison work, heavy metal inks that left thick and blurry lines on the skin.

The tattoo etched across Mentor's arm fell somewhere in the middle of the spectrum, the work neat enough to have been done in a shop, just marred enough to denote that it wasn't a top dollar establishment.

Clicking on an icon, Reed pulled up the Columbus Police Department Gang Unit database, entering his badge number and password. A few clicks got him into the repository for emblems and markings, the screen split between Mentor's arm and every known insignia in central Ohio.

Twenty minutes of scrolling revealed nothing, none of the stored images even close to the symbol he was searching for.

"Well, I'll be damned," a voice shot across the room, a mocking tone bore of faux surprise and condescension. "Look at this guy in here playing detective."

A sense of dread passed through Reed as he shifted his attention away from the screen. He remained silent as he glared at the pair of men waiting in the center foyer, both with cups of coffee in hand, smug looks on their face.

"I guess making the lead story on the evening news and the morning paper was enough to finally get you to work, huh?" Iaconelli asked, the look growing more pronounced on his face.

Since the last time Reed had seen him he had swapped out shirts for a solid red number buttoned to the lower chest, the effect making him resemble a balding Kool-Aid Man.

"I thought you guys had gone home for the night?" Reed asked. "Couple of regular nine-to-fivers around here?"

A momentary look of surprise seemed to pass between them as they exchanged a look, Iaconelli extending a hand towards him. "Nine-to-fivers. If you think such a thing exists in here, no wonder you haven't solved this thing yet."

Heat rose along Reed's back as he stared at the men, his heart rate rising, pulse starting to pound through his temples. Beside him Billie picked up on the change, pulling her chin from the floor and raising herself to a seated position.

"Could be that, or that thing he calls a partner there," Bishop said, motioning at Billie with his coffee cup, a look on his face that was almost hopeful, an attempt at humor in front of his partner.

"Yeah, well, after what happened, is it any surprise?" Iaconelli said, the two conducting the conversation as if Reed wasn't sitting nearby, couldn't hear every word they said.

The statement was more than he could bear.

Reed snapped himself up from the chair so fast the back of his knees hit against the seat, sending it hurtling backwards across the floor. The moment it happened Billie was on her feet beside him, a low growl rolling out, her fangs exposed.

"She," Reed corrected, standing off across from them, both men frozen in place. Along the back wall Jackie seemed to have assumed the same position, nobody expecting the sudden outburst.

"Not *it*, not *that thing*, she," Reed said, letting malevolence drip from the words. "Her name is Billie, she is a veteran and an officer in the Columbus Police Department."

Still every other person in the room remained in place, unmoving.

"And as for my last partner," Reed continued, his voice lowered, the tone unmistakable, "if either one of you ever say another word about her, I'll set my new one loose on you."

He stood peering across at them, checking each one in turn, almost daring them to respond.

"Got it?"

Both stood in complete silence, coffee cups in hand, jaws slack. Reed waited for any sign of a response and when it become apparent none was coming, snatched up the files from his desk.

"Come on, Billie, let's go."

Chapter Thirty-Two

Any hope at meaningful rest was short lived, Reed's phone ringing at ten minutes after six, Grimes on the other end. In no uncertain terms he was told to get down to the precinct for a six-thirty meeting, his brusque manner and clipped words suggesting it wouldn't only be the two of them sitting down together.

Allowing just enough time to let Billie out the back door and jump in the shower, the two of them met back at the car eight minutes later, both of their hair still wet from their respective chores.

Another eight after that they were parked outside the precinct, one of the first to arrive for the day, neither of them happy about it.

Taking the stairs two at a time, Reed made it to Grimes's office two minutes before directed, finding the space already full, a trio of bodies inside. None said anything as he approached, wearing dour expressions as they turned to face him.

Behind the desk sat Grimes, his standard frown on full display. On the other side were two people Reed had seen before but never met.

To the right was Oliver Dade, senior media correspondent for the CPD. Unlike the other two he was not in uniform, dressed in chinos and a dress shirt, the sleeves rolled three times each. Approaching sixty he was one of the oldest employees in the system, his thinning grey hair belying that fact.

Beside him sat Eleanor Brandt, Chief of Police for the entire Columbus force. Perched on the edge of her seat, she sat ramrod straight, only her bottom touching the chair. Her dishwater blonde hair was pulled up tight and her lips were pursed before her, not a trace of makeup anywhere.

Though seated, Reed guessed she couldn't have been more than five-foot-three at full height.

"Detective, thank you for joining us," Grimes said, motioning towards the door for him to close it. Stepping inside, Reed did as asked, the sound of wood rattling through the room.

With both chairs already occupied, Reed moved to the table against the wall and leaned against it, folding his arms across his chest. He stared back as all three seemed to measure him, waiting for someone else to open up the discussion.

In a move that didn't surprise Reed in the slightest, Brandt took the floor.

"I want to pull you from this case," she said, the words flat, her voice honed of any trace of femininity. "Your captain seems to think that would be hasty. You have three minutes to explain why you should stay."

The air slid from Reed's lungs as his mouth fell open. He instantly felt his wet hair begin to itch as blood rushed to his scalp, sweat appearing on his upper lip.

"You called me in here this morning to tell me I'm being punted?"

Nobody in the room moved, or made an attempt to answer the question.

"Two minutes and fifty seconds."

Reed opened and closed his mouth twice as he looked at her perched on the edge of her seat, a tiny flicker of rage welling within him. As the Chief of Police, it was well known that she had the authority to assign cases and had on many occasions. The fact that half the precinct was now working the Near East Side murders proved that.

This though, calling him first thing in the morning and making him beg for a case, was too much.

"Why the hell would you pull me off now?" Reed asked, hostility apparent in his tone.

"Two and a half minutes," Brandt said, raising her voice to match his own.

Breaking eye contact, Reed glanced over to Grimes, who remained behind his desk, his fingers laced over his stomach. The scowl on his face was a little deeper than usual, but otherwise there was no reaction at all.

"I knew it," Brandt said, shifting her attention back to Grimes, "this high school gym teacher you've assigned the case to is out of his league. I'm bringing in the big boys."

The backhanded comment at his appearance coupled with the blatant questioning of his capability brought the feeling of indignation higher in Reed's chest, pressing down on his torso so hard he had to force air in and out. The sound of his breathing echoed through the room as he pushed his hips against the table, dropping his hands by his side, both curled into fists.

"I'm not even going to dignify this little charade you're trying to play with an answer," Reed asked, heat flushing his features, his voice just south of a yell. "I am an experienced detective with this department and I don't have to beg for cases.

"I will tell you this though, in the last twenty-four hours I've made more progress working with a dog than your damn *big boys* will make in a week. I know this case, and I know these streets, and I know for a fact I will catch the sonuvabitch doing this."

For so long Reed had felt pinned up, forcing himself to bite his tongue. Lashing back at Iaconelli and Bishop the night before had felt good, but this was on an entirely different level. Months had passed of his feeling repressed, going through the motions, not sure of himself or his abilities.

Now, that feeling was gone.

The looks on the faces of both Brandt and Dade bore that he was walking a fine line between confidence and insubordination.

At the moment, he didn't much care.

He inched forward another half step, far enough away not to be threatening, but close enough to make Brandt look up at him.

"How much time do I have now?"

The flinty veneer of the chief's face broke just a bit as her lips parted, a muted sound passing over them. She stared at him a long moment, not saying a word.

"That's what I thought," Reed said.

In the background, the sound of Billie barking from the parking lot could be heard, no doubt a reaction to the sudden explosion from Reed. For a moment he fought back a smirk before turning and exiting the room.

Nobody said a thing as he left.

Chapter Thirty-Three

Less than four miles separated the 8th Precinct from the Columbus department headquarters, an easy drive through the pre-rush hour streets of downtown. The entire ride Reed sped with both hands gripping the steering wheel, twisting it so tight shreds of rubber peeled away, dropping onto his jeans.

In the backseat Billie paced back and forth, an animal in perpetual motion, feeding off the change in Reed.

Both were ready for movement, springs that had been coiled tighter and tighter, ready to burst forward at the first available target.

Eight minutes after leaving the 8th, Reed pulled to a stop outside the headquarters. Different in every way from his home precinct, it was a sprawling structure made entirely of grey stone, resembling the kind of thing he once saw on a class trip to Washington D.C.

Standing three stories tall, an arched rotunda rose from the middle of it, a flag pole extended high, the colors already flying for the day. Across the street pale sunlight reflected off the Olentangy River, early morning joggers dotting the landscape.

Eschewing the visitor lot a story underground, Reed pulled to the curb on the opposite side of the street. He knew his police issue plates would be enough to keep him from getting a ticket in the metered space, climbing straight out and clipping the short leash onto Billie.

He had made the mistake of leaving her behind once already on the morning, he wouldn't do so again.

Side by side they jaywalked across Marconi Street to the front of the building, falling in with a steady flow of foot traffic. At the front door Reed flashed his badge to the guard on duty who barely noticed it, instead focusing on Billie as he waved them through.

The front door opened up into the main of the rotunda, an enormous circular space with hallways shooting off in various directions. Filling them were scads of people in both uniforms and suits, all holding coffee, their gazes aimed down at the floor.

Using a directory affixed to the wall, Reed determined they were headed to the second floor, the first floor reserved for administrative personnel, the top for ranking officers.

Bypassing the elevators for the stairs, together he and Billie ascended to the second floor and found the office they were looking for, a pair of glass double doors in the center of the building welcoming them in. On the frosted panels were the words **COLUMBUS POLICE DEPART- MENT - GANG UNIT**, all etched on with uniform height and thickness.

The front desk sat empty as they entered, a glance to the clock on the wall showing it was still just shortly after seven. With Billie pressed against his leg he leaned across and confirmed the computer had not yet been started for the day before raising a hand to his mouth and calling, "Hello?"

Movement sounded from the back as a moment later a middle-aged man with sandy brown hair and a matching mustache emerged. Standing a few inches shorter than Reed he was dressed in jeans and a sports coat, wiping his hands on a paper towel.

"Hello," he said, a single word relaying the exhaustion Reed knew most middle-management police officers were perpetually under. "Detective Mattox?"

"Yes, sir," Reed said, making sure to clear any lingering hostility from his voice. He had a feeling it would be a long time before it left his system, though he needed to be sure not to level any at others, especially someone whose help he needed.

"Sergeant Brooks Morris," the man said, shaking Reed's hand and looking down at Billie. He regarded her a long moment before asking, "Belgian?"

"She is," Reed said, his eyebrows rising a bit in surprise. "You K-9?"

"In a previous life," Morris replied. "Never seen one all black before. Good looking girl you've got there, must scare the hell out of perps."

For the first time in days a smile hit Reed's face as he nodded. "Yes, that she sure does."

"Come on back," Morris said, waving a hand at him. "I apologize for the early hour, but I'm in task force meetings most of the day."

"Not at all," Reed said, "just appreciate you making the time."

He followed Morris into a small, square office with windows on one wall and a standard pattern of government issue furniture filling the space. A desk, chair, computer, book case sat on one side, a couple of chairs and a small table on the other.

Different arrangement than Grimes's office, but the same allotment of goods.

"So, what can I do for you this morning, Detective?" Morris asked, lowering himself into his seat.

Across from him Reed did the same, Billie going flat to her stomach as well. Reaching into the pocket of his sweatshirt Reed extracted a color printout of the image on Edwin Mentor's arm, passing it across the desk.

"I know you've got a ticking clock, so I'll get right to it. You know that murder at Midwestern Paper the other night?"

Morris winced as he accepted the paper, the thick folds in it keeping it bent at an odd angle. "Yeah?"

"Well, it's starting to have all the earmarks of a serial. More just like it, praying every second that I don't get a fourth."

The wince remained in place as Morris stared at him, not yet having looked down at the paper. "And you suspect gang activity?"

Reed raised his right hand and laid it flat on edge, wagging it at Morris, his face scrunched up. "Possibly? I've got a lead on something that I strongly suspect of at least affiliation, but I can't be certain."

"And that's why you asked to see me?"

"It is," Reed said, motioning to the picture still grasped in Morris's hand a few inches above the desk. "That insignia has been found on the forearms of all three victims so far. I ran it through the system last night, but nothing came back."

The explanation was a slight exaggeration of the truth, though close enough Reed felt reasonably certain sharing it.

Smoothing the paper down flat, Morris leaned forward and stared at it a long moment before shaking his head. "Can't say it looks familiar, but I'm sure you can imagine how many of these cross my desk in a given year."

"Probably more than either of us would want to admit," Reed said.

"Not just probably," Morris corrected, pushing himself back upright in his chair. "And certainly more than the guys upstairs would ever confess to."

A reflexive smirk slid from Reed as he thought of his encounter that morning with Brandt, though he remained quiet.

"That's part of why this task force was put together," Morris said, resting his elbows on the arms of the chair and folding his hands in his lap. "These groups are popping up and dissolving faster than we can track. One day, a handful of guys get together, design a logo, start knocking out crimes like they're a damn small business start-up.

"A year later they decide they've had their fill, go back to whatever life it was they were living beforehand."

Reed nodded, not so much surprised at the sheer volume of such occurrences but at the sudden disbandment of them.

"So just like that, they fall apart?"

"Just like that," Morris said. "Usually happens when one of two things occur. First, they finish whatever it was they set out to do. That's not as common, as more likely they get a taste of success and keep going. Few ever just stop.

"The second, which is the complete flip side, is something happens to divert them the opposite direction. Somebody gets hurt, gets pinched, gets shot."

"The proverbial scared straight," Reed said, his gaze shifting to the window, thinking of everything he'd just been told.

"Exactly," Morris said.

If whatever group this emblem belonged to fit the profile Morris was describing, it made sense. Reed had seen ample sign of the major outfits in the area before, plastered onto every flat surface in The Bottoms in various shades of spray paint.

Until the day before, never once had he seen the script K.

"Can you tell me," Reed asked, shifting his attention back to face forward, "is there anywhere that image might be stored outside of the general system? Maybe someone undercover or something be keeping it off the books?"

A long moment passed as Morris stared across at him before the left corner of his mouth turned upward in a weary smile.

"I honestly wish it were that easy, but the truth is I could have saved you trip this morning. If it isn't in the general database, we don't have it."

Chapter Thirty-Four

The old man had said late afternoon, but the Boat Man didn't have that kind of time to wait. Already he had put his plans on hold for a day, a pause that could potentially undo everything he had worked so hard for.

In the months that led up to the commencement of action, there was no predetermined time frame. It could have started in April or August, rain or shine, weekday or weekend. The only thing of paramount importance was that once the initial strike was made, once dominos started to fall, they must do so with speed and precision.

The damage to his blade was a fluke accident that was unforeseeable. It had cost him a precious day, one that could have sent his targets into hiding, disappearing into obscurity or raising their security to a level that would have ensured the Boat Man's mission became a kamikaze run.

His observations the night before had showed they either hadn't yet put together the connection or had failed to give their enemy his proper due.

Either way, he couldn't risk waiting any longer and letting them come to their senses.

The bell above the door to the Japanese man's shop rang once as the Boat Man stepped inside, the scent of incense engulfing him. It was so strong it brought a sheen of moisture to his eyes as he turned away, moving down the first aisle, feigning interest at the items on the shelf as the man rang up an elderly couple at the front counter.

The Boat Man could hear them talking as he pretended to browse packets of dried spices, knowing each one by name, all reminders of a life he once knew.

Would never know again.

Tucked away in the back of the store he waited until he heard the bell a second time before traversing up through the second aisle, the old man standing at the front counter, both hands pressed into the glass, waiting for him.

He wore a dour expression as he watched the Boat Man approach, shaking his head.

"*Nintai ha iwa o mo toosu,*" he said in his native tongue, his voice conveying his age, the grave nature of the words he was reciting.

The Boat Man felt his eyebrows come together as he reached the front counter, resting his wrists on the edge of it. "Meaning?"

"Patience will pierce even a rock," he replied. "Japanese proverb."

It was plain what the old man was trying to say, but the Boat Man had no interest in hearing it. He had a plan to complete, a promise to fulfill. Either the old man could help with that, or he could get out of the way and let the Boat Man find somebody that could.

"Ain't nobody got time for that," the Boat Man replied. "Sweet Brown."

A moment passed as the two stood off from each other, neither blinking, the sweet smoke of burning incense rising between them.

"Is it done?" the Boat Man asked, trying to mask the anxiousness, the anticipation in his tone.

Still the old man remained frozen a long moment before stepping back and bending at the waist. The Boat Man fought the urge to lean forward for a better look, waiting until the old man emerged, the *ken* sword stretched across the same green cloth.

The air caught in the Boat Man's chest as he looked down at it, the notch now indecipherable in the polished steel. He felt his heart beat increase as he leaned forward, wanting so desperately to run his fingertips along the gleaming blade, to feel and know it was whole once more.

"Thank you," he whispered, his attention aimed downward. "You do good work, sir."

Remaining a step back from the case, the old man bowed forward a few inches at the waist, turning his head in acceptance of the praise.

"You are welcome."

Sliding his hand forward and wrapping his fingers around the base of the weapon, the Boat Man hefted it upward. He extended it to arm's length and looked down the extent of it, the design as straight and true as the moment it had first arrived to him.

Every fiber in his body wanted to twist the blade through the air, turning it in a slicing pattern, already envisioning his targets, his plans for the evening now complete.

Digging into the pocket of his pants, he extracted a large roll of cash and placed it on the table, the implication obvious that it was all in appreciation for work well done.

"I do not know where you got this sword or what purpose it truly serves," the old man said, "but it was an honor to work on it. I only hope I did it justice."

A cruel smile stretched across the Boat Man's face as he slid the sword back into its scabbard, slinging it across his back.

The meting of justice had only just begun.

Chapter Thirty-Five

Something didn't sit right with Reed. He couldn't pinpoint exactly what it was, more a conglomeration of a lot of different comments and misshapen facts that were aligned in a jumble in his mind. At this point, given the kind of information he'd gleaned out in the last day, things should be coming together. The finish line itself might not be in sight yet, but he should at least be seeing the connective threads that tied things to one another.

Thus far, that wasn't happening. Instead, the pile of mismatched facts was getting bigger.

Added to the mix just that morning was the discussion with Morris. There was apparently no mention of whatever group the tattoo on the victims belonged to anywhere in the Gang Task Force system, yet somehow they had done something bad enough to earn the spite of someone in the community.

A full day of digging through the precinct records had also turned up blank on the insignia. It was as if it didn't exist, or somehow had never once surfaced on the radar of law enforcement in the area.

In a space as small as The Bottoms, that seemed almost impossible.

Late in the afternoon Reed shut his computer down, leading Billie out to the parking lot, ignoring the sideways glances from coworkers as he went. Once loaded into his sedan he drove eleven blocks and parked along the street, leaving his partner behind and walking the last two on foot.

Halfway between four and five o'clock he stepped onto a sagging front porch and knocked on a door, the screened top of it shaking with the impact. He took a step back and waited, hearing the sound of a television on inside, the approach of footsteps.

A moment later the door swung open, the top half of Gale Pearlman visible on the other side. If she was surprised in the slightest to see him she didn't show it, wiping her face with a cloth napkin as she appraised him.

"Mrs. Pearlman, I'm sorry to show up like this," Reed said, "but I had a couple additional questions and I thought you might be the best person to answer them for me."

Taking a step forward she looked through the screen in either direction before stepping back, offering a slight nod. "Thank you for not parking in front of the house. Will keep the lookey-loos from getting too fired up."

Reed took the statement as an invitation, stepping inside, and pausing on a small linoleum foyer. He glanced down at the three pairs of shoes lined by the door and pushed his from his feet, stepping on their heels without bothering with the laces.

"I hope you don't mind, I was just having my dinner and watching my stories," Pearlman said, moving straight back for the couch. In front of it stood a wooden folding TV stand, a plate of pork chops and gravy half-eaten atop it.

The smell filled the air as Reed moved for the arm chair sitting perpendicular to it, his stomach clenching but remaining silent.

"Please, continue," Reed said, watching as Pearlman took up her utensils, intent to move on with or without his permission.

"You know, I figured you'd be back," Pearlman said, starting again on the meat.

"Why's that?" Reed asked, masking his surprise at the statement.

"Because the last time we spoke, it was plain as day that you were just getting started," Pearlman said, cutting a chunk of meat free from the bone and stabbing it with her fork. "Hard for a man to know what to ask when he doesn't know what he's looking for."

She forked the oversized bite into her mouth and chewed loudly, Reed looking away as he considered the statement.

Very little actual time had passed since their last meeting, though she was right in assessing his position was radically different. No longer was he solely focused on whoever might have committed a heinous act or two, now pulling on the common thread between them, determined to see what had driven someone to do so.

Only then would he be able to figure out who he was searching for.

"That's quite astute," Reed said, nodding, forcing a small smile. "And quite accurate, I have no problem admitting."

Continuing to chew, Pearlman nodded in approval at his humility.

"Today I only have a single question for you," Reed said, reaching into his pocket and extracting the same photo, still folded into quadrants. "If the answer is no, I will be on my way with my sincerest apologies for interrupting your dinner."

Across from him, Pearlman seemed to sense what he was trying to say, placing her utensils down and pushing the plate a few inches away.

"And if I say yes?"

"Then I will probably have a few more questions to ask," Reed said, still holding the sheet between his thumb and forefinger, resting it against his thigh.

Raising a hand to him, Pearlman flicked her fingers back towards herself, motioning for him to pass over the paper.

"Are you sure?" Reed asked. "You might not have much of an appetite afterwards."

The right side of Pearlman's face curled up as if she was offended, her head rocking back a few inches. "Boy, one thing you ain't ever got to worry about with this old woman is her appetite."

There was no doubt in Reed's mind about the veracity of the statement, the corners of his mouth both turning upward. He rolled his body forward and raised his backside from the chair, extending the paper out to her, before dropping himself back down against the green upholstery.

One corner at a time Pearlman unwrapped the image before setting it flat on the TV stand beside her dinner, brushing it smooth with both hands. Once she had done so she stared down at it a long moment, her face unmoving.

More than once Reed wanted to ask if she recognized it, prompt her to search back in her mind, but he remained silent.

Anything she had needed to come from her own recollections, an organic response not persuaded by him.

Seconds seemed to crawl by as Reed forced himself to remain motionless, his elbows resting on his thighs, his fingers laced and hanging down between his legs. He turned his gaze to the side so he wasn't staring straight at her, a muted episode of the newest cop procedural playing on the screen.

The irony was almost too much to ignore.

"Yes, I remember this," Pearlman said, snapping Reed's attention back to her, palpitations racing through his chest.

She reached out and traced each of the letters with her fingers, her movements slow and deliberate. "They called themselves the KOTB. Kings of The Bottoms."

The simplicity of it was almost too much to bear, Reed biting his tongue to keep from cursing his own fallibility.

"They were here for a total of maybe two, three years," Pearlman said, her voice far away, her mind in another place. "Dropped out of sight for good a little over two years ago."

His breathing picked up as Reed stared at her, resisting the urge to start jotting notes down, not wanting to interrupt her thoughts.

"Two years ago? You're sure?" Reed asked.

"Yes," Pearlman said, her eyes growing glassy as she rocked her head up and down. "I know because that's when my Henry passed away. I remember at the time being worried they might start messing with me, but they never did.

"They were gone by then."

Warmth crept up Reed's back as he added the information to what he already knew. Not only did he now have a name, but he had a specific time frame to work from.

"Why were you concerned? Had they ever bothered you before?"

"No," Pearlman said, "but like I said, Henry was still here. He'd been in the Navy before we got married, knew how to shoot a gun."

She left the end of her statement dangling, allowing Reed to ascertain that it was common knowledge he wasn't afraid to fire it either.

"So, two years or so?" Reed asked.

"Yeah," Pearlman said. "They just kind of showed up one day, all with those tattoos you've got here. Started messing with folks, stealing things, being a general nuisance to everybody."

The last sentence brought disdain to her face, the sheen of moisture on her eyes at the mention of her late husband now gone.

"Were the police ever notified?" Reed asked, again wondering why his search had revealed nothing.

"Never by us," Pearlman said, shaking her head. "But I imagine by somebody at some point."

Scads of questions came to Reed's mind as he tried to get a handle on what Pearlman had just said. Most of them were things he knew she couldn't speak on, but that he needed to find the answers to fast.

His pulse pounded through his temples as he ran his hands down the front of his jeans, fighting not to jump up and run straight back to his car, set to digging on a new line of inquiry.

"Just one more question, if you wouldn't mind," Reed said. "How many people in total would you say was involved with this gang?"

The right side of Pearlman's nose pulled up in a snort, the sound sharp and derisive. "Gang? Oh no, this was barely enough kids to be called a group. Maybe a half dozen or so, tops."

Chapter Thirty-Six

"Kings of The Bottoms."

"Kings of The Bottoms," Grimes repeated, looking down at the picture in his hands, the creases in it growing wider with excessive use. "Not a real original bunch, are they?"

"Were," Reed corrected. "Past tense."

Grimes looked up from the photo and tossed it onto his desk, the paper landing near the middle intersection and rotating once before resting on a side. "As in they no longer exist?"

There was no attempt to hide the smirk on Reed's face as he rocked his head back, letting the full effect of it hit Grimes. "If our database is any indicator, they never existed at all."

The eyebrows on Grimes's forehead rose a bit higher as he opened his mouth to speak, paused, then started again. "Really? There's nothing in there anywhere?"

"Not about that emblem or any complaints, arrests, warrants, anything ever associated with them. Like I said, it's as if they never existed."

"Yet you're sure they did?" Grimes pressed.

"Yes," Reed said, motioning at the photo. "That tattoo proves they existed, the statement of Gale Pearlman confirms it."

A moment passed as Grimes lowered his shoulders deeper into his chair, his chin receding back into his chest. Thick folds of skin gathered along the bottom rim of it, one layered atop another.

"I feel like you're taking this somewhere, Detective, I'm just not sure where."

The question was one Reed had expected when he first requested the meeting with Grimes, knowing full well the conclusion he was fast drawing towards would not sit well with the captain.

"Figuring out what these guys did will enable me to figure out who's going after them now."

The frown remained on Grimes's face as he kept his fingers laced, the pads of his thumbs tapping together above his belt. "But you can't do that now, because...?"

"Because somebody is hiding something," Reed said, pushing the words out in one quick breath. "*Something* happened that made these guys suddenly disband two years ago. And it was something bad enough that now someone has taken it upon themselves to rectify the situation."

Without even realizing it, Reed had slid to the front edge of his chair, the same one that Brandt had been perched in that morning. His heart rate and breathing patterns were both high, his brow wet with perspiration.

"So you're saying we've got a mole?" Grimes asked, his face, his voice, relaying the displeasure he felt at the mere insinuation.

"That I don't know," Reed said, moving back an inch, forcing his hands to remain flat on his thighs. "What I do know is somebody worked damn hard to scrub these guys from the system."

He paused for a moment, collecting his thoughts, thinking of a new way to approach things.

"Think about it, Captain. Have we ever had a gang before, no matter how small, no matter how short lived, that didn't pop up on somebody's radar? That didn't piss off the wrong neighbor, or try to rob the wrong old lady, or something that got them at least a warning?"

On the other side of the desk the look of discontent softened a bit, Reed knowing he had struck pay dirt. Both of them had spent far too many years with the department to believe that any group just came together, acted as proper citizens, and dissolved without the slightest hint of mischief.

Especially not someplace like The Bottoms.

"What are you asking me to do?" Grimes said. "If something is in there and isn't coming up because it was expunged, you know there's nothing I can do about it."

The response too was something Reed had come in anticipating. There were only two logical explanations he could conceive for the Kings having been nowhere in the system. One was a dirty uniform, which would take an unheard of level of deceit from both them and their partner to pull off.

Possible, but not likely.

The other was that for some reason the charges had been redacted, expunged from the permanent record by a judge and therefore untouchable by someone like him.

"I know," Reed said, settling his gaze on Grimes, hoping the look alone was enough to relay what he was trying to say.

A long moment of silence passed between them as Grimes matched the stare, realization settling over his features.

"So you came here to tell me, not ask me," he finally said.

"No," Reed replied, pushing himself to a standing position. "I came here so if Brandt and her watchdog show up here again in the morning you'll have enough to keep them off my ass."

Chapter Thirty-Seven

There were two rules that were non-negotiable at the place Reed was headed. The first was to never, ever arrive empty handed. If services were to be performed, payment must be made.

The second was if a job well done was sought after, never let that payment be in cash.

The full handle of Jack Daniels was stowed away in a gym bag as Reed walked up to the front door, the weight of it resting against his hip. He could sense the liquid inside sloshing back and forth with each step, though his shoes scraping against the sidewalk masked any sound.

The place was somewhere he hadn't been in many months, not since before everything changed. In the time since he hadn't been avoiding the place, no reason to, but as he grew closer he could sense he hadn't made an effort to seek it out either.

Like most of the other things from his life just six months before, it had been purged away, just one less reminder of the way things were and could never be again.

The sound of the doorbell echoed through the house as Reed pressed it and stepped back, waiting as feet shuffling over tile grew louder within. A moment later the corner of the curtains over the glass top of the door peeled back, the porch light coming on simultaneously.

The glare from the light caused Reed to take another step back, raising his hand to his face as the door wrenched open, a rush of warm air escaping.

"Can I help you?" an elderly woman asked, suspicion in her voice. Despite the hour she was already in pajamas and an oversized pink bathrobe, her short grey hair in tight curls around her head.

"Good evening, Mrs. Chamberlain," Reed said, moving back a few inches out of the direct light. "Is Deek home?"

The suspicion in her voice spread to her face as she looked at Reed, peering down her nose at him. "So you've been here before?"

It was at least the tenth time Reed had stood on the front porch, though the first time he had ever been scrutinized so closely. On previous trips Riley had handled the interactions with Mrs. Chamberlain, the two falling into friendly banter before being welcomed inside.

Apparently now those days were gone, Reed just another potentially nefarious character looking to corrupt her grandson.

Reaching into his sweatshirt, Reed pulled out his badge, letting it slap against his chest. "Yes ma'am, I'm here on official police business. I need Deek to run some records for me."

All concern bled away as she looked from the badge to Reed, a faint smile crossing her lips. There seemed to be no notice of the duffel bag over his shoulder as she stepped aside, extending an arm towards the door.

"Oh, I'm so sorry, Officer. One can never be too certain these days."

"Not a problem, Mrs. Chamberlain," Reed said, stepping through and heading straight for the doorway on the opposite side of the foyer. "Thank you so much."

"That's quite alright, you just go on down. Derrick is always happy to help!"

Her voice carried through the door swinging closed behind Reed as he descended a set of wooden stairs, a two foot swath of carpet covering the middle portion, bare blonde pine on the outside. They creaked heavily beneath him as he trudged downward, the sound of video games growing louder with each step.

Fourteen rungs after passing through the doorway, Reed found himself on the basement floor, a contrast in every way to the scene upstairs. What had been a scene out of Country Living magazine, filled with light blue and cranberry red, had been replaced by an exaggerated dorm room, the entire basement turned into an enormous den of arrested development.

One half of the basement was a living space, with a king sized water bed and a kitchenette, both illuminated by neon signs that had once hung on the walls of some nearby tavern. Across from it was a makeshift living area, the centerpiece an eighty inch television, towering speakers and subwoofers on either side.

Parked in front of the television was a single black leather recliner, its occupant extended back as far as the chair would allow. From where he stood Reed could see only the top of his head, most of it covered with a headset, and a pair of feet silhouetted against a war video game.

"Damn it, where is my sniper!" the occupant shouted, a male voice, slightly pinched. "Sniper! Where the hell are you?!"

Reed arched on eyebrow as onscreen the main character took one bullet and then another, digital blood spatter shooting into various directions.

"Get them off my ass!" the voice yelled, a note of fear and desperation present, before a final kill shot struck home, the top of the main character's head exploding in vibrant color.

The screen froze as the game was paused, the headphones pulled down over a shock of thick dark hair.

"Grandma, how many times have I asked you to not come down uninvited while I'm working?"

An air of annoyance was unavoidable.

"I came down because *I'm* working," Reed said, putting a bit of extra bass in his voice for effect.

The reclined portion of the chair snapped down in response, the man in the chair springing to his feet. He turned with a look of pure shock on his face, his jaw hanging open, the chair rocking back and forth between them.

Derrick Chamberlain was a friend of Riley's from their time at Ohio State together, an odd-duck pairing of neighbors that somehow became friends, even now ten years removed. One had gone on to the police academy while the other returned to his grandmother's basement, content to do just enough cyber sleuthing to pay the bills.

The rest of his time was spent in a fog of Red Bull and first-person video games, insisting that everyone call him Deek.

At six feet tall, he was about the same height as Reed, though the similarities stopped there. Waif thin from an existence of energy drinks and fruit rollups, his boxer shorts and t-shirt hung from his frame, a pair of wool gym socks pulled to mid-calf. His hair rested in a misshapen tangle atop his head and several days of growth dotted the underside of his chin.

"Detective Mattox," he said, the words almost a whisper. "Damn, I haven't seen you in..."

"A long time," Reed finished for him. "Too long."

"Yeah," Deek replied. "Didn't even see you..."

Reed nodded, breaking eye contact as he glanced at his toes. "I know. I was there, I just couldn't..."

An air of awkward silence fell between them a moment, both averting eye contact.

It was no secret that the two had never been especially close, the connection always coming through Riley. Reed had gone along with it because Riley vouched for Deek, who in turn provided a good work product. Deek went along with it because Riley told him to.

Never before had Reed come to him without his partner, hoping the arrangement still stood.

"Look," Reed said, shifting his focus back, praying the sincerity he felt was evident in his posture. "I know it's been a while, and I know we haven't had the greatest relationship in the past, but I could really use your help right now."

The approach seemed to throw Deek off a moment, his jaw rising and falling a few times in silence. "Oh," he managed after a moment, not moving.

Seizing the small opening, Reed pushed ahead. "Riley always said you were the best, the guy who enjoyed digging up stuff nobody else could or that others thought they had buried."

The situation seemed to resonate a bit with Deek as he thought on it, finally nodding once. "So it's something big?"

"You been watching the news at all lately?" Reed asked, still remaining in place, no more than a few feet removed from the stairs.

"On occasion," Deek replied. "Grandma always has it on. I hear it when I go upstairs sometimes."

"Seen anything about the killer loose in The Bottoms?"

Deek's eyes bulged as he looked at Reed, a lump traveling the length of his throat. "Damn. That's you?"

"That's me," Reed confirmed. "And I could really use a hand."

Without breaking his gaze he slid his fist into the duffel bag and extracted the whiskey, pulling it out and wagging it in front of him. "I even brought full payment. No pro bono work. I remember the rules."

A crack of a smile showed just a sliver of teeth as Deek looked at the bottle and up at Reed. "You didn't have to bring that, I would have done this as a favor to Riley. Since you did though, and grandma won't let me bring it into the house myself..."

His voice trailed away, letting it be known the token would be accepted and appreciated.

Reed walked forward and extended the bottle butt first across the recliner, hanging on to it as Deek grasped the opposite end. "Before you take this I should probably tell you, I need you to hack into the expunged records of the Columbus Police Department for me."

The half smile grew into a full grin, a jack-o-lantern opening spread across Deek's face. He shook the bottle twice and brought it over towards himself, looking down at it but refraining from diving right in.

"I almost feel bad now. I would have gladly done that job for free."

Chapter Thirty-Eight

Sitting in a parked car would have been too obvious. Even on a street as dilapidated as this one, it would have been glaring. Not only was it far too nice to even be in the neighborhood, anybody that owned it would know better than to just leave it on the street, seated behind the wheel or not.

Instead the Boat Man opted to leave it parked ten blocks away at a McDonald's, covering the remainder of the distance on foot. Sticking to alleyways and the long shadows afforded by the street lamps throwing bright orange light down in misshapen cones, he was able to move in virtual invisibility.

Most people, no matter how secure, tended to feel a bit of fear in the darkness. There was something about the unknown, of never being quite sure what could be lurking just beyond the sightline, that petrified them.

Society as a whole tended to rely far too much on their eyes for their sense of self. They used it to dictate how they regarded themselves and how they shaped their place in the world around them.

Two years before, the Boat Man had been one of those people. He had lived in a comfortable home on a comfortable street in a comfortable suburb. He had felt the tingle of fear rise along the nape of his neck whenever he was forced outside that comfort zone, always worried of what he couldn't see, wondering what might be lurking in the dark.

Unlike most other people though, he had found out first hand. He had discovered the horrors that could be found in the shadows, had experienced the violence they could produce, far beyond anything he could have imagined.

The doctors after the fact had said he was lucky, that his life had almost been taken. What they didn't realize was how wrong they were, how every iota of his old life had been stripped away, shattered in an instant.

In its place was what he had now become, a man that no longer feared the shadows. A person that had made peace with them, felt most at ease in their presence.

No longer was he afraid of the shadows. He was something to be feared in the shadows.

The Boat Man's shoes made no sound as he picked his way through the back alleys, coming up on the opposite side of the intersection. Less than fifty yards away he could see the glow of the diner he had spent the previous evening in, the lights spilling into the darkness, illuminating much of the area.

His back pressed against the outer wall of an abandoned building that had once been a pawn shop, the Boat man tucked himself behind an overflowing dumpster, his body hidden from view. Bags of rubbish were piled around him, the stench of rotting food filling the air, providing him the perfect cover as he sat and waited.

Fifteen yards in front of him Scanson and Duvall Streets intersected, two thoroughfares that fifty years ago had served as the hub for The Bottoms. Now more of a cautionary tale of what had been lost, they were home to dozens of buildings just like the one he now leaned against, a refuge for the poor and destitute.

On the opposite side of Scanson was a corner schoolhouse, closed down decades before, the windows gone, standing like gaping sores on its façade. The far corner was the diner, the sole survivor of the four, the thin crowd visible through the front window showing it too fought a daily battle for survival.

The final corner of the intersection was what the Boat Man had come for, the spot he had trained most of his surveillance on the last few months. He knew that it was only a matter of time before his marks arrived, just as they had the night before, just as they did most every night.

Until then he only had to sit and wait, alone in the shadows, allowing the city to continue its slide into slumber.

Chapter Thirty-Nine

After a full hour of digging, Deek was able to only find a single mention anywhere of the Kings of The Bottoms. It was attached to a complaint from a local business owner that had since closed shop and moved across town, a citation being the only thing that had come from it.

The fact that someone had gone to the trouble of having a citation redacted seemed odd as Deek first read it off, even more so as time passed. It clearly seemed someone was going to extreme lengths to keep the gang off the books, though their motivations for doing so still eluded him.

More important at the moment though was that the citation had yielded a name, William Pryor.

Using Deek's computer they had moved into the general police database, finding Pryor had two previous convictions for assault, both bar fights that had the charges dropped. A bit more digging proved there was nothing else on him, in the general record or expunged.

The address on file was on the edge of Franklinton, a block or two outside of The Bottoms, though on visual inspection very much in line with its close neighbors. Most of the homes seemed to range from disrepair to condemned, trash and weeds piled high.

Under the angry glow of streetlights the situation looked even uglier as Reed rolled to a stop, long shadows cloaking most of the property in darkness. Two automobiles sat on blocks in the driveway and a sofa rested across the front lawn, all three looking like they had been there a long time.

"I'm thinking you might join me on this one," Reed said over his shoulder, shutting the car down as Billie raised herself up onto her front paws. She remained that way, waiting as he clipped on the short lead, both of them making their way up the front walk to the door.

The porch sagged beneath their weight as they stepped up onto it, paint peeling away from the floorboards. A pair of folding lawn chairs was placed off to the side, a plastic table between them, an ashtray overflowing with cigarette butts perched atop it.

The scent of cigarette smoke was strong, like someone had just been outside, as Reed raised his fist and smacked it against the metal outer door. The entire thing rattled loudly on contact, Reed pausing before pounding once more and stepping back.

"Yeah, I hear you out there!" a female voice called, annoyance, frustration in her tone.

A moment later the inner door was pulled open, a wheeze escaping from the rubber stripping encasing it. On the opposite side of the door stood a woman in her mid-forties, her hair frizzed out away from her head in a lopsided afro. She wore spotted sweatpants and a tank-top, a small boy of no more than two perched on her hip.

"What?" she asked, spitting the word out. Reed sensed there was more she wanted to add, most likely a comment on his skin tone or the fact that he was in the wrong part of town, but she refrained.

"Good evening, ma'am," Reed said, holding the badge up from its chain around his neck. "I'm Detective Mattox, I'm looking for a William Pryor."

A sour expression crossed her face as she stared at him, her eyes flashing hatred. "What you want with Willie?"

Again Reed got the impression there was more she wanted to add, realizing from her repeated glances to the side that her restraint was for the benefit of the child, not respect for his badge.

"I need to ask him some questions about a crime that has been committed," Reed said, keeping his answer vague, trying to follow her lead on deferring in front of the child. There was no need to mention the word murder, the effect only serving to evoke a response from the both of them.

"Willie didn't do it," the woman snapped. "He's been cleaning up his act, got himself a job now."

Reed nodded, pretending it wasn't the same story he had heard a hundred times before, all from an angry spouse or parent.

"Don't you guys have nothing better to do than be hassling people in the middle of the night like this?"

Reed knew from the clock on the dash in his car that it was still not even nine o'clock in the evening, though her crack was meant more for dramatic effect than accuracy.

"Ma'am, I'm sorry to show up so late," Reed said, forcing his voice to remain even, "but I really need to speak with Mr. Pryor. We don't believe he has done anything wrong, just that he may have information about something that has happened."

The anger retreated a bit from the woman's features, her gaze flicking to the child and back again. "Information? What kind of information?"

Taking the cue, Reed paused, selecting his words carefully. "Information from his past that might be able to help us with something occurring presently."

He widened his eyes a bit to try and let her know he was insinuating something more, waiting a full moment before a bit of dawning set in. Her mouth dropped open and she nodded, drawing in a short breath.

"Oh, you mean..."

"I do," Reed said. "And it's imperative I speak with him immediately. He might be in trouble."

The move was one Riley had been famous for, being able to take the anger of someone and turn it around on them. Three minutes before the woman had hated the police, all but tried to come through the door and throw Reed off her porch. Just by telling her that William wasn't in trouble and might himself be in danger her entire tenor had changed.

Reed only hoped it was enough to extract what he needed from her.

Almost a full minute passed as the woman chewed on the information before finally nodding once. She tilted the top of her head towards the boy on her hip and said, "This is his son, Willie, Jr. For his sake, I'll tell you Willie still spends most of his evenings down at the old Mobil station. Don't do nothing wrong, just him and some friends like to get together and talk.

"Been doing it for years."

Chapter Forty

Reed thought of leaving the short lead attached to Billie's collar as he pulled away from the Pryor residence, but decided against it. She was trained to react to the sound of his voice and he wanted her to have the freedom to rove if need be.

He wasn't sure what he would find in the gas station lot, but felt reasonably certain there would be some posturing once he arrived. In his experience, rare was the time when a group of young men didn't try to hassle an officer at least a little, even when there was no reason to.

He understood it was all part of the imagery of being affiliated with such a group, but that didn't mean he had to make it any easier on them.

Reed knew the way to the place even before the woman had told him, it being the same parking lot he had met with McMichaels and Jacobs in just a couple days before. The added benefit of the location was that Billie had already searched it—an odd bit of luck.

Without any real reason for it, Reed felt his pulse rise as he drove towards the location. He knew there was an eatery nearby with a full visual, and that it was still early, though walking up on a group that may or may not have been a gang in recent years left him feeling uneasy.

The thought of calling for backup occurred to him, dispelled just as fast by the knowledge that showing up with an entourage would likely only escalate any potential confrontation.

A pair of cars was parked in the center of the lot as Reed approached, both long bodied cruisers, each looking to have been constructed in the seventies. Against either of them leaned a single individual, both openly staring as he pulled into the lot and parked perpendicular to them, the nose of his car aimed out towards Scanson Street.

"Come," Reed said, his voice sharp, letting Billie know they were on-duty the moment they exited the car. She responded in kind as he climbed out and opened the rear door, her ears raised, her body poised.

"Hey man, you lost?" a voice called out to him, a trace of amusement, a bit more of a challenge in the tone.

Reed ignored it as he walked around the front of his car, letting Billie and his badge both be seen at the same time. On sight both men exchanged a glance, shifting a bit, placing the brown paper bags in their hands at arm's length away from them.

What good they thought that would do Reed wasn't sure, though at the moment he didn't much care what they were drinking.

"William Pryor?" Reed asked, moving forward and coming to a stop at the end of the two cars. On his right was the tail of a Buick Skylark with a faded orange paint job. To the left was the front grille of a purple Pontiac Tempest.

Both looked like they had at one point had a great deal of money sunk into them, though years of abuse and neglect had ebbed away their potential luster.

At the sound of his question one of the men snorted, the other scowled. He cast a sideway glare at Reed before looking across at his cohort, the same look still in place.

Taking the look as a cue, Reed shifted his focus to him, his hands shoved into the pockets of his sweatshirt, trying to seem as unimposing as possible.

"I take it you must be William?" Reed asked.

Again the man to his right started laughing, raising a hand to cover his mouth. He was lean, his hair shaved tight to his head, skin dark black.

A diamond stud was in the ear closest to Reed, a thick braided chain flashing around his neck.

"Man, ain't nobody named William here," the man on his left said. Anger was apparent in his posture as he said it, continuing to glare at Reed. "My name is Dub-P."

It was a common form of slang Reed had learned over the years, using initials for a moniker. In the case of the letter W the word dub was inserted, making William Pryor now Dub-P.

Why he couldn't have just answered the question, Reed wasn't sure.

"Alright," Reed said, moving on without acknowledging the name. "Do the names Edwin Mentor, A.J. Wright, or Mason Durell mean anything to you?"

The mirth faded from the man on the right's face as the two exchanged a glance, neither saying anything.

"Is that a yes?" Reed asked again.

Sidestepping the question, Pryor made a face, pushing himself up from the hood of his car. "Man, what the hell is this? We're not doing anything wrong here. You can't roll up and start heckling us, hiding behind some damn badge."

"Yeah, I think you might be best served to take your dog for a walk somewhere else," the other man added, raising his head to look down his nose, trying to appear tough.

Reed had seen both of the moves so many times before it almost brought a chuckle to his lips. Normally he would go back and forth with them for a while, letting them think they had the upper hand, trying to get them talking by placating.

Tonight, he had neither the time nor inclination.

"Alright," he said, the jovial manner gone, his voice and features both hardening, "here's how this is going to go. I tried to be nice, but at this point I need information and you're going to give it to me."

"And if we don't?" Pryor asked, taking another half step forward.

Reed had anticipated the move, responding by raising his fist by his shoulder, a lightning quick movement that he had practiced a hundred times but never performed on the streets before.

It had the intended effect as beside him Billie lowered herself into a crouch, her teeth bared, all four legs bent, ready to burst forward.

"If you don't, my partner here will tear you apart," Reed said, letting them know he was enjoying the sudden shift in power.

"What you see beside me is a Belgian Malinois, sixty-five pounds of pissed off canine with a bite so tight they nicknamed her breed Maligators. If my fist drops she will be on you in point two seconds, thrashing and shredding every bit of exposed skin she can find."

Pryor stopped where he stood, unsure how to proceed. He glanced to his friend, neither saying a word.

"And since I've come here with information that could save both your asses," Reed continued, "how about you cut the tough guy bullshit and we get this over with?"

Both men kept their attention on Billie as she quivered with anticipation, waiting for him to give her the green light to move on them. Reed could almost feel it rolling off of her like electricity, her body aching to explode forward.

After a long moment they both seemed to sense there was no bluff in Reed or Billie, each taking a step back and resuming their pose against the cars.

"Alright, let's get this over with," Pryor said. "Just call that damn dog off before she does something stupid and gets herself hurt."

"That dog is an officer of the law," Reed corrected. "Touching her would be the something stupid."

Again they seemed to consider the information, both looking at Billie.

"Yeah, I knew them, why?" Pryor finally managed, the answer slow and begrudging.

"Kings of The Bottoms, right?" Reed asked, jumping straight to the conclusion, watching as both men's eyes bulged with surprise.

"Man, how the hell..." Pryor started.

"Did you know we have no idea what you're talking about?" his friend finished, reaching out a hand towards Pryor to stop him from speaking further.

"Oh, come off it," Reed said, leaving his hand raised, letting the threat of Billie stand a few moments longer. "This isn't a very big community. People see stuff, they talk."

Another glance was exchanged as Reed pushed forward, feeling his own ire rise. "Yeah, somebody near here gave you guys up. You all did something to piss someone off and they ratted the first chance they got."

The only reason Reed felt remotely safe saying such a thing was he knew there was no way the men would ever piece it back to Pearlman. As far as they were concerned people like her didn't exist, just faceless entities in the crowd.

"My question is, what happened that was so bad you guys decided to disband all of a sudden? Just one day you're there, the next you're gone."

"Man, we didn't do shit," Pryor snapped, malevolence on his face.

"And we ain't telling you shit," the other man added.

For a moment Reed considered asking the man his name, certain that if he raised the sleeve on his right arm a matching tattoo would be evident. He was just as sure though that whatever the guy told him would be a lie, just one more way to try and mess with the police.

Instead he would run his license plate the moment he got back in his car.

"Alright, fine," Reed said, "be that way. Just stand there and keep your mouths shut while I tell you something instead then.

"Whatever happened a couple years ago, whoever you did it to is back, and they're pissed. I'm sure you've figured out by now that your boys are being picked off, and I'm sure you even think that what you're doing out here, making yourself open targets, is a way to lure them to you.

"Let me tell you though, that would be a mistake. This guy is on a mission, and he is much, much smarter than you."

Reed lowered his hand, careful to drop it in a slow circular pattern so as to not incite Billie. Beside him the growl ceased as her jowls lowered back over her fangs, her legs losing just a bit of tension.

"If you guys know anything, you'd better get your ass down to the precinct and ask to see me, Detective Mattox."

He looked at each of them in turn, their anger having receded a bit.

Both held their mouths drawn into tight lines, waiting for him to continue.

"I've processed three of the most horrific crimes scenes I've ever seen in the last four days. I hope I don't soon have to do yours too because you were too damn proud to ask for help."

Chapter Forty-One

The Boat Man could feel his pulse quicken. The car wasn't familiar, though if it were coming to meet the others at the corner lot it was a fair assumption that whoever was driving was affiliated with them.

The details from that night were still a bit fuzzy, his own scattered consciousness making the last few months so much more difficult than necessary. Everything still drifted back to him in spliced snapshots, a combination of what happened and his natural defense mechanisms trying to cope by blocking it out.

Had there been more for him to go on, an official report of any kind, his task would have been so much easier. By the point he was able to deliver a statement or pursue the matter so much time had passed it had become a losing proposition.

Besides, doing so might have had the unintended consequence of protecting those responsible. Society's idea of justice was to take perpetrators such as them and lock them away, letting taxpayers provide for their food and clothing, provide them with cable television.

It had taken a long time for the Boat Man to prepare, the only way to ensure that true justice was ever really served. Once that moment of inception hit there became no doubt in his mind about what must be done, his entire life becoming a mission hell bent on setting things right.

For that reason, the surge of adrenaline that first passed through his system fell away just as fast as he saw the gold badge swinging from the man's neck as he exited the car, bits of light from the diner across the street reflecting off it. The intense sense of dread flooded in right behind it as he beckoned the oversized police dog from the back seat, both looking determined and capable.

The mishap with the blade had cost him, wasting precious time, allowing the police to finally catch up. Somehow they had managed to put together what each of the victims had in common, finding their way to the abandoned parking lot, there to warn the vagrants congregating every night of what was going on.

For the briefest of moments the Boat Man raised his right hand behind his head, squeezing the handle of the sword tight. Just touching it filled him with resolve, his knuckles whining as they flexed around the black fabric encasing it. He left his arm raised by his ear, his bent elbow resting against the brick wall beside him as he watched the scene across the street.

The opening between him and the small gathering was no more than twenty-five yards, an easy distance for a man in his position, well hidden in the shadows. He could clear half of it before anybody so much as looked his way, their own conversation serving as the distraction he needed to close the gap.

At that though, the numbers game was overwhelmingly stacked against him. One on one, he armed with his *ken* blade, there was no way any of the men could best him. Even two on one, knowing that all three were carrying weapons, he liked his odds.

Three on one would be long, even for the best of swordsmen. Adding in the presence of the dog, itself appearing to be a small wolf, all black, trained to react in such instances, would make any move the Boat Man made a fool's errand, a kamikaze run he couldn't hope to return from.

Slowly he released his grip on the handle, lowering his arm back to his side. As much as he ached to rush forward and complete his vow, make right a wrong that had been done years before, he couldn't allow himself to do something foolish.

The objective would not, could not, be completed tonight, regardless how things went with the two men standing across from him.

Settling himself back against the trash piled around him, the Boat Man remained tucked in the shadows, watching as the encounter played out beneath the street lights. He watched as the cop approached and the two sides conversed, saw as the men seemed to give him a hard time, their standoffish demeanor showing as little respect for the law as they had for him.

He observed as the man flipped the power dynamic on them, setting his partner at the ready, an oversized animal bred for the purpose of handling criminals such as them.

A thin smile grew on the Boat Man's face as he watched the rendezvous grow tense, the meeting clearly not planned, neither side one wanting to interact with the other. It grew a bit larger as the officer finally called the tension from the animal by his side, both parties climbing back into their cars and driving away.

This had merely been a warning shot, a courtesy call to let the two men know that they could be next in the line of fire, counsel that they had obviously cast aside.

His opening still existed. Even as both men waited until the officer drove away before climbing into their own cars to leave, the Boat Man knew just as surely that his opportunity was coming.

It was obvious from the body language of the impromptu gathering that the cop would not be back.

It was only a matter of time before he would be.

Chapter Forty-Two

Traffic was lined up nose to tail on the opposite side of the median, just a thin band of grass separating Reed from the early morning gridlock. Brake lights flaring as far as he could see, the cars were stretched in a serpentine pattern, the entirety of the freeway reduced to a parking lot, the early morning crowd rushing in from the suburbs for the start of a new day.

Having bypassed another potentially awful coffee-based experience, Reed raised a bottle of Mountain Dew from his thigh to his lips, a wet ring of condensation left behind. Taking a long pull, he shook his head at the sight of the people jockeying to get somewhere they had no desire to be, his continuing battle with his body clock only serving to make his mood worse.

In the back seat Billie seemed to be fighting the same war, her usual early morning patter reduced to nothing, her body laying flat on the cool plastic. Not once since leaving home had he heard the telltale squeak of the cover as she adjusted her body, her entire form going limp upon entry.

Reed knew the feeling.

After leaving the gas station the previous evening he had again driven by the homes of Edwin Mentor and A.J. Wright, trying to pretend that he was hoping to spot something, knowing more than anything he was just hiding.

From the precinct and the chance of running into Iaconelli and Bishop, from home and the stack of case files strewn across his table, from sleep and whatever horrors his body continued to play out every night but refused to let him see.

Shortly after midnight he gave up on the voluntary patrol, having passed three blue-and-whites in the process, the chatter over the line no doubt thick wondering what he was up to. The entire time he had ridden with the radio off and the book on tape left on the floor, trying to collect his thoughts, formulate some sort of cohesion to what he knew.

As best he could tell, the things he had to follow up on were both numerous and ethereal. He knew for a fact that the Kings of The Bottoms had existed and that all three victims were once affiliated. He also knew that William Pryor was at one time a member.

A quick call to Jackie the night before had shown the man with Pryor to be Marcus Knighton, who Reed also suspected was an active participant.

Beyond that, the complete lack of mention of the Kings in the system left him puzzled and with precious little to follow up on. Both men the night before had shown signs of recognition when he asked, but shut down tight when he tried to press the matter.

Their reaction, taken with the statement from Pearlman, proved that they had existed. The fact that there was so little mention of them in the system was something Reed could only speculate at, his morning venture an exercise in trying to do just that.

The sole mention Deek had been able to ferret out of the system about the Kings was a complaint from a shop owner named Fareed Rasul. He had owned a convenience store in The Bottoms for six years, a search through local records showing his permits to run from 2005 to 2011. In May of that year he had filed a formal complaint against the Kings, citing theft and vandalism on multiple occasions.

Two weeks later all charges were dropped.

Three weeks after that he chose not to renew his lease, moving across town and opening a similar establishment in Gahanna.

The address for the new shop was scribbled across the top of a sheet of paper in Reed's spiral-bound notebook, a quick series of directions jotted down beneath it. The blue ink of the lettering stood out against the white paper as he glanced down every few minutes, following the freeway across town before exiting onto smaller side streets, avoiding the main boulevards.

The journey from one side of Columbus to the other took him a full thirty-five minutes, the first half a crawl with the incoming traffic, the backend opening up as he crossed downtown. By the time he arrived the entire bottle of soda was gone and nestled on the floor against *Crime and Punishment*, the jolt of caffeine just beginning to take hold.

He could feel his neurons beginning to fire and his heart rate increasing as he pulled up in front of Rasul's shop, Billie remaining prone in the back.

The convenience store stood as the end unit in a small strip, fifth out of five moving left to right. The outer shell of the structure was made of brick, though the storefronts were mostly glass, a few steel bars interspersed for support.

Most of the window space for Rasul's was covered in advertisements for various products, the goods offered ranging from cigarettes and beer to cereal and cookies. A neon sign flashed that the establishment was open as a pair of middle-aged women stepped out the front door and walked in the opposite direction.

Parking in the front stall, Reed turned off the ignition and surveyed the place, comparing it to what he had seen in The Bottoms the night before. Despite just fifteen miles separating the two geographically, they were different in virtually every way. Gone were any traces of graffiti on the walls, any need for bars on the windows.

Glancing over his shoulder, Reed saw Billie raise her eyelids towards him, questioning if her presence was required, her chin pressed flat to the seat relaying she was less than enthused by the notion.

"Stay here, girl," Reed said, wrenching the door open and stepping out, the smell of coffee and pastries hitting his nose. Behind him he could hear the sound of a school bus pulling to a stop on the corner, air brakes engaging and the muted din of children laughing.

The sound fell away as he stepped through the front door, the smells of breakfast on-the-go hitting him full in the face. A reflexive groan from his stomach cried out as he stepped to the front counter, a young girl in her early twenties behind it, head aimed down at the cell-phone in her hands.

"Good morning," Reed said, his voice just a little bit higher than necessary so as to be heard over the enthrallment of the phone.

"Uh-huh," the girl said, the sound coming out as a low garble, delivered without looking up.

A bevy of smart remarks came to Reed's mind as she continued punching at the phone with both thumbs, but he let them go. "I'm looking for Fareed Rasul, please."

"In the back," the girl replied, snapping the top of her head to the side, directing him towards a door along the far wall. Just as fast she returned to an upright position, a ponytail of thin blonde hair swinging behind her.

Having no desire to continue the conversation any further, Reed moved on without thanking her, following her directions towards the back wall and knocking on the door there twice before pausing and pounding once more.

"Yes!" a heavily accented voice said from the other side, traces of irritation present as Reed shoved it open and stood in the doorway.

In front of him was a small office, barely large enough for a desk, a computer, and a file cabinet. Behind it was a short man that looked to be from somewhere in southwest Asia or the Middle East, his skin stained dark brown. Most of the hair on his head had migrated out to the sides, though it still appeared dark, his features dominated by a pointed nose and chin.

On the wall above him was a pair of security monitors, showing everything occurring inside the shop in muted black-and-white.

"Fareed Rasul?"

"Yes?" the man repeated, his eyes narrowing slightly. "Who are you?"

Raising the badge from inside his hooded jacket, Reed wagged it once and said, "Detective Reed Mattox, Columbus PD."

Rasul nodded once, unease on his face, and motioned across his desk. "I would ask you to sit, but as you can see, there is no room for a chair in here."

"That's alright," Reed said, resting his shoulder against the door-jamb, the wood groaning a bit in protest. "This shouldn't take too long."

The look of discord remained on Rasul's face as he nodded, the corners of his lips turned downward.

It was not a reaction Reed, or any law enforcement personnel he had ever known, wasn't familiar with. Just the way every driver that ever saw a cop in the rearview mirror became nervous, he had found the vast majority of people he spoke with to be uneasy, even when there was no call for it.

That was one of the chief reasons Reed preferred wearing his badge inside his sweatshirt.

"I'm from the 8th Precinct," Reed said, "covering the part of town known as The Bottoms. I understand you're familiar with the area?"

A long moment passed before Rasul responded, Reed sensing the wheels turning in the man's head as he tried to determine where this was going.

"I am," Rasul said, adding nothing more.

Pushing a loud breath out through his nose, Reed deciding to nudge things along, hoping to bypass any trepidation so he could get to the information he needed.

"Mr. Rasul," Reed said, "I am not here because of you or anything you have done. I am simply here to ask about an incident that occurred while you conducted business in The Bottoms."

Another moment passed as Rasul stared at him, a bit of color returning to his cheeks. Reed could see his chest begin to rise and fall as he resumed breathing normally, the top of his head rising an inch in recognition.

"You're here because of the complaint I filed against them," Rasul said, his voice low.

Reed felt a stab of adrenaline in his stomach as he stared at the man, fighting to keep his features even. Not once had he made any mention of who or why he was there beyond mentioning a prior complaint, but already the man knew what he was referring to. "I am."

"So am I," Rasul said, reaching out and extending a hand towards the door, folding his fingers back towards himself. "Please, come in."

Reed cast a glance over his shoulder to see the girl behind the counter still engulfed in her electronic conversation, the remainder of the store lifeless. Shifting himself inside the door, he swung it closed behind him, resting his back against it.

"What do you mean, so are you?"

One at a time Rasul brought his hands up onto the desk and laced his fingers together, leaning forward so his wrists pressed against the edge of it. "Tell me, what did you see when you drove in here this morning?"

The word *traffic* was the first thing that came to mind, but Reed let it pass, content to allow Rasul to continue.

"Or perhaps, what didn't you see?" Rasul asked, the stare remaining affixed to his face.

"I'm not sure what..." Reed managed, letting his voice trail off, uncertain where the question was meant to go.

"Crime," Rasul answered for him, the word coming out harsh and bitter. "Poverty. Vagrancy."

He rattled the terms off one at a time, each with more acrimony than the one before.

"Those are the reasons I am here, on this side of town, a long way from The Bottoms and everything found there. The higher rent, the nervous staring, the snickering at my accent, all worth it to be here."

Finally what the man was saying fit into place in Reed's mind, bringing with it understanding of what he was being told, why Rasul seemed so angry.

"At night I leave, I lock one door, I walk to my car and I drove home. No looking over my shoulder, no wondering if this place will be here in the morning."

It was apparent from the growing animosity, from the rapid-fire cadence the man was employing that it was a speech that had been said many times, one with no apparent denouement in sight.

"What happened in May of 2011?" Reed asked, hoping both to stem the monologue before it went any further and to channel the already apparent frustration into answers.

At the mention of the incident Rasul paused, his mouth still open, ready to deliver more, before a sour look passed over his face. He worked his mouth up and down twice as if trying to take the taste from his tongue before beginning anew.

"Gangs weren't new to me, you know," he began. "I had been told many times when I decided to open the shop that they were down there, but the city was so eager for businesses to come in that they were practically giving floor space away.

"I figured if I could just make a go of things for eight, ten years, I would have enough put back to go elsewhere, pay cash for something better, maybe even open a couple of shops."

Again Reed waited as Rasul collected himself, content to let the man finish whenever he was ready. Handfuls of questions came to his mind, wondering how the man had ended up in Columbus and why he thought being a shopkeeper was his life's calling, but each one he let fall by the wayside.

"The first five years or so, there were incidents, sure," Rasul said, scrunching his face and wagging a hand at Reed in a dismissive nature, "but nothing too bad. A few sodas here, a candy bar there. The occasional bum wandering in looking for a handout."

It was apparent the man was working towards something, his meandering back story headed on to information Reed needed. For that reason he let him keep going without interruption, nodding as if every detail was important.

"Little less than a year before I shut down, those bastards started showing up," he said, a harsh glower crossing his face.

The feeling in Reed's stomach kicked up at the mention of the men in question, his senses rising, fueled by the carbonated caffeine. "And?"

"And..." Rasul said, muttering to himself, collecting his thoughts. "At least most of the people that stole tried to hide it, you know? These guys just walked in and grabbed whatever, started saying they were the Kings, could do as they wanted."

As he spoke, Rasul waved his hands in front of him, his expression becoming more animated.

"At first it was just one or two of them, but pretty soon it was all of them, grabbing things by the handful, threatening the girls behind the counter if they said anything. Got to the point where I couldn't even find people to run the register. Was just me and my wife, and she was afraid to be there alone.

"They made me a slave to the place."

With each sentence Rasul said, Reed forced his expression to remain even, allowing his brain to soak up the new information, fill in the cracks of everything he already had.

"Is that why there aren't more complaints against them?" Reed asked. "People were afraid to say anything?"

"You damned right!" Rasul shouted, the words sounding distorted through his accent. "After my inventory started coming up so short my suppliers thought I was lying to them, I had no choice but to file an insurance claim. They said I needed a police report to process it, so I called the station and asked someone to come out."

He paused there, his gaze turned towards the wall beside them. "Best and worst thing I ever did."

This was the part of the story Reed had come for, of that there was no doubt. He kept his hands balled into the front pockets of his jacket and moved an inch away from the door, anticipation gripping him.

"What happened?"

Rasul glanced up at him and back again, shaking his head from side to side. "One of them happened to be driving by, saw me talking with the cops. That night they came by just before closing time, trashed my store, threatened to kill me, have their way with..."

He stopped midsentence, Reed knowing where he was going with the statement, not willing to make the man say it aloud.

"And so a few weeks later you moved out?"

Once more Rasul shifted his attention to Reed before looking away, the corners of his eyes now damp. "A few hours later I moved out. It was just a few weeks before I stopped having to pay rent."

More questions came to Reed's mind, but he let them pass. There was no point to inquire why the man had not filed another report or done anything else, Rasul's shame already apparent. Instead he extracted a hand from his sweatshirt and reached into his rear pocket, pulling out a thin stack of papers folded into quadrants.

Smoothing them out against his thigh, he turned the stack upside down to himself and spread them out in front of Rasul, five sheets of paper in total.

The crime scene shots of Mentor, Wright, and Durell were too outrageous to show an informational witness, so Reed had pulled DMV photos for the three of them, along with Pryor and Knighton. Lined up together they resembled mug shots, all five young men in their mid-twenties, menacing looks on their faces.

"Are these the young men you named in the complaint?"

Shifting his attention from the wall to the desk in front of him, Rasul raised himself to a standing position, pressing his palms into the desk and looking down at the photos. Moving his weight onto his left hand, he extended his right towards them, using his index finger to nudge them forward.

"This one, this one, these two," he said, moving all pictures except for Knighton. "This last one I recognize, he was with them, but nobody knew his name at the time so we didn't include it."

Reed nodded, the data fitting with why Deek found Pryor's name in the file but not Knighton's.

"But you're missing one," Rasul said, lowering himself back into his chair and looking up.

"I am?" Reed asked, looking at the sheets, running over each one in his mind.

Pearlman had said the number was something like a half dozen, though no mention of a sixth member had ever been made.

"Are you sure?"

"Very," Rasul said, nodding his head in an exaggerated fashion. "I know this because he was the only one that was white."

Chapter Forty-Three

Mrs. Chamberlain was dressed the same exact way she had been the night before, the pink bath robe still encasing her body, the same fuzzy slippers covering her toes. She walked without raising them from them floor as she moved, their soles scraping against linoleum, announcing her presence long before she got to the door.

It took her a moment to place Reed despite their recent interaction, standing and blinking into the morning light. "Can I help you?"

"Good morning, Mrs. Chamberlain, Detective Reed Mattox," Reed said, reaching into his sweatshirt and exposing his badge out of pure habit. "We met last night."

A long moment passed as she stood and stared at him, her eyebrows pulled together in thought, trying to place him.

Not fourteen hours had passed since their last encounter, though to watch her try to remember it was something akin to seeing an animal attempt to decipher trigonometry.

"I came by for Deek's help?" Reed added, the words coming out as a question, meant to jog something in her memory.

Another moment passed before she pulled her mouth into a tight circle and said, "Oh, yes, that's right, I remember now," though it was apparent from her tone that she didn't.

Despite the obvious lie Reed used the opening to shove out his request. "Is he home this morning? I know it's early, but I really need him to take a look at one more thing for me."

For the first time Reed saw some semblance of the woman he had spoken to the night before, the same look of pride sweeping over her features. "Oh, yes, yes. You go right on down. My Deek's such a good boy, always ready to lend a hand to the police when they need it."

She added a wink to the last line, letting Reed know it was a playful jab. Out of courtesy he offered a small chuckle, the barb just one more in an endless string that had come his way over the years.

At least she had the good sense not to say she was just making breakfast and try to offer him bacon.

The entirety of the basement was dark as Reed descended the stairwell, running a hand along the walls, groping for a light switch. When none came he removed his keys from his pocket and snapped on the pen light clipped to them, the glow doing little to penetrate the vast space.

"Deek? You down here?" Reed called, raising his voice a bit more than necessary, making sure to be heard. "It's Detective Mattox, I need another favor."

Remaining at the foot of the stairwell, Reed rotated at the waist, the small light doing little to illuminate the room. To the left the entirety of the entertainment system sat dark and silent, nothing more than hulking shapes.

On the opposite side the neon lights from the night before were blacked out, the scent of whiskey thick in the air. Remembering the gift he brought, Reed shook his head, only hoping the whole bottle wasn't now working its way through Deek's digestive system.

"Deek!" Reed called once more, his voice gaining a few more decibels, the word coming out in a sharp crack.

A moment later a groan was heard from deep in the recesses of the room, the sound of springs creaking as Deek rousted himself from the depths of slumber. "Good God man, what time is it?"

The words came out low and raspy, the sounds of someone clearly in pain.

"It's going on ten now," Reed said. "You decent? I'm going to turn on a light."

"For the love of God, no," Deek said, his voice still contorted. "And why the hell are you here so early?"

There were a dozen retorts Reed could have stated in reply, but he held back. He knew he was seeking the help of someone that was unaffiliated, this time coming empty handed, hoping that residual goodwill from his previous offering was enough to cover the slight gaffe in protocol this morning.

"I need you to go back into those files," Reed said. "You're the only one I know that can get in there or that knows I found them."

"Christ," Deek muttered, lying silent for a moment before rolling across his bed, the sound of his bare feet thumping against the floor ringing out.

Remaining in place, Reed stood and waited as a silhouette emerged from the darkness, a thin pair of shoulders with an oversized head, a hand outstretched before him. The stench of booze seemed to hang around him like a halo, burning Reed's nostrils.

More than once he had the thought of inquiring how much of the bottle Deek had put down the previous night, but opted against it.

"Please kill that damn light, will you?"

A click of the plunger extinguished the bulb as Deek moved past him, using the same shuffling gait as his grandmother until dropping his weight unceremoniously in his desk chair. A moment later the monitor before him came to life, pulling a wince to his face as it bathed him in light.

"This better be important," he muttered in a mock whisper, pretending his voice was lowered but purposely leaving it loud enough to be heard.

"Extremely," Reed said, choosing to say as little as possible, not trusting what might come out if he began commenting on the man or his lifestyle. Instead he stood and waited, watching as Deek slowly went to work.

"Okay," Deek said, "what am I looking for?"

Reed felt his eyebrows rise a bit on his forehead in surprise, taking a step forward towards the computer monitor. "Just like that?"

"It's a lot easier when you've already been inside," Deek answered, lacing his fingers and stretching his arms up high, both shoulders letting out a series of popping noises.

"I need a name," Reed said, taking another step forward and immediately regretting it as the stench of booze rolled off of Deek's exposed skin.

"I gave you the only name there was last night," Deek said. "Prince or Peters or something like that."

"Pryor," Reed corrected. "And I don't mean in the complaint, I need to know who entered it in the system."

Stifling a yawn, Deek shrugged his shoulders and typed in a few keystrokes, his eyes pinched to almost slits as he read. "Nothing doing, man. If it was ever here, it's gone now too."

"Damn," Reed muttered, shaking his head, staring over into the darkness that he knew housed an oversized television and gaming system. He remained that way a long time, thinking about everything he knew, about the gaps that still existed.

Somebody had gone to a lot of trouble to keep a simple complaint out of the books, so much so that even the officer filling it out had been redacted as well. To pull something like that off took a lot of juice, clout that originated pretty high on the justice system food chain.

High enough that somebody would remember something from the incident, no doubt finding it as odd then as he did now.

"What about a judge?" Reed asked. "Does it say who it was that ordered the records sealed in the first place?"

Another clatter of keystrokes could be heard in the darkness as Deek went to work, stopping a moment later, his voice just audible as he mumbled to himself, reading off the screen.

"Good call, man," Deek said, stopping and looking up at Reed. "Looks like some guy called the Honorable Jackson Bennett."

Chapter Forty-Four

In the time since the complaint was expunged from the record, Jackson Bennett had moved on from presiding over the Franklin County Municipal Court. Appointed a year earlier by sitting United States District Judge Bryan Hansen, he had become the newest United States Magistrate Judge in the state, sailing through the confirmation vote from the other judges in District Six.

After moving over he had served strictly in an overflow capacity from Hansen, seeing almost no new business, being used only to cull the mass of cases that were hitting the federal desk. A quick search had shown many of them to be fairly benign in nature, agriculture and interstate commerce being the biggest two. Only a few were even remotely interesting, though Reed found nothing in them that connected to his case in the slightest.

The conglomerated information on Bennett, including the case files, was printed out and sitting on the passenger seat as Reed drove. Every few moments he glanced over, somehow hoping a breakthrough would work its way to the surface, shouting for him to notice it.

Instead it remained as dull and lifeless as Deek no doubt already was, making it very clear when Reed left what he considered acceptable business hours.

In the back seat Billie had regained a bit of spring, a nap while Reed was tucked away in Deek's basement having rejuvenated her. Reed could hear paws squeaking against the plastic cover as she moved about, her constant motion arising from a host of possibilities, the top two on the list being hunger and the need to use the restroom.

Reed felt pangs of the same two things as he maneuvered his sedan back across town, pulling up in front of the U.S. Southern District Court.

Just one block down from the CPD headquarters, it had the same style architecture, the entire thing cut from grey stone. A little boxier in shape, it stood four uniform floors in height, even rows of windows lining each of the sides. A pair of gleaming brass flagpoles extended up from the roof of it, the United States flag on one, the Ohio state flag on the other.

Given that the man he was going to see was a judge long familiar working with law enforcement, Reed opted to bring Billie along, attaching the short lead to her collar. As they made their way to the corner and used the crosswalk, he pulled his badge out from the folds of his sweatshirt, careful to make sure it was seen as they approached.

While his particular manner of dress was a personal choice, it wasn't hard to see how it was viewed by the public at large. Brandt's comment about him resembling a gym teacher was hardly the first he had heard, Riley herself having made similar comments on an almost daily basis.

Looking as he did, walking up to the front door of the courthouse and asking to meet with a federal judge would prove an almost impossible task. Working without a partner would be an oddity someone like Bennett would seize on.

Bringing Billie and making sure his ID was visible would save him a lot of time and questions at the very least.

Given the potentially testy nature of what he was there to inquire about, any help at all would be appreciated.

A pair of U.S. Marshals in matching sports coats nodded to Reed as he entered, motioning him to the side of the line moving through the metal detectors. As an officer of the law he was allowed to wear his sidearm inside the courthouse, a rule that made scanning him for anything else futile.

He waited a long moment along the side as the Marshals screened the few people in front of him before coming over with a clipboard and taking down his name and badge number. Each made a few idle inquiries about why he was there, losing interest when he mentioned only needing to speak with Judge Bennett for a few minutes, wrapping the conversation up with a few scratches behind Billie's ears.

Just ten minutes after parking Reed found himself on the third floor, passing through a glass door, the title of the office embossed on it in gold overlay, a small sense of déjà vu setting in from his meeting with Morris the day before. The only major difference was this time the desk was manned by a blonde in her late thirties, two even rows of blinding teeth smiling as he approached.

"Well now isn't she just gorgeous?" the woman said, folding her hands in her lap and raising herself from her chair, bent forward at the waist. The smile remained as she looked down at Billie, completely ignoring Reed.

It was the first time anything even approaching that reaction had ever occurred, Reed content not to interrupt it, watching as Billie seemed to enjoy the attention. She glanced up at him for only a moment before inching forward, her backside just a few inches above the floor.

Sensing this might be his best chance to get past the gatekeeper, Reed silently urged Billie forward and said, "Is Judge Bennett in? Just need to ask him a few quick questions."

"Yeah, he's in his chambers," the woman said, coming out from around the desk, still turned down at the waist.

Reed paused a moment, watching as she approached by showing Billie the back of her knuckles, allowing the dog to get her scent before attempting to pet her. Having confirmed that the woman knew her way around animals, he dropped the leash to the floor beside Billie, passing through an open door into the chambers behind the desk.

At first glance, Jackson Bennett was a big man, much larger than Reed expected. Most of the judges he had encountered over the years were of a stooped variety, made that way from advanced age and decades spent bent over a desk.

The one before him was different in every way, standing several inches taller than Reed, outweighing him by at least a hundred pounds. The effect was made even more pronounced by the robe he was fitting into place as Reed entered, the black material offset by his white hair and red face.

"Judge Bennett?" Reed asked, tapping on the door with a single knuckle as he passed inside.

At the sound of his voice the judge turned, his hands by his neck, working on a paisley tie. "Yes?"

"Hi," Reed said, moving forward without being invited, "I'm very sorry to drop by unannounced like this, but my name is Detective Reed Mattox and I had a few questions I was hoping you might be able to answer for me."

Cinching the tie into place, Bennett lowered his hands and turned, taking in the badge and Reed's attire. "What's this about?"

Taking another step forward, Reed came to a stop behind a pair of wingback chairs, the furniture meant for guests sitting opposite the judge's desk. On the walls around them was a menagerie of outdoor landscapes, most of them wooded scenes that Reed guessed to have been from the central Ohio area.

"I understand you used to preside over much of Franklin County," Reed said, starting vague.

"I did," the judge replied, walking over and placing a hand on the back of his chair, choosing not to sit. "What is this about?"

Drawing in a breath, Reed paused a quick moment, contemplating the best approach. The last thing he wanted to do was sound accusatory, needing to frame it so that the judge knew he was in need of help, nothing more.

"Two years ago, when you were still in that capacity, you expunged a complaint from the record. I need to know why."

As much as his intent was not to inflame, he couldn't help but notice how harsh the words sounded, even to his own ears.

A shadow passed over Bennett's face as he stared back at Reed, a bit of color flushing his cheeks. "Officer, as I'm sure you're already aware, if those records were sealed then it was with good cause. Confidentiality prohibits me from ever speaking of it."

Three minutes before the judge had heard Reed introduce himself as Detective. His choosing to address him as an officer was obviously a move to try and seize control of the conversation, letting Reed know he didn't appreciate where things were headed without saying as much.

"I do understand that, Your Honor," Reed said, adding the title in hopes of using it to diffuse things. "And I wouldn't be here asking unless it was a vital matter."

"Let me guess," Bennett interjected, cutting him off. "Life and death?"

The tone of his voice and the flat look on his face relayed he was being facetious, trying to make Reed feel a fool, blowing things out of proportion, asking for things that simply weren't possible.

"Three deaths," Reed replied, using the same demeanor as the judge, turning the dynamic back on him. "In a rather horrific manner, using a broadsword. Dismemberment, disembowelment. I'm sure you've seen it on the news at this point."

Not once did Reed raise his voice or challenge the judge in any way, though it was clear his words had found their mark. Bennett shifted a few inches to his right and cupped both hands atop the chair, all hue fading from his cheeks.

"The Bottoms."

"The Bottoms," Reed echoed, nodding. He didn't feel the need to elaborate on which complaint he was referring to, the immediate reaction from the judge making it clear he was already familiar with the one in question. "So far every one of the victims has been individuals whose records you wiped clean that day."

He paused, making sure his words were heard, before adding, "Now, I know the enormity of what I'm asking, but there really are lives at stake here. Who leaned on you to make this go away, and who were they trying to protect?"

Color had continued to recede from Bennett's face until all that was left was a ghostly pallor. He stared at Reed a long moment, his body rigid, before glancing at the miniature grandfather clock sitting on a table along the side of the room.

"I need to be in court in three minutes, so I'll have to give you the abbreviated version. I'm sorry, but if you want more it'll have to wait."

"I'll take anything you can give me," Reed said.

Bennett nodded once, folds of skin along his jaw line bunching and uncoiling like an accordion. "I'm not even going to bother asking how you come to have the information you have. At this point, I'd say there are more important matters to focus on."

"But you remember it well?" Reed asked, wanting, needing Bennett to give him something to work with before leaving.

"What I remember," Bennett said, his voice getting a bit softer as he looked past Reed to the wall above him, "was how mundane it was. Basic filing for public nuisance, barely a misdemeanor. There was no need for it be wiped away, certainly no call for pressure from on high to be exerted."

A tiny bit of what Rasul had mentioned lined up in Reed's head. The report he filled out had been for the bare minimum, wanting solely to file an insurance claim, pressing no major charges.

"So then why...?" Reed asked.

"Not why," Bennett said, "*who*. Who would have had so much to lose at that particular moment in time that they would do anything to protect it?"

Reed knew Bennett was trying to tell him something monumental, was giving him the key piece of information he needed without having to condemn himself in the process. His brow furled tight as he met the man's gaze, trying to piece it together.

"Who would have been so threatened by a mere vagrancy complaint in The Bottoms that they would lean on a judge to wipe it clean?" he asked aloud, letting Bennett know he followed the line of reasoning, even if he hadn't quite come to the conclusion yet.

"Two things," the judge replied, again glancing over at the clock beside them, "and then I'm sorry, but I really do have to go."

"First, I never said I was leaned on. There wasn't outright pressure for me to do anything."

"But you were rewarded just the same," Reed finished.

Bennett held his hands out to his side, motioning to the office around them. "Six months later I moved in here. I won't say it was a direct cause, but the glowing letter of recommendation sure didn't hurt.

"Second," he pressed on, picking up an iPad and a legal pad from the desk in front of him, "you've already figured out I can't tell you who it was. What I can do is tell you if word ever got out that this conversation took place, *she* would be flat pissed."

Chapter Forty-Five

There was an itching sensation crawling the length of the Boat Man's back, an insatiable tingling that he couldn't scratch, couldn't shake no matter what he did. It started at the nape of his neck, extending down to his waist, feeling like a whisper of cool breath against his skin. Every few moments it kicked up again, becoming more pronounced, goose pimples standing out along his forearms.

Things were not going the way they were supposed to. Months of planning, waiting, watching, had led him to a plan that was perfect, that was infallible.

That was fast becoming useless.

The first mistake had not been his own. It had been the finished corpse of Mason Durell's, the spastic gasp of a body that didn't quite realize it was done, jerking away in the warehouse three nights before. That one movement, that one unforeseen spasm had ruined his blade, and with it any chance he had at continuing with his scheme as directed.

Had he known then what he did now, he might have forged ahead anyway, using the damaged weapon, making it work for the sake of finishing what he had started.

Instead, the second mistake had been his, pausing for a moment, waiting until his equipment was perfect before pressing on. In doing so he had underestimated the stir his actions were causing in The Bottoms, had discounted how fast the police would be on to him. Now they were about, they were patrolling the streets, they were watching for him.

Worse still, they had warned his targets that he was coming.

The truncated timetable he was on, the sudden change in his circumstance, had switched the rules. No longer was he far out in front of everyone, working in complete obscurity, needing only the shadows to mask his movements.

As much as he hated what he was about to do, what it represented, there was no way around it.

Sitting behind the steering wheel of his rented Dodge, the Boat Man watched as a faded green pickup pulled into the lot, parking three stalls down from him. For a long moment neither party emerged, both glancing to each other, watching the deserted park for signs of life.

The meeting had been arranged through an online chat room, the kind of place where rednecks frequented to discuss the end of the world and what they were doing to prep for the day when all mankind became zombies. Just logging into it had brought a feeling of revulsion to the Boat Man's stomach as he typed out the simple request, pushing it into cyberspace, waiting less than five minutes for a response.

The man's online handle was The Joker, his avatar an emblem from a deck of Royal playing cards. He claimed to have exactly what the Boat Man was looking for and a willingness to part with it for the proper price.

It took just three emails for the two parties to come to an agreement on all relevant terms, the exchange set for four hours into the future. What the man had on his plate that needed so much time to clear the Boat Man didn't feign to know, going about his own tasks until the time was right before making the fifty mile drive west of Columbus.

The state park that the man had suggested seemed suitable for such an exchange, lending the impression it wasn't the first time he had done so. Upon agreeing to the arrangement the Boat Man had thought for sure the guy was trying to lure him into a trap, arriving a full two hours early, bringing along some reinforcements just in case.

After one hundred and ten minutes in complete silence he was content things were clear, the location chosen because it was remote, nothing more.

The park in its entirety looked to be little more than ten acres, a turnout from a state route running diagonal away from the interstate to the south. The back end of it was a pond with a dock on one end, a playground opposite it.

Bisecting the area between them was a small asphalt parking lot, spaces marked out for six cars.

The only two in use were occupied by the Boat Man and his one-time business partner.

"Let's get this over with," the Boat Man said to no one, pushing the driver's side door open, again feeling the tingling run down the back half of his body. He came to a complete stop as he exited the car and shut the door behind him, raising his hands to either side, showing he was unarmed.

A moment later the sound of the truck's door opening could be heard, the vehicle shifting as a man climbed out on the opposite side of it.

Built like a soda machine, the man walked around the side of the truck and came to a stop behind his tailgate, his thick arms hanging six inches from his sides on either side. He was dressed in jeans and a sleeveless Henley, thick red hair covering every visible bit of skin save a small oval around his eyes.

"You Boat Man?" the man asked, jerked his chin upward as he spat out the question.

"I am," the Boat Man replied, choosing not to comment on inanity of the question. "The Joker?"

"Mhmm," the man grumbled, going for the rear latch on his tailgate and jerking it open.

The heavy green metal fell with a rumble, the Joker stepping forward and sliding a vinyl gun case over onto it. Starting at the far end he unzipped it in one long movement, peeling back the top flap and stepping to the side.

"As requested, a forty caliber sniper rifle," Joker said, lifting it from the oil cloth it was resting on, his hand finding the trigger guard, the barrel pointed towards the sky. "Fiber optic scope mounted to the barrel, spring loaded feed capable of pushing out a hundred rounds per minute."

He tipped the gun down to parallel and supported it with his left hand, peering down the barrel, his left eye pinched closed as he looked through the scope with his right. "Sighted in up to five hundred yards, capable of hitting targets as far out as a thousand."

The Boat Man kept any sort of reaction off his face as he looked at the weapon, the matte metal finish polished clean, the smell of lubricant and oil finding his nostrils. He watched as the Joker handled it like a man that had been doing so most of his life, he himself keeping his hands in his pockets.

"It's a beautiful weapon," he said. "It will do nicely."

"The back story is completely clean," the Joker replied. "There is no serial number, no history whatsoever. Anybody coming across this gun or a shell it fires will find nothing as to where it came from."

The Boat Man nodded, glad that the man had taken care of that aspect without being asked.

The man again raised the front end towards the sky and extended the butt towards the Boat Man, only to be met with a twist of his head.

"That won't be necessary," the Boat Man said. "This is merely for precaution, meant as a scare tactic. Just looking at it I can tell it will more than fit that job description."

The man narrowed his eyes slightly at the explanation but said nothing as he lowered the weapon back to its case and zipped it closed. When he was finished he turned towards the Boat Man, the same wary expression in place.

"Don't take offense to this, but for my own purposes I have to ask," he said.

Already the Boat Man could tell something was coming he didn't especially want to hear, but again chose not to let it show.

"You're not one of those sick bastards are you? Am I going to read tomorrow about you going into a schoolhouse or a movie theater and going ape shit on the place?"

To the Boat Man the question was humorous, though there was no outward show of it. There were certainly people in the world that needed to fear his having the weapon, though none of them were of the sort that frequented schools or cinemas.

With his left hand he extracted a roll of cash from his pocket, extending the money in front of him.

"Would it matter if I was?"

A long moment passed as the man looked from the money to the Boat Man before reaching out and accepting the bills. "Only if you were foolish enough to say where you got it."

This time the Boat Man allowed the corner of his mouth to turn up in a smile, nodding towards the money he'd just handed over. "Look at how much cash I just gave you. That was to buy your silence as much as the gun."

Shifting his gaze downward just briefly the Joker fanned the money out before shoving it in his pocket, nodding in affirmation of their transaction.

Without another word he reached out and took up the case, extending it towards the Boat Man.

Four minutes later they were both back on the road, headed in their respective directions.

Chapter Forty-Six

For the third time in recent days, Reed found himself sitting back in Grimes's office. As someone that had gone out of his way in the preceding months to stay as far off the grid as possible, the amount of face time he was putting in around the precinct was fast growing uncomfortable.

Especially considering a lot of it was during the busiest daylight hours.

Unlike the previous two trips, this meeting had been called by Reed. Not quite a demand, but definitely far north of a request, he had contacted Grimes on his direct line and told him he would be in shortly.

They had things to discuss that could not wait.

At the time Reed could tell Grimes wasn't especially fond of being told by a detective what was going to happen, a fact that was now made even more apparent by the glower splashed across the captain's face. His jowls hung on either side of his face and tiny red lines crossed over the whites of his eyes, the telltale signs of a man that hadn't been sleeping well.

Reed knew the feeling.

"I hope to hell you're here to inform me that you've got this thing figured out," Grimes opened with, assuming his usual posture behind the desk, his fingers lined up over his abdomen.

"Pressure coming down from on high?" Reed asked.

"High, low, kidney shots, you name it," Grimes said. "Your outburst at Brandt yesterday bought you some time, but I don't need to remind you that it is running out fast."

The words had not been stated out loud, or if they had Reed had left too fast to hear them, though he had suspected as much. A woman like Brandt was too concerned with her own image, both within the community and the organization, to let either this case or Reed's outburst go for long.

What he was about to share certainly wouldn't help either.

"Media?" Reed asked.

"Every hour on the hour," Grimes said. "Which means we have about ten minutes here before I'm sure somebody will start calling again."

He leaned forward a few inches in his chair, his head extended at the neck. "Trust me, you don't want to be here when that happens."

Taking the hint, Reed launched forward with everything he had discovered in the previous twenty-eight hours, beginning with his trip downtown to meet with Morris and the gang task force and ending with his encounter with Judge Bennett right next door to headquarters.

He delivered the entirety of the update in a straight ahead style, rattling it off like a reporter reading from a teleprompter, even managing to keep his tone neutral as he delivered the punch line. When he was finished he fell silent, waiting as his captain processed the news, the internal sequence playing out on his features.

A full minute of silence passed as Grimes made sense of what he'd been told, his chin receding back against his neck, his breathing growing more pronounced as he did so. By the time he spoke he appeared to have aged several years in just a span of seconds.

"So he never actually said..." he began, his voice trailing off.

"No," Reed said, shaking his head. "I think it's pretty obvious where he was going, though."

"Very obvious," Grimes said, "but he was smart to give himself plausible deniability. If we pursue this and it blows up, you know this is entirely on us."

Twice in his response Grimes used first person plural pronouns, a fact that was not lost on Reed.

"Any idea why she might have done it?" Reed asked. "Maybe if we can figure out her angle it will dictate how we approach it."

"I think the obvious answer is just as the judge intimated, which is this all went down at a time when she could ill afford a scandal. Whatever it was must have been big enough it made her concerned about her new post as chief."

Already having considered it, Reed nodded in agreement. "My next move was going to be digging around and seeing what kind of connections she has to The Bottoms, seeing what she might have been trying to cover."

He paused a moment, considering how to best put the next sentence.

"That's part of why I came here first. If somebody figures out I've been snooping through the chief's laundry..."

The statement was left there, Reed feeling he didn't need to take it any further.

"So if your ass gets burned I'm going with you," Grimes said, his expression even. "Gee, thanks."

There was no way of telling if the comment was an attempt at levity or the truth so Reed let it go, waiting for some clear directive.

Another moment passed as Grimes peered across at him, his lips pursed, wrestling with the position they were in. There was no clear answer and both of them knew it, each trying to weigh the politics of the force with the greater ramifications of the crimes being committed.

"Go," Grimes said. "Do what you have to. Right now we're lucky to have this mess in the Near East Side dominating most of the headlines, but the longer this goes unsolved the more heat it's going to pick up."

"You think she's going to be alright with us doing this?" Reed asked.

"Definitely not," Grimes said. "In fact, we should both be prepared for her to sweep in here like a hurricane the second she finds out we're looking her direction, but right now we don't have a choice."

A sardonic smile picked at the corner of Reed's mouth as he thought about it. "So we're going after this thing, even it costs us both our careers."

The same look fell over Grimes's features as he glanced to his phone. "Didn't I just tell you I've got the media calling me all hours? We solve something this big it'll be all over the state in minutes, she won't be able to get rid of us."

Chapter Forty-Seven

The thought of paying Deek a third visit crossed Reed's mind after leaving Grimes's office, though he decided against it. There was little doubt the overgrown child was still curled up in bed, sleeping off the remains of a massive hangover, having already given Reed a lecture on the state of any future working relationship.

Instead Reed went straight for the bullpen, bringing Billie with him as he ascended to the second floor. Still several hours before Jackie came on he made a hard left at the top of the stairs without glancing over, weaving his way through an odd assortment of people and chairs en route to his post in the corner.

Much like it had a few nights before at Midwestern Paper, the weight of stares seemed to burn on his back as he went, though he pretending not to notice. For months his presence had been an oddity around the precinct, something he knew others spoke about, though with the exception of Iaconelli nobody dared voice.

Now that he was the attached lead to the biggest case in the region, he could only guess how much the speculation surrounding him had grown.

"Down," Reed said as he reached his desk, Billie going to her stomach beside him as he fell into his chair. Seeming to sense the demeanor of the room she kept her head upright as he went to work on the computer, poised like a solid black sphinx watching over him.

"Good girl," Reed whispered without looking down at her, his face partially hidden from view by the computer screen in front of him. Still he could feel the occasional glance lobbed his way from the small handful of men working nearby, though not once did he meet their gaze.

The first place Reed looked was in the CPD personnel database, getting as far as the entry for his name and badge number before balking. If there was any way to obtain what he needed without setting off warning flags in the system he would prefer to do so, minimizing the screen and bringing up a basic internet search engine.

Beginning with "Eleanor Brandt," the site spit back over half a million hits, the top links being for Facebook and LinkedIn profiles. Scrolling down through the list he saw a row of pictures of women of various ages, many of them grainy black-and-whites, appearing to have been from the first part of the century.

The fourth picture in the row was a uniformed shot of Brandt taken several years before, the link an article from *The Columbus Dispatch* announcing her appointment as the new Chief of Police.

Pulling the story up, Reed browsed down through it, the bulk of the text providing an overview of her previous career stops, postings in precincts around the city, service on different task forces. Nowhere did it make any mention of family or personal history, Reed backing out from the story to begin anew on the search engine.

For a second stab he added the words "Columbus Police Department" to the end of Brandt's name and set it to searching, the number of responses swelling considerably. The top result was the personal bio for Brandt on the CPD website, a condensed version of everything the news article had just stated.

"Shit," Reed muttered, feeling his heart rate begin to rise, a film of sweat starting to pop up on his skin.

Pulling back a final time Reed erased any mention of the department and simply attempted "Eleanor Brandt The Bottoms."

Once more the website returned a host of options, though a quick pass through confirmed that none of them were what he was looking for.

In addition to the same profiles he had bypassed a moment before were now a litany of mentions about horse racing and fishing, though nothing pertaining to even the state of Ohio, let alone the woman he was searching for.

On the floor beside him Billie lifted her body onto her front paws and moved a bit closer to him, settling herself down again just inches from his feet. Leaving the search engine in place Reed looked down at her, watching as she settled in, looking out over the room before twisting her head up to look at him.

"Yeah," Reed said, nodding in agreement with his partner's assessment.

At this point, the fact that somebody was terrorizing the area they were meant to protect far outweighed any potential for inflaming one public official.

Drawing the personnel database back up, Reed entered his name and badge number, the front screen dissolving, bringing up a searchable site that resembled the public one he had just been using. Without delay he entered the chief's name and began to search, the file coming back to him in under five seconds.

The top page of the report was the basic info sheet made for every cadet upon enrollment. It showed a photo of a twenty-two year old Brandt, her hair much longer, her features softer. Below it was all vital information, including her height, weight, and blood type.

The second page was her personal history, showing she had earned a BA in criminal justice from Capital University in Bexley before receiving a Master's in criminology from Ohio State.

The last entry on the page was her family history, showing her father to be deceased, her mother living at an address in Worthington. Below it were listed two siblings, both younger, a brother and a sister.

A thought sprang forth in the back of Reed's mind, his breathing picking up a bit more, the cotton t-shirt beneath his hooded sweatshirt now sticking to the small of his back. Dropping the personnel database from sight he pulled up ViCAP and the NCIC, entering both of the sibling's names into the system.

Both results came back negative.

"Son of a..." Reed whispered, closing both the programs.

Never during her time with CPD had Brandt worked in The Bottoms. With no husband or children of her own, the only people she could have been protecting were her siblings. The odds of anybody being important enough to earn her coverage, or potentially inflammatory enough for her to offer it, had to have been family.

Once more he went back to the search engine and entered the name of her brother, adding "Columbus, Ohio" to the end of it. On cue, a website listing came back for a dermatology practice in Dublin, the pictures therein showing a man that vaguely resembled the chief, his arms spread wide around a wife and two children well into their teen years.

Retreating away, he erased the man's first name and inserted the sister, clicking it to search.

The first image that came up was a shot of a servicewoman in an Air Force uniform, her appearance a carbon copy of her older sister. She had the same short hair and flinty features, her narrow form swallowed up by the blue uniform she was wearing.

In the photo she wore a medal around her neck, Reed recognizing it as a Governor's Service Award, the time stamp at the bottom showing the photo to be from eleven months before. On sight he felt his mouth go dry as he stared at the image, blowing it up to full screen, leaning in so close his nose almost touched the glass.

His interest had nothing to do with Bonnie Brandt, not the uniform she wore or the award she'd be given.

Instead he was focused solely on the young man beside her. With short dark and smooth skin he appeared to be somewhere in his mid-twenties, smiling as he draped an arm around his mother's thin shoulders.

An arm that had just the hint of the KOTB tattoo Reed had been chasing for days extended beneath the rolled up sleeve of his dress shirt.

Chapter Forty-Eight

"Tell me something, do *you* have the Chief of Police on speed dial?" Pierce Brandt asked, an eyebrow cocked upward at Reed as he settled down into his chair on the opposite side of the interrogation table. "Because I do."

A smirk was the only response Reed offered as he dropped the stack of case files he had amassed onto the table and lowered himself into his chair.

The reaction wasn't out of amusement at the vague threat that was being lobbed his way, he had heard much worse over the years. It wasn't in the cocksure manner with which Pierce carried himself, the kind of kid that was used to getting away with things. That too he had seen more times than he could count.

What got him, bringing on the smirk, making him take on an almost jovial tone, was that the kid had no idea what was about to hit him. He had no clue that encased in the files between them was enough concentrated information to wipe the conceit from his system, reducing him to nothing more than babble.

An hour ago, the thought would have never crossed Reed's mind. He had no ill will towards Pierce, had not once even heard his name before today. Never before had the two crossed paths, Reed willing to overlook whatever he had gotten into in the past for the sake of dealing with whoever was picking people off in the present.

When he pulled up to the two story ranch Pierce lived in his only intention was to have a civil conversation, ask a few questions, determine what he needed to know so he could finally get out ahead of the killer.

Pierce had made sure things didn't go quite so easily.

A sharp knock on the window behind him drew Reed up just a moment after touching his chair, rising to full height and turning towards the door. He purposely left the files out in the open as he went, almost daring Pierce to take a look through them, passing out into the hall without looking back.

Standing just feet outside the door was Grimes, a frown so deep it almost touched his jaw line on either side. His arms were folded across his chest as he looked at Reed, his eyebrows raised, forming deep creases across his forehead.

"You brought him here?" Grimes opened, no lead-in, no preamble. "When I gave you the green light to pursue this, I guess I erroneously believed you would exercise some level of discretion."

Keeping his hands plunged into the pockets of his sweatshirt, Reed shrugged, rotating at the waist to see the young man inside the room. True to form he was sitting and staring at the window, posturing for them to see.

"Believe me, I tried," Reed said. "He didn't want to talk and he sure as hell didn't want to cooperate. Started in with all the usual pig jokes, followed it up by telling me to get off his porch, lot of profanity thrown in just to prove how tough he was."

The same expression remained on Grimes's face as he looked past Reed, taking measure of Pierce through the glass.

"Got so damn ugly after I threatened to bring him in I had to go get Billie," Reed added. "That shut his ass up right quick."

Only Grimes's eyes moved as he shifted them from Pierce to Reed.

"After that he just kept mentioning over and over again who his aunt was, like that was supposed to be enough to make me go away."

"You know she's probably en route as we speak," Grimes said, keeping his focus on Reed.

236

"She probably is," Reed said, "but the kid has the same tattoo as all three of our victims. If nothing else we can tell her we're just trying to protect him."

"Yeah, that'll work," Grimes groaned, raising his wrist and pushing back the cuff of his shirt to reveal a wristwatch on a battered leather band. "My guess is you've got less than ten minutes. You'd better get in there."

For the second time on the day Reed understood the unspoken statement that Grimes would support him as much as he could, turning on his heel and walking right back into the interrogation room. He slammed the door behind him harder than necessary as he went, the metal-on-metal contact echoing off the concrete walls.

At the sight of him Pierce opened his mouth to speak but Reed cut him off, waving a hand at him. "Yeah, I know who your aunt is, and no, I don't care."

He went straight to the table and slid the chair in flush against it, remaining standing as he spread the files out three across.

"What I do care about is that tattoo on your forearm."

The statement was left vague on purpose, floated out there as Reed positioned the files in the correct order, the new jackets they were in void of any identifying marks. The odds were good that Pierce was already intimately familiar with what was going on, but in the event he wasn't, Reed didn't want to give him any chance to steel himself.

Any reaction that was evoked needed to be spontaneous.

"My tattoo?" Pierce asked, a half-smile on his face. He raised his right forearm above the table top and pulled back the sleeve of the plain blue sweater he was wearing, the script K and block OTB Reed had grown so familiar with coming into view.

"This?" Pierce asked, his voice relaying his surprise. "You hauled me down here to talk about some ink I had done a while back? Well hell, why didn't you say so? Could have saved us all a lot of time."

Most people inside the interrogation room fell into one of a few distinct categories. People like Lucy Barr were a wreck, too emotionally damaged by whatever happened to be of any use. Those like Hank

Winters knew they had nothing to hide, people that just wanted to get things over with, get on with the lives they had waiting for them.

Pierce Brandt fell into another group that Reed had seen many times, those that used false bravado. The move was so overplayed, so patently over-the-top, that Reed had to stop himself from laughing.

"Pierce, what did the Kings of The Bottoms do two years ago that was so bad you guys immediately disbanded?"

As he spoke Reed leaned forward, pressing his palms flat against the table, looking across at Pierce.

The same half-cocked smile remained on Pierce's features, the thin bit of stubble covering the lower half of his face twisted up to the side. "Officer, I have no idea what the hell you're talking about."

Reed knew that his time was running short, that any moment the door behind him would fly open, the chief herself storming in. Vitriol sprouted deep in the pit of his stomach for the entire Brandt family, sweat starting to form in all the usual places.

"Detective," Reed corrected, "and you mean to tell me you just went out and got a shitty tattoo on your forearm for fun? Just picked four letters at random and had a buddy with an ink pen and a needle carve you up?"

"Yeah, you look like a dick," Pierce replied, seizing on Reed's amendment. "And what's it matter why I got this tattoo? Lots of people have even crazier stuff that doesn't make any sense. Buddy of mine has that girl with black hair pulling the football out from Charlie Brown across his back, doesn't mean a thing."

It was clear Pierce wasn't going to give anything up on his own. For whatever reason, whether it be a sheltered life or a supreme belief that he was above everyone else around him, he had truly started to believe the aura of faux invincibility he had created for himself.

The time had come to shake that out of him.

"Tell me though," Reed said, "did somebody take a sword and slice your buddy's Charlie Brown tattoo in half?"

Starting with the file on his left, Reed jerked back the top cover of it, revealing an 8x10 glossy print from the crime scene. "Cause somebody sure as hell did that to your friend Edwin Mentor."

Two feet away Pierce's jaw dropped open, the ghastly image hitting him full in the face.

"But they weren't done there," Reed said, moving to the next one in order, "after that they paid your buddy A.J. Wright a visit."

He extended an index finger down at the image, and said, "Messed him up so much his own dog mistook him for Puppy Chow."

The color drained from Pierce's face as he turned his head to the second image, the mangled forearm of Wright visible.

"Definitely wasn't done there though," Reed pressed on, feeling adrenaline surge through his system as he opened the third file. "This guy hates you all so much he even risked walking in to Midwestern Paper to get rid of Mason Durell."

No sound crossed Pierce's lips as he looked from one image to the next, shaking his head in disbelief. "No. This isn't them, this is you messing with me."

Reed opened his mouth to reply but was cut off before he got a word out, the door behind him exploding open, the sound so sharp it caused Pierce to jump in his seat.

Chapter Forty-Nine

"What *the hell* do you think you're doing?" Eleanor Brandt snapped at Reed, her entire body quivering, one finger extended in front of her, just inches from Reed's face.

Reed opened his mouth to respond, but Brandt continued before he could get a word out.

"It's bad enough you were digging through my personnel records, but now you've gone and brought my nephew in for questioning?!"

This time Reed knew better, keeping his mouth shut, waiting for her tirade to pass.

"Well?" she snapped, swinging her hands out from her sides, letting them fall with a slap against her hips.

Reed was acutely aware that Grimes and Oliver Dade were both standing right beside them, watching things unfold like spectators at a tennis match. While he couldn't see them he was also near certain various personnel from the precinct were nearby listening, the entire station having gone quiet.

"I'm following the evidence," Reed said, fighting a losing battle to keep the anger he felt from his voice. "It led me to you, which led me to him."

"Led you to me which led you to him," Brandt muttered. "Are you listening to yourself? How stupid are you, Detective?"

Fire flashed behind Reed's eyes as he stared across at her, feeling his body temperature rise, knowing that an explosion he may soon regret was lurking just beneath the surface.

"I should have thrown your ass off this case yesterday," Brandt said, shaking her head. "I got conned by your little display so I told Grimes to leave you on another forty-eight hours just to see where things went. What a mistake that was."

On pure reflex Reed glanced over to Grimes, his arms still folded over his torso. Not once had he mentioned the ticking clock hanging above, giving Reed the autonomy he needed to work.

"No," Reed said, iron in his tone, "not letting me finish my questioning in there right now, that would be the mistake."

This time it was Brandt's turn to try and respond, Reed cutting her off before she had the chance.

"And let me save you the time of your little three minute game you put me through yesterday.

"So far, all three victims have the same tattoo on their forearm, all marking them as a group called the Kings of The Bottoms, a group that did something so heinous that just killing them isn't enough, someone is going out of their way to chop their arms off and destroy the brand forever.

"A brand, I might add, that your nephew in there has on his forearm."

Brandt's face went stiff, her breath catching in her throat as she tried to fire back at Reed.

There was so much more Reed wanted to add, to stand in the precinct and yell at the top of his lungs. Things such as how the sole mention of the Kings was a complaint that had been covered up because the incoming Chief of Police was worried about a scandal. Facts such as the judge that wiped the record clean was able to parlay that action into a United States Magistrate chair.

He didn't though.

As much as he wanted to, as much as every impulse told him to lash into her, he held back. He had done enough to make his point. There was still a case to solve and deriding the chief in front of everybody would get him no closer to it, potentially making his life that much more difficult in the process.

Opposite him Brandt seemed to sense everything Reed was thinking, somehow working back in her mind how he had gotten from The Bottoms to her nephew. Bit by bit the flush of her face receded, her hands falling slack by her side.

"He's not going to tell you anything," she said, shifting her head at the neck to look through the window.

On the other side of the glass everybody could see Pierce looking through the files, his hands shaking as he took in the carnage of the photos.

"The little prick has spent a lifetime being sheltered," Brandt said, the fury gone from her tone, her demeanor all business. "You're going to need me in there to prove to him he can't hide from whatever happened."

It took a moment for the sudden downshift to catch with Reed, his eyes widening a touch before he too settled back into a professional stance. "Okay. I'll follow your lead."

"No," Brandt said, shifting away from the glass to look up at Reed. "You've been working this thing and clearly have reasons for bringing him in. You do it, I'll back your play."

Deep in Reed's stomach something twisted tight, a roil that felt like barbed wire within him. It was the first time since Riley that he had had a human partner on anything, this one a woman too, though only a shell of the one he had worked with and trusted months before.

The tangle gripped him so tight it forced the air from his lungs, suffocating him inert for a long moment before he nodded, moving back into the interrogation room without speaking.

Seated on the other side of the table, Pierce looked up from the photos as he entered, his eyes wide with fear. He kept his gaze on Reed a long moment before shifting his attention to Brandt, sliding in and closing the door behind them.

"Aunt E?"

"Hey, Pierce," Brandt said, taking two steps towards him before stopping, her hands remaining by her sides.

"What's going on here?" Pierce asked, keeping his attention on Brandt. "Are these pictures true? Did this really happen?"

The chief flicked her gaze to Reed, who nodded just slightly.

"Yes," Brandt said. "You haven't heard from any of these people?"

"No," Pierce replied, pleading in his voice. "We haven't spoken since everything happened. Things were already bad after what you did, and then after..."

He let his voice trail off, his gaze reaching past Brandt, focusing on nothing along the back wall.

"But I didn't have anything to do with this," he whispered. "I saw on the news something had happened, but I swear to God, I had no idea."

"We don't think you did," Reed said, raising his voice just slightly, enough to be heard through the daze Pierce was fast falling into. "But we do think whatever it is you're talking about is the reason this is all happening now."

Chapter Fifty

"It was right after the thing with the mini mart," Pierce said, his eyes unfocused, his attention aimed at the table in front of him.

"Some of the guys didn't like the way things had gone down, with the owner calling the police on us and then the whole thing getting wiped clean. They thought for us to really take hold, for us to make a name for ourselves in The Bottoms, we needed to make a statement.

"Having my aunt take care of the first thing we ever got busted on didn't exactly do that."

Positioned on one corner of the table, his arms crossed, Reed glanced to Brandt. She was posted on the corner opposite him, looking down at Pierce between them.

As the young man spoke Brandt drew her mouth into a thin line, Reed able to see tendrils of guilt creeping into her visage. In trying to help, in trying to protect her family and her own career, she had potentially set something in motion that was now much, much worse.

"So we needed to do something big," Pierce said. "Something to get noticed by some of the other groups in the area. There were only six of us, but we wanted to prove we were hard, could stand toe-to-toe with anybody."

It took everything Reed had not to shake his head in disgust as Pierce spoke, listening to the misguided delusions of young men, their notions of toughness.

"Night after night, we started hanging out down in the old gas station lot. Somehow one of the guys, I don't remember who, got his hands on a couple of guns. They were old as hell, rusted out, probably wouldn't even have fired, but we were all convinced that's what we needed to show we were legit."

He paused a moment and swallowed hard, a lump traveling the length of his throat.

"There were only two of them, so they went to Mase and Eddie. The rest of us did what we could. Dub-P and Mac got knives, I had a set of brass knuckles. I'm sure A.J. had something, but I can't remember what."

Reed had made a point of keeping the files open in front of him, using the photographic carnage to force complicity, leaning on the young man by assaulting his senses, making him realize that the people he was speaking about were no more.

"We spent a good month or so out there every night, nothing really happening. We'd all show up around dark, drink some beers, take turns passing the guns back and forth, running into the diner whenever we got hungry.

"Wasn't like there was anybody else around, the cops sure as hell weren't patrolling the area."

More than once Reed wanted to urge Pierce forward, get him to divulge the punch line, jump straight to the part they needed to hear. Pulling in long breaths through his nose he remained silent, feeling his heart rate pick up as seconds ticked off.

"After about a month, I thought things were chill again. All the talk of needing to do something big had died down, most of the guys content to hang out every night.

"Of course, that was before they showed up."

At the sound of the last sentence Reed and Brandt exchanged a look, nothing more than a quick meeting of gazes before focusing back on Pierce.

"They?" Reed asked.

Pierce's head shifted an inch or two from side to side as he continued to stare straight ahead, his voice just a decibel above a whisper. "Had to be the only two people in The Bottoms more out of place than I was. Young couple, thirties maybe. Both nice looking, driving a decent looking car, the kind of thing you never saw down there, definitely not after dark.

"They rolled up at some point late in the evening, just after the diner closed. We saw them as they pulled onto the curb outside and both hopped out, running up to the door hand in hand, laughing and falling against each other when they found it locked up."

His eyes narrowed a bit, the skin around them tightening as he continued. "At the time we thought they were drunk or high or something, but now looking back I think they were just enjoying themselves, out having fun together."

He said the words as if such a notion were completely foreign to him, something that he never would have considered before that very moment.

"We all sat there and watched as they stumbled back towards their car when Dub pulled back the slide on the gun he was holding, said it was time we got ours."

A veneer of moisture came to his eyes as he pressed on. "The rest of us, hell, we just jumped up and went along with it. We didn't think he was actually going to hurt anybody, just thought we'd scare them, leak the story out, let people know not to mess with us."

Again he paused, his lips moving, but no sound passing over them.

"What happened next?" Brandt said, her voice the tone of an investigator, not a concerned family member.

"Dub and Mac, they told me and Mase to hold the guy while they went for the girl. Made us stand him up while they started touching her, doing things to her."

Moisture pooled at the bottom of his eyes before gravity finally won out, pushing twin tears down his cheeks. Long gone was the cocky, conceited young man Reed had brought in an hour before, replaced by a scared kid, still in his mid-twenties, for the first time realizing just how bad what he had done really was.

Of the consequences it was now bringing down on them.

"The guy fought against us for a while, and he was strong too, hell of a lot stronger than he looked. About halfway through he stopped fighting as hard, started crying, us forcing him to stand there and watch what was happening to his girl."

Twice he blinked, each time forcing more moisture down his cheeks.

"That was when I couldn't take it anymore. I slipped my hand into my pocket and pulled out the brass knuckles. One shot to the temple, put the poor bastard out of his misery.

"The guys, they all thought it was because I was sick of restraining him, starting whooping it up like I'd done a hell of a thing. At that point I just wanted to go home, be done with it all."

Reed had to force his mind to slow down, to stay in the moment, to focus on what Pierce was telling them and not jump too far ahead. He had just been handed enormous chunks of information, things that finally confirmed he was on the right trail, that every supposition he had was correct.

At the same time, he couldn't allow his thoughts to retreat into themselves. He had to stay alert, to hear everything Pierce had left to share.

"What happened after that?" Reed asked.

For the first time since beginning his narrative, Pierce looked up at him. No longer was he in the past, now in the room, the spell having been shattered.

"The car we left sitting on the curb. Both of them we loaded into Mase's van and drove down to Grove City, dropped them in a park.

"The guys worked them over a little bit more before we took off, but by that point I was pretty out of it. I was sick to my stomach and wanted to go home."

He shifted his attention from Reed to Brandt and said, "Two days later I moved back in with mom. This is the closest I've been to The Bottoms or the Kings since."

Dozens of thoughts sprang to Reed's mind, all of them things he now needed to check up on, new angles that had to be considered. Before he could though he had one last thing he needed to ask Pierce.

Flipping to the bottom file of the stack he'd brought in, Reed pulled a single sheet of paper from it. On it was the pencil drawing the sketch artist had made from Hank Winter's description, the image that had been generated taking up the entirety of the sheet.

"The man you held that night, was this him?" Reed asked, turning the paper so it faced Pierce and sliding it across.

Offering a quick look to his aunt, Pierce shifted his stare down at the sheet, his head beginning to bob up and down almost immediately.

"Yeah, that's him. His hair wasn't like that. It was shorter, not as curly, but that's his face. I'll never forget that face."

Upon receiving confirmation, Reed pulled the image back to himself and reinserted it into the folder, piling the stack back atop one another.

"Go," Brandt whispered, watching as he collected his things. "I'll take care of this here. You just go do what you need to, Detective."

Chapter Fifty-One

An overcast afternoon had brought with it a heavy cloud cover, blanketing all of central Ohio, blocking most sunlight from getting through. By five nightfall was already well on its way, more than an hour earlier than usual.

At six The Bottoms were completely dark, nothing but street lights and long shadows over everything.

The bit of meteorological luck fit the Boat Man's plans perfectly, most of his day spent in the rear of his home, alternately oiling and checking his weapons.

Still perched on its stand was the *ken* blade, its blade polished to a gleam, the new finish on it free of any imperfections. Laid before it on the ground was the rifle, the body of it pulled free from the gun sleeve, stretched across the black vinyl.

If the man was to be believed, the weapon was completely untraceable. That made it imperative that no matter how badly the Boat Man wanted to fire it, regardless of how much he wanted to check the accuracy, to feel the interworking of the mechanism pressed against his shoulder, he couldn't risk it.

Already he knew the police were starting to close in. Leaving a trail of spent shell casings or slugs to be dug out of trees somewhere would not behoove him or the goal he was so close to accomplishing.

Even with the noise suppressor on the end, no gunshot was ever truly silenced. They had a distinctive sound that people would hear, would remember, that they might even come to investigate for themselves.

The targets of his mission were a very distinct list of people, a list that would be two shorter in just a few hours. There was no need to put anybody else in the compromising position of becoming collateral damage, no point in forcing himself to become like the men he was hunting.

Fighting his every inner desire, the Boat Man refrained from practicing with the gun, trusting it was ready to go as he now toted it up to the fourth floor of the abandoned schoolhouse, the same one he had sat and observed so many nights before.

Despite having spent countless hours in direct eyesight of its crumbling edifice, it was the first time ever having set foot inside.

The body of the building was laid out much the way the outside would suggest, a central staircase crossing back and forth through the middle, a wide landing encasing it. Four classrooms made up the bulk of every floor, one in each corner.

Sticking to the stairs, the Boat Man ascended through near darkness, just a faint ambient glow cast through the south facing windows, residual light from the diner nearby. The rest of the building remained dark, the doors to most of the classrooms closed tight.

Behind each one the Boat Man could envision stray vagrants, or even families of homeless huddled together, whatever possessions they'd managed to salvage heaped into a pile. With every step he could imagine them hearing the tread of his boots hitting the wood floor, hunkering down low, beseeching each other to be quiet.

Much like the people he might have encountered in the woods, the Boat Man wished them no harm. Their plight was difficult enough, he had no reason to add to it. He was only passing through for a short period of time, just long enough to do what he must before moving on.

Coming to the top floor, the Boat Man found all four doors open, a telling sign that it was deserted. Large water spots and bits of rotting plaster dotted the floor, pulling his gaze to the ceiling. Overhead he could see small pockets of the night sky peeking through, feel the cold air of the outer world on his cheeks.

A faint smile traced his lips as he thought of the building's state of disrepair aiding him, pushing away any squatters that might have been camped out, the universe assisting his quest for justice.

Using the light from the diner as a guide, the Boat Man slipped into the southwest corner classroom, a tangle of desks reserved for children in their early years still inside. Most of the wood had long since been stripped away from them leaving only misshapen metal skeletons behind, their bodies tossed on a side.

Careful to step around them, the Boat Man picked his way to the closest window, nothing more than a gaping hole, the glass shattered away, lying in large shards across the floor. Sliding the rifle from its case, he rested the front of the barrel on the window casing and checked his view, a series of green halogen scale markers visible.

The Boat Man felt his heart rate increase as he stared through the scope, feeling like a military sniper as he checked over the area. Across from him he could see the diner at work, a half dozen regulars scattered amongst the tables. To his right, he could just make out the dumpster he'd used for cover the night before, trash still piled high around it.

The last place he looked was down at the abandoned gas station lot, at the open expanse of concrete providing an easy target. No more than twenty-five yards away, the Boat Man sighted in on small objects scattered on the asphalt, curling his finger around the trigger guard, imagining himself tugging it backwards, almost feeling the weight of the stock kicking against his shoulder.

Just as fast the Boat Man lowered the weapon, the smile remaining in place.

Leaning it back against the wall, the Boat Man lifted the shell of a desk from the ground nearby and placed it perpendicular to the window, using the metal as a makeshift frame. He rested the weapon across it, only the butt and barrel touching, both ends extended far out in either direction.

There he left it, just inches from his fingertips, as he took a few steps back from the window to ensure he was out of direct eyesight. He shoved his hands into the pockets of his pants, his fingers curling around the obols lodged deep in the cloth sacks. He lowered his chin to his chest, his body going into a low power state as he focused in on his target.

All he had to do now was wait.

After two years, the Boat Man was good at waiting.

Chapter Fifty-Two

Reed's cell phone was out before he crossed the threshold from the interrogation room, already scrolling through his recently dialed calls. He thumbed to the top entry in the list, a string of digits so new that a name had not yet even been attached to it, and pressed send.

"What the hell just happened in there?" Grimes asked, his attention still on the glass, the question aimed in Reed's direction. Beside him Dade stood in a trance that was somewhere between awe and a daze, staring through the glass, watching Brandt and her nephew on the other side.

"What just happened was our case just got blown wide open," Reed said, raising the phone to his ear. "Hopefully in a few minutes we'll have a name to go with that story and we'll be off and running."

While listening to Pierce's tale, a number of loose strings Reed could pull on had come to mind. The obvious place to start was figuring out who the couple was and where they were, the odds being overwhelming that they or someone affiliated with them was now going after the Kings.

It hadn't taken a great deal of sleuthing to get the story out of Pierce, the photos having the effect of bringing a harrowing reality to the situation, stripping away his veneer. In its stead he had gone straight to that incident, the last and presumably worst thing that occurred during the existence of the gang.

The murders now occurring had to be connected.

If not, the reality was Reed had no idea what to pursue next.

The line rang three times before going to voicemail, an automaton telling him to leave a message. "Deek, this is Reed. Call me back, now."

Looking up at Grimes, Reed said, "Whatever you hear me say in the next few minutes, I need you to agree to."

Holding the phone out in front of him, Reed counted off six seconds before it erupted in his palm, the sound shrill through the hallway. Accepting it, Reed switched it to speakerphone.

"You know, man, when I gave you my number this morning that was so you wouldn't wake me up anymore, not so you'd be calling again already."

There was a slight hint of annoyance in Deek's tone, though unlike their previous encounter he did sound awake and alert.

"Deek, I'm standing here right now with Captain Wallace Grimes," Reed said, bypassing Deek's comment. "We need some serious cyber digging done this second, and we're willing to pay you as a special consultant to make it happen.

"Isn't that right, Captain?"

Grimes's eyes grew larger as he reached out and covered the receiver on Reed's phone. "We have people on the force that do this sort of thing. They can be on it in minutes."

"Sir, with all due respect, we don't have *anybody* that works like this guy does. He'll have me an answer by the time they even start looking."

It was apparent from the look on Grimes's face that he didn't like it, was even less comfortable with being put on the spot, but he let it ride. Slowly he pulled his hand back and said, "That's correct. As this is a time sensitive matter in a high visibility case, we will compensate you for all assistance rendered."

A moment of silence passed, Reed and Grimes looking at each other, before Deek asked, "The usual form of currency? Or actual cash?"

"Whichever you'd prefer," Reed said, waving a hand at the confused look on Grimes's face.

Another moment passed, this one filled with the sounds of feet shuffling over a bare floor, followed by the plastic wheels of a desk chair doing the same.

"Alright man, hit me when ready."

"I need you to look at May of 2012," Reed said. "Check the hospitals in the area, starting with Grove City, for a pair of people being admitted. One male, one female, both assault victims, the woman a possible rape victim."

Even as he rattled off the information, Reed knew how thin the data he had was. It was a good start for establishing motive, but still a long way from securing an identity.

The sound of keys moving quickly rang out, all three men in the hallway staring down at the implement in Reed's hand.

"You got anything else for me, man? Over the course of a month we've got eleven different rape victims and twenty-seven assaults."

Aside from the sketch artist picture, there was precious little Reed had to work with.

"I know the male was Caucasian. That help any?"

More keys sounded out. "Fourteen. Cut it almost in half."

"Damn it," Reed said, looking up at Grimes and Dade, both wearing the same strain he felt on their faces.

He looked a question to each of them, hoping for some bit of guidance, but both seemed as stumped as he was.

"Alright, let's try this again," Reed said. "Is there any way to determine if the victims were found in a park?"

"Found in a park?" Deek asked. "I'm looking at hospital records right now, not housing reports."

Reed gave a bitter nod, his head moving no more than a few inches, as he agreed with Deek's assessment.

Once more he ran the story back through his head, starting with the Kings hanging out in the gas station parking lot and taking it up through the moment when they dumped the bodies. Start to finish it took him just over a minute, everyone watching him, waiting in silence.

"The car," he said, his attention focused on Brandt and Pierce still talking on the other side of the glass, the elder now having reached across the table, holding her nephew's hand. "He said they left the car."

Both Grimes and Dade continued to watch him, neither saying anything.

"Deek, can you determine if a car was towed from in front of the All-Nite Diner at any point that month? I don't have an exact address, but I know it's on Scanson."

"Hold on," Deek said, his voice distracted as he went to work. He continued to punch hard for thirty seconds, paused, and then went back again.

When he was done, a low, shrill whistle sounded out over the line.

"Well, I'll be damned."

"What?" Reed asked, looking up at Grimes, not wanting to allow hope to creep in, but feeling it doing so just the same.

"Riley was right. You are good."

The feeling of hope grew a little stronger as Reed focused in on the phone, squeezing it so tight in his hand the plastic threatened to explode at any moment.

"Deek, what'd you find?"

"On May 18th, a solid black BMW registered to a Michael Rigas was towed from that corner. Thing sat in impound for two and a half months before it was ever claimed."

"How about the hospital records?" Reed asked. "That name come up?"

"No," Deek replied, his voice again growing distant as he searched. "But four of them were admitted as John Doe's."

"That's got to be our guy," Reed said without looking up, staring at his phone. "Is there an address?"

"This your cell?" Deek asked. "I'll text it to you right now."

Chapter Fifty-Three

The first thing Reed thought as he pulled up in front of Michael Rigas's home was that Pierce had been correct. Quite possibly the only people more out of place than him in The Bottoms at that time of night would have been the owner of this home and his lady.

Located in Worthington, the house was tucked away in a cul-de-sac, a few miles away from the outer belt encircling the city. Leaving behind any of the noise or traffic of the freeway and the collection of restaurants and shopping centers it supported, the street was a bucolic look into residential living.

Generous lots lined either side of the street, equally spaced out, homes situated in the middle of them. All looked to be newer in manufacture, constructed from brick or cedar, only a couple using vinyl siding. Every last one of them stood two stories in height, towering oak and elm trees just starting to bud, their limbs extended out over the street.

As he sat and stared out at it, Reed could almost imagine the place in the summertime, the sort of street where impromptu barbecues and games of street baseball were common.

The images seemed almost a cruel juxtaposition from the reason Reed was there, at the very least at what had befallen Rigas.

"You ready?" Reed asked over his shoulder, taking up the short leash as he climbed out, clipping it to Billie's collar so they could both approach the front door together.

Under different circumstances, he might have been more cognizant of the neighborhood dynamics at play. He may have tried less to alert any neighbors that might be watching, been sure to leave Billie behind so as to not arouse suspicion.

At the moment though he had ample reason to believe the man that was terrorizing The Bottoms fifteen miles south called this location his home. At the very least, he had direct knowledge of something horrific the victims had done, something so vile the likelihood of it not being connected was almost non-existent.

Given all that, there was no way he was leaving Billie behind.

The house appeared deserted as Reed approached, no car in the driveway, no lights in any of the windows. The front lawn had not yet been cut for the spring, errant tufts just starting to sprout up in odd places.

On the whole, the home stood two stories tall, a mixture of brick and white vinyl siding. The combined effect made the house look much brighter than many surrounding it, the place almost appearing inviting as Reed and Billie approached.

Again Reed could feel his heart rate increase, his pulse pushing through his temples as he came near, Billie sensing the physiological change in him, her demeanor shifting in turn. His breathing picked up as he ascended the front two steps and rang the doorbell, waiting a few moments before curling his hand into a fist and pounded on the frame of the door.

Thirty seconds of standing confirmed his original assumption. No lights came on from within, no sound of footsteps approaching, not even the slightest creak of the home to indicate someone might be moving around within.

Had any of the previous things occurred, Reed might have been able to claim probable cause and forced his way inside, feigning that a suspect was hiding, refusing to answer. As was, he had no reason to believe that to be true.

All forcing his way inside now would accomplish would be to bring down a firestorm of bad press for the department.

"Come on," Reed said, turning on a heel and starting back down the front walk, pulling Billie along. When they got to the end of it a thought occurred to him and he kept moving forward, crossing over the street and walking to the door of the home directly opposite them.

With lights spilling through the front windows, the home could be seen as a near copy to Rigas's. The only difference Reed noticed as he approached was the siding painted blue instead of white, an inconsequential detail as he rang the doorbell and stepped back.

The echo of the bell had no more than died away when heavy footsteps approached, the door pulled open a moment later by a woman with thick blonde hair. Somewhere in her late-thirties to early forties, smile lines had just started etching themselves around her eyes and mouth. Dressed in jeans and a turtleneck, the majority of her frame was covered in a red and white apron, a dish towel in her hands.

A look of concern passed over her face as she looked at Reed and his enormous partner both standing on her porch.

"Yes?" she asked, her voice a bit deeper than expected.

"Good evening," Reed said, reaching into his sweatshirt and removing his badge. "My name is Detective Reed Mattox, and this is my partner Billie."

The look of concern faded a bit, though she remained silent.

"I'm sorry to bother you, but I'm looking for Michael Rigas," Reed said, hooking a thumb out by his side and twisting so as to motion to the house across the street. "You wouldn't happen to have seen him tonight, would you?"

The woman glanced past Reed to the home sitting dark and shook her head, a tight, curt movement. "No, I haven't. What's this about? Has something happened...?"

He got the impression from the way her voice tailed off at the end that she had wanted to add "again," but had stopped herself short.

"Not at all," Reed said. "In fact, there's been a bit of a break in a previous case and I was hoping to ask him a few questions."

Even as Reed gave the response, he knew it sounded hollow. The woman before him seemed to as well, her stance remaining aloof, guarded.

"No," she said, again shaking her head. "To be honest, we haven't seen a lot of Michael in quite some time."

The statement struck Reed as a bit off, something in her tone suggesting she was trying to tell him more than she was saying.

"He does still live here though?" Reed asked.

"Far as I know," she replied. "I still see his car pull in and exit from time to time, but it's been ages since any of us actually interacted with him."

She paused, seemingly hoping Reed would pick up on what she was saying, only continuing once it was clear he didn't.

"At first, after what happened, none of us really knew how to. After a while it became apparent there was no point, he didn't want to anyway."

The familiar feeling of pressure returned to Reed's stomach, again bits of prickly heat accompanying it as it climbed his back.

"Really? That was almost two years ago, nobody has spoken to him since?"

The woman looked from Reed to the house again, a bit of wistfulness crossing her face, before finally shrugging.

"Best guess? Try the church down on the corner of Knox and Edgewood. Sometimes I see his car parked there. Maybe you'll get lucky, or find somebody that knows where he's been."

Chapter Fifty-Four

The name Rigas should have tipped Reed off, though for whatever reason he never once thought the church he was being sent to was Greek Orthodox. Not until he pulled up in front of the white stucco building, twin spires on either front corner extending up into the darkened sky, did it even occur to him.

"Well, this is different," Reed whispered, turning the engine off and climbing out, leaving Billie behind.

A quick scan of the parking lot showed there to be only two other cars on the grounds, both of them a long way from BMW's.

Had he any other leads at the moment, if he had not already invested so much time and energy into finding Rigas, he would have gone somewhere else. As it stood, he didn't. If this too turned out to be a dead end he would have no choice but to slink back to the precinct, call in a BOLO for Rigas's car, and hope Brandt could wrestle something useful from her nephew.

The thought made Reed shudder, his heart continuing to race, his body somehow knowing that he was close, that at any second the last bit of information he needed was going to fall into place.

The front door was thick and heavy, made of wood and painted white, as Reed tugged it open and stepped inside. The smells of incense and candle smoke assaulted his nose simultaneously as he entered, his feet sinking into heavy carpeting.

Pausing just inside the door, Reed took stock of the small front holding room he found himself in, a second set of doors standing open before him, beckoning him into the main hall of the church. Glancing to either side he made his way forward, stepping through as the space opened up before him, bright light and color almost blinding him.

The space was much larger than it appeared from the outside, over twenty rows of pews lined on either side of the main aisle, all painted white with red seat cushions. Overhead massive chandeliers hung down, their lights twinkling through ornate crystal arrangements.

One step at a time Reed moved forward, heading towards the front altar. In the center of it rested a wooden pulpit with a Lent banner draped over it, an organ rising along the back wall. Standing silent to the side was a table for the necessary implements of communion, a half dozen miniature pews set aside for the choir.

"Hello?" Reed asked, his voice echoing through the room.

"Hello," a voice said beside him, jerking his attention to the left.

Tucked along the wall was a pair of confessional booths, both standing just seven feet tall, constructed from the same wood painted white, a latticed screen covering the length of the doors. Kneeling at the foot of them was an older man in slacks and shirtsleeves, a paintbrush and bucket by his side.

"Good evening," Reed said, sliding himself through the second and third rows of pews, making his way towards the man. "My name is Detective Reed Mattox and I was told I might be able to find Michael Rigas here."

At the mention of Rigas's name the man's face fell flat, his shoulders slumping by his side. Carefully he sat his brush down atop the can of paint and stood, his total height falling six inches shorter than Reed.

He walked forward and met Reed before he reached the end of the pew, extending a hand. "Peter Galanos, priest here at the church."

"Father," Reed said, reciprocating the handshake.

Galanos waved a hand at him and said, "That won't be necessary, but thank you. Please, have a seat."

The urge to tell Galanos he didn't have the time to be sitting and engaging in idle chit chat crossed Reed's mind, but he opted against voicing it. He could tell from the man's demeanor, from his instantaneous reaction to Rigas's name, that he had something to be shared.

He only hoped it would help with what he needed to do.

"May I ask," Galanos said, "why it is you wish to speak with Michael?"

Reed opened his mouth to give the same canned response he had given the woman a few minutes earlier, but closed it just as fast. Something about the gravity of the situation, of the clock he knew was ticking, of sitting in church speaking to a priest, just wouldn't let him.

"We have reason to believe Michael may be involved in a series of murders that have taken place," Reed said, his voice low, careful to ensure anybody else that might enter would not hear.

Beside him Galanos's eyes slid shut, his shoulders somehow falling another inch in height. "The Bottoms, right?"

Feeling his heartbeat rise again, Reed nodded. "That's right."

A mournful sound passed from the man as he remained with his eyes closed, his entire upper body jerking with a shudder. He remained that way a long moment, his body fighting off the sobs in the silence, his cheeks growing wet with tears.

For three minutes Reed let him continue without a word before reaching out and touching his shoulder. "Why do I get the impression you're not surprised to see me here?"

Galanos passed the back of his bare wrist over his face, wiping away the moisture, before shaking his head. "You have to understand something. The Michael that exists today, the Michael that you're now looking for, isn't the same Michael that I know.

"What happened that night was monstrous. It changed him. I truly believe it broke his spirit."

All Reed knew about that night was what Pierce had told him, which was bad enough on its own. There was no doubt though that enormous chunks of it had been left out, parts that only someone as terrified, as helpless as Michael was to stop it, would understand.

"So he spoke to you about it?" Reed asked.

"No," Galanos whispered. "Not really. He didn't have to though. The things he did talk about made it clear what was in his heart, what he was thinking on."

At that he started to weep again, his voice dipping lower. "I tried to talk to him. I thought I was getting through to him, but it's clear I wasn't."

Unsure how to respond, Reed reached out and laid a hand on the old man's back. There was much he needed to know, many questions desiring to be asked, but he knew this wasn't his interview to conduct. He was at the mercy of Galanos's emotions.

"Maybe he was right," Galanos whispered. "Maybe it would have been better if they'd killed him, too."

Too.

The word shot Reed's eyebrows up his forehead, his eyes opening wide. In his ears he could hear Pierce saying some of the guys had done things in the park, though he hadn't taken part.

"They killed her," Reed whispered.

For the first time since sitting down Galanos turned to look at him, his mouth formed into a perfect circle. "You didn't know?"

All Reed could manage was a shake of his head, no words escaping him.

"Janice Rigas was a beautiful person, in every sense of the word. The daughter of a Japanese father and a Greek mother, she was hopelessly devoted to Michael, to God, to everything that was right in this world."

He paused again, fresh moisture coming to his eyes. "The injuries she sustained were just too much though, the stab wound, the slices across her stomach..."

Fireworks exploded in Reed's mind as he heard the words, realizing that Pierce had lied about the end of that night. The visceral reaction he had to the pictures wasn't from seeing his friends, it was from seeing those wounds, so similar to what had happened before.

"By the time that jogger happened by, she was already gone."

He looked at Reed a long moment before turning to face forward. "They did the same to Michael, but somehow, whether it was the grace of

God or a cruel trick of the Devil, he hung on. Spent over two months in a coma, didn't even get to go to her funeral."

It had taken almost a solid week, a lot of false starts, a serpentine route, but finally Reed understood what this was all about.

"He never took it to the police?" Reed asked.

"No," Galanos said. "By the time he woke up, he was a different person. Gone was any of the baby fat he once had, the jovial nature that colored his cheeks. In their place was a hardened man, someone that spent a lot of time asking me questions about vengeance."

Vengeance. The word resonated through Reed's mind, linking back to so many conversations he'd had in previous days.

"Charon."

Raising a gnarled, paint-splotched hand, Galanos pointed to a stained glass window high on the wall beside them. Following the direction with his gaze, Reed raised his attention to find the same image Jim Shatley had showed him stretched over six feet in height, depicted in vivid color.

"I tried and tried to get him to talk about what happened, to come to grips with all of it," Galanos said, "but it never took. Instead he wanted to discuss God's wrath, to hear what the heavens had to say about justice.

"To find out everything he could about Charon, the Boat Man, the one responsible for escorting souls into Hell."

Chapter Fifty-Five

Reed bypassed the cell phone, going straight for the radio hanging beneath the dash. One hand he kept draped over the steering wheel, the other he used to hold the microphone just an inch from his face, his fingers squeezing the spring loaded release on the side.

"McMichaels? Jacobs? Gilchrist, you there?"

If anybody else was listening on the line they might have balked at the complete lack of protocol, but it was the furthest thing from Reed's mind as he sped down the freeway, his front lights flashing. He released the lever on the side of his radio for a long moment, fuzz coming in over the line as he waited for a response.

"Come on, come on, come on," he muttered, glancing into the rearview mirror to see Billie pacing as much as the confines of the car would allow. The sound of her paws working over the plastic filled his ears, her hot breath fogging up the rear windows as they drove.

"McMichaels, Jacobs, Gilchrist, you there?" Reed repeated, his tone relaying the urgency he felt.

Everything he had learned in the last few hours, both from Pierce and Galanos, proved that Michael Rigas was their man.

Two years before, the Kings of The Bottoms had attacked he and his wife, unprovoked. They had killed her and left him for dead, putting the man in a coma that he was two months coming out of.

Once he did wake, he was no longer the same person, not interested in forgiveness or even society's general idea of justice. As far as Reed could tell, no police report had ever been filed about the incident, no formal investigation launched.

Instead, the man had shown up talking to his priest about notions of wrath, about Greek mythology and the purveyor of souls into Hell. That very same purveyor was known to require a toll for passage, a toll that was found in the throat of previous victims.

Whether they realized it or not, the Kings had turned Michael Rigas into the Boat Man.

"Yeah, this is Jacobs and McMichaels, go ahead," the voice of Jacobs called over the line, pulling Reed from his thoughts.

"Gilchrist, Greene, you guys out there too?" Reed asked, keeping the receiver pressed tight against his lips.

"Yes, sir. That you, Reed?" Gilchrist responded.

Nodding grimly, Reed pressed the plunger and said, "Yes, everyone, this is Reed Mattox. I am currently tearing down I-270 with the flashers going, making like hell for The Bottoms.

"I have strong reason to believe that Michael Rigas, the man responsible for the murders there this week, is en route if he is not already on site."

Over the line he could hear somebody mutter, "Jesus," though nobody addressed him directly.

"Suspect is to be considered extremely armed and dangerous. His targets are a pair of African-American males in their late-twenties to early-thirties named Willie Pryor, aka Dub-P, and Marcus Knighton, aka Mac."

Reed paused a moment as he glanced over his shoulder, making sure the lane was clear before drifting off the freeway, hitting the exit ramp at seventy miles an hour. As the car drifted he could feel Billie sliding for purchase, her tail slapping against the passenger door.

"I could use all of you, and anybody else from the 8th that is listening, at the abandoned Mobil station on the corners of Scanson and Duvall. Right now I am just leaving the freeway, ETA eight minutes."

"Roger that," Gilchrist said. "We just left the station, be there in five."

"On the opposite end," Jacobs added, "be there in the same. Please advise on how to approach upon arrival."

Reed answered without pause, almost yelling the response into the receiver. "Take targets into custody. Once scene is secure, will begin immediate sweep of the area."

Both parties confirmed and signed off, Reed dropping the microphone onto the passenger seat beside him.

For the last few nights Pryor and Knighton had both been baiting Rigas, standing out in the open, daring him to act on them. Even if he wasn't there at the moment, Reed still had to get them off the streets and out of sight until he could be brought in.

Something told him though that wouldn't be an issue.

Chapter Fifty-Six

The Boat Man ran his hand up under the black knit fleece he wore, letting his fingertips trace over his stomach. Moving slow, he inched them just past his navel, to the ridge of furrowed skin that ran from his midline to his ribs. Rough and uneven, the healed flesh made a clear line across him, separating his navel into two parts.

In the preceding months, the Boat Man had come to think of the scar as a metaphor for his life as well, severing it into two parts. On one side of it was Janice, their years together, the future they had planned for. On the other was nothing, an empty shell of an existence, a life that was predicated on only one thing.

A single thing that was now just hours away.

What the world held for him after the task was completed, or even if there would be any place for him in it once it was, didn't much matter to the Boat Man. Everything he had done, from the months of rehab, to exhaustive physical training, to the tedious research and preparation, had been with an eye to this.

It was for that reason that he had not gone to the police, had not been able to open up to Father Galanos about his true intentions. This was his task to complete, his oath that he had sworn to the memory of his wife.

Stepping forward from the shadows of the room, the Boat Man could see the twin cars of Willie Pryor and Marcus Knighton parked in the Mobil parking lot, just as they had been the night before, just as they had been most nights for the previous three months.

In either of their hands was a bottle wrapped in brown paper, each taking occasional sips as they leaned against their respective front hoods. He was too far away to hear what they were saying, though he could see them gesturing as they spoke.

The mere sight of them brought a white hot rage to his chest, gripping his entire body, causing his every nerve ending to twitch with fire. The fingers on either hand curled into tight fists as he stared down at them, remembering their faces so clear from that night, having waited so long for this time to come.

Hefting the gun up from its makeshift hold, the Boat Man rested the barrel of it onto the edge of the window sill and lowered himself to a knee. He braced the stock of the gun against his shoulder and slowly exhaled, again sweeping the area through the magnified lens of the scope.

Sweat droplets formed along his brow, streamed down the side of his face as he inched the barrel forward out the window, feeling the cold night air flush on his skin.

From where he was positioned both cars were parked at an angle, Knighton's back to him, Pryor facing forward. One at a time the Boat Man settled the lowest range sight of the scope on each of them, counting off the seconds in his head, imagining the first shot and then the second.

It was time.

Setting his aim on Pryor, the Boat Man curled his finger around the outside of the trigger guard, feeling the cold steel against the pad. There he left it for a long moment, drawing in deep breaths, making sure his hand was steady, before shifting it to the inside, flush against the trigger.

The first shot made only a slight popping noise, the sound swallowed up by the light evening breeze. A single flower of orange was emitted as the muzzle flashed, his round drawing center mass, the target crumpling to the ground.

Beside him the Boat Man watched as Knighton grew rigid, too stunned to move, the bottle falling from his hand. A second squeeze of the trigger punctured his back in the same spot as Pryor, the impact of the blow knocking him forward, draping his body over the front of the opposite car.

Keeping his sight focused in on them both, the Boat Man drew one more deep breath, watching as Marcus Knighton's body rested atop the hood, his arms outstretched beside him.

With one last curl of his finger he fired a solitary parting shot directly through Knighton's right forearm.

Chancing a few last seconds, the Boat Man watched through the scope as Knighton's body slid down the side of the car, a trail of smeared blood spatter in his wake. The entirety of his corpse disappeared from view between the automobiles, hidden from sight, tucked away beside Pryor.

A feeling of deep satisfaction settled into the Boat Man's chest as he pulled back from the window, lifting the barrel of the gun away and carrying it from sight.

Sliding his left hand down the barrel, he gripped the weapon with one hand, using the other to dig deep into the pocket of his pants. There he found the twin pair of metal discs lodged in the corner of the cotton material, the interior of the pocket matted by sweat against his thigh.

Gripping both between his middle and forefinger, he tossed both the obols out through the open window, watching them each catch a tiny flash of light before disappearing into the darkness.

Chapter Fifty-Seven

A pair of blue-and-whites was already on the scene as Reed pulled to a stop, parking at the same odd angle he had two nights before. He left the front flashers on his car going as he climbed out, their fluorescent light illuminating the intersection, bouncing off the nearby buildings, tossing long shadows out over the street.

Side by side at the front of the lot were the Pontiac Tempest and the Buick Skylark, the majority of their frames blocked by the twin police cruisers, blue-and-red flashers working overhead. Moving like silent silhouettes through the lights was a small handful of officers, traveling fast.

"Oh, shit," Reed muttered, breaking into a run, feeling his badge bounce against his chest. As he moved he drew his weapon from the holster on his hip, shifting into a shooter's stance, the gun trained in front of him.

Bright light flashed in his eyes, momentarily blinding him as he passed by the cruisers, coming up on the tail of Pryor's Buick.

"Oh, shit," he whispered again.

Tucked away behind either end of the Tempest were Jacobs and McMichaels, their weapons extended over the dented metal frame.

Behind them Gilchrist and Greene were crouched low, attention aimed in the opposite direction, using the Skylark as a shield.

Filling the space on the ground between them was two inert objects, recognizable at a glance as the two men Reed had spoken to just two nights before.

Keeping his weapon drawn, Reed slid on a knee between the two groups, coming to a stop just inches from Willie Pryor. Lying flat on his back a single entry wound was present in the upper right side of his chest, the circle no larger than a nickel. A single trickle of dark blood ran sideways from it, already beginning to congeal in the cool night air.

Beside him on the pavement was a circle of blood the size of a basketball, the shape of it smeared, most likely by the first arriving officers rolling him over to check for vitals.

"What the hell happened?" Reed asked, remaining in a crouch, hopping over Pryor and moving to Knighton.

"This is what we found when we got here four minutes ago," Jacobs yelled, turning his head an inch to the side but keeping his attention aimed forward.

"Nobody saw anything?" Reed asked.

Knighton had been rolled flat onto his back, the collar of his puffy jacket pulled back to expose his jugular. Unlike his friend, a gaping hole four inches in diameter was cleaved through the middle of his chest, blood and tissue spatter coating the glossy yellow fabric.

Also different from Pryor was his right arm, the lower half of it hanging at an angle, a second shot placed right through the meat of the forearm.

"Nothing," Gilchrist said in front of him. "We got here just a second after they did. Found them already like this."

"Shit," Reed muttered, looking at the two bodies, raising his attention to the cars around him.

It was clear from the entry wounds that Pryor had been shot in the chest, Knighton in the back. That likely meant a single shooter getting both as they were positioned against their cars.

Risking standing almost to full height, Reed checked over each of the hoods, seeing two distinct blood sprays along the front of the Skylark, none for the Tempest.

"Shots were fired from the southwest," Reed said, shifting over between Jacobs and McMichaels, looking out over the roof just behind the driver's seat. The combined red, blue, and white lights of the three police vehicles bathed everything in an odd assortment of colors as his gaze traced over the intersection, settling on the enormous brick edifice across from them.

"The school," he whispered. "The son of a bitch was tucked away in there, firing down on them."

Dropping back down, Reed pulled his radio from his waist, raising it to his lips.

"Dispatch, this is Detective Reed Mattox," he barked in clipped words, "I need a full tactical assault force on the corner of Scanson and Duvall Streets right now. Target is an abandoned school house that served as the hide for a shooter in a double homicide.

"Assailant may or may not still be inside."

He lowered his radio a moment, glancing to either side. "You guys good here?"

"Yeah," McMichaels grunted, his body still tense, his head moving from side to side, checking every shadow.

"All set," Jacobs said, his mouth pulled into a tight line across his face.

"Greene, Gilchrist?" Reed asked, raising his voice just a bit.

"We're good," Gilchrist replied.

"You sure you don't want us to go in right now?" Greene said, looking back over his shoulder to Reed. "Three of us could clear it, leave two here to secure the scene."

"Roger that, Detective," Jackie's voice sounded over the radio. "Units have been dispatched and are en route. Be on hand in under five."

Reed nodded without responding.

"No," he said, his attention aimed at Greene. "I'm not sending you guys in there against what looks like a 30-cal undermanned and under-equipped."

He shifted and looked back through the hull of the Skylark, the double layer of windows distorting the image just a bit. "Besides, I'd be willing to bet all they're going to find is a bunch of homeless people scared shitless."

"Yeah?" Jacobs asked.

"Yeah," Reed said, nodding, running back everything he'd learned in the previous hours on a fast loop. "This guy isn't on a suicide mission, he has a job to do and he's going to get it done. The fact that he shifted from a sword to a long-range rifle, something he could fire and still make a getaway, proves he's in the self-preservation business, at least a little longer."

"What do you mean a little longer?" McMichaels asked, glancing over at him, a tiny bit of tension easing from his body.

Reed met the glance a long moment, a thought coming to his head. Without responding he raised the radio back to his face and said, "Jackie, who's on standby tonight?"

There was a brief pause followed by Jackie bursting back on the line, panting as she spoke. "Iaconelli and Bishop. You need them, too?"

Chapter Fifty-Eight

Two distinct options had presented themselves to Reed.

The first was that he could wait for the assault team to show up and clear the schoolhouse, telling him what he already knew, which was Rigas was long gone. The fact that he had chosen to go with shooting Pryor and Knighton from afar proved he was cognizant of Reed getting closer, had chosen an attack method that allowed him to be far away by the time police arrived.

Otherwise, he would have stayed with his traditional MO, using his sword, inflicting on them the same wounds they had on him.

Once the building was cleared, Reed could use Billie and her other-worldly gift of scent to track his movements, hoping they led him somewhere besides the place where he had parked before driving away.

The second option, the one that Reed had begrudgingly gone with, was to wait for Iaconelli and Bishop to arrive at the scene, responding to Jackie's call. When they did, Reed flagged them down the moment they stepped out of their car, telling them to fall in behind him. He didn't allow Iaconelli to get out a word as he lumbered out, pretended not to notice the grimace on both their faces.

As much as he hated to admit it, as sour as the words tasted on his mouth, he needed them as backup.

Retracing the route he had taken just a quarter hour earlier, Reed left the front lights flashing, tearing back towards the freeway. In the back seat Billie had worked herself into a lather pacing, knowing that Reed, the situation, had both escalated, fraught with pent-up energy ready to be expended.

Taking up his cell phone from the passenger seat, Reed dialed and dropped it into his lap, the sound of ringing echoing through the car. In his rearview mirror he could see the flashing lights of Iaconelli's matching sedan, the back end of it drifting a bit as they followed him onto the freeway.

"Grimes," the voice of the captain growled, little more than a grumble.

"Captain, it's Mattox," Reed said, his words, his tone, both clipped.

"Holy hell, Mattox. You've turned my whole precinct on its head tonight. What's going on out there?"

The red speedometer needle pushed its way above ninety as he headed north, Iaconelli keeping pace behind him.

"William Pryor and Marcus Knighton are both dead," Reed said without preamble, his voice even as he relayed the information.

A long breath of air was audible before the captain asked, "Same guy?"

"Same guy," Reed said, "but not same MO. This time he used a rifle big enough to take down an elephant. Looks like he was holed up in that old school house across the street, you know the place?"

"Yeah," Grimes said, a tinge of weariness in his tone. "People have been clamoring for years for that place to be torn down, saying it was nothing but an eyesore and a homeless commune. They'll have a field day with this one."

Reed moved on past the statement without comment, having neither the time nor inclination to debate local politics.

"Despite the change in nature, I've got no doubt it's the same guy," Reed said. "Shot them both right through the chest, put a round through Knighton's arm right on the tattoo, almost took the damn thing off."

"Sure sounds like the same guy," Grimes agreed.

"Anyway, I'm calling you now to let you know I'm on my way to Worthington. Iaconelli and Bishop are in the car behind me."

"Worthington?" Grimes almost spat, the word coming out in one sharp crack. "Why the hell aren't you on the scene?"

"Because he's not there anymore," Reed said. "So I'm going to his house to tear the place apart. Can you get on the horn and clear the way for me?"

As a detective, Reed was given a certain amount of latitude throughout the greater Columbus area. It was a generally accepted practice though that if discovering a crime having been committed or going to question a hostile witness an alert was given to the locals out of professional courtesy.

Reed didn't have the time to issue one himself, trusting that the captain could handle the matter.

"Also, I'm not bothering with a warrant," Reed said. "There's probable cause aplenty already, but I just wanted you to know in case the media starts bitching again."

"Don't you worry about them," Grimes said, the previous steel returning to his tone. "I'll bother with the media when and if I need to. You just find this asshole, and fast."

"Thanks," Reed muttered. "And the local guys up here?"

"I've got you covered there, too," Grimes said. "You need any more manpower with you?"

"No clue," Reed said, "but having a couple of uniforms on standby just in case couldn't hurt."

Both sides signed off the call without farewell, Reed again feeling his heart rate spike as he exited off the freeway. Cool air streamed through the front dash but did little to sate the sweat pouring from his skin as he turned on to Rigas's street.

Chapter Fifty-Nine

"What the hell was that?" Iaconelli asked, his face red, as he spilled out of the sedan. His shirt was untucked and his hair askew as he walked forward, wagging a finger at Reed. "I told you I'm on my last days here, so whatever cockamamie scheme you've got cooked up here, I want no part of it."

Reed had expected, even anticipated the outburst, cutting him off before he really got going.

"Shut the hell up, Iaconelli. I'm not here to mess with your pension, I just needed backup and you're the crew on call night."

The complete dismissal of their role seemed to throw Iaconelli off, his face again swelling with rage.

"This is the home of Michael Rigas, the man that as of tonight has killed five people in The Bottoms and may be going after more. I can't storm his house alone, so I brought you along."

The explanation deflated some of the steam rising from Iaconelli, Bishop stepping up beside him, his pale skin flashing in the darkness.

"So there were two more back there?" Bishop asked.

"GSW's," Reed said, nodding. "High-powered, long-range. MO didn't fit the previous incidents, but the victimology matches. He knew we were getting close, so he was taking preventive measures."

"You sure he's in there?" Bishop asking, motioning towards the house ahead.

"No," Reed said, "in fact I'm almost certain he's not, but I need to know where he's headed next."

"What makes you so sure there is a next?" Iaconelli asked.

A grim look was all Reed offered in response, the simple fact being he wasn't sure. All he had was a feeling, an inkling, that whatever else Rigas had planned ended tonight.

Things were getting too close for him to continue indefinitely, something he was acutely aware of. If there was anything else left on his agenda now that Pryor and Knighton were dead and Brandt was in custody, it had to happen soon.

"We'll take the back," Reed said, going to his rear passenger door and jerking it open, Billie spilling out onto the pavement. He didn't bother clipping her to a lead, letting her bounce on the balls of her feet, unbridled energy rolling from her in waves.

"Two minutes," he added, turning and jogging off into the night, coming up through the neighbor's yard and circling around the back of the house. Beside him he could sense Billie matching his movements, holding herself back from sprinting on ahead, her black body little more than a shadow.

The back of the house matched the layout of the front, the bottom level brick and the top half white siding. A carport and free standing garage were situated to the side, connected by an extra wide brick walkway.

"Slow," Reed said, using his command tone, but keeping the volume low. Dropping into a crouch he drew his weapon and crept towards the back door, Billie just a few feet away, a low growl rolling out over her exposed teeth.

Counting off seconds in his head, Reed made it to one hundred before moving up the three brick stairs to the back door and driving the heel of his foot between the handle and the jamb. On contact the heavy wooden door swung open, splinters of wood spraying the floor, bits of sawdust hanging in the air.

"Clear," Reed said, Billie bolting through the opening at the sound of his voice, disappearing inside.

Veins stood out on Reed's forearms and the backs of his hands as he moved through a small mudroom and into the kitchen, everything dark and empty.

"Michael Rigas! This is the Columbus Police Department! If you are here you need to make yourself visible, approaching with your hands raised!"

On the opposite side of the house he could hear the front door breached, the sound of wood shattering, Iaconelli issuing the same warning he had just made.

Remaining in place, Reed stood and waited as the voice fell away, the only sound Billie's nose and toenails as she moved across the hardwood floor.

Going past the kitchen, Reed entered into a dining room, the elongated wooden table and chairs appearing to have not been used in ages. Thick cobwebs connected the three bulbs of the light fixture hanging down, a bouquet of dried flowers occupying the centerpiece area.

At the far end of the room Bishop appeared in the doorway, his ghostly pallor giving him an ethereal glow in the house. "We're going upstairs. You good?"

"Good," Reed said, a curt nod to reinforce the response.

Just as fast Bishop disappeared from sight, a moment later the groans of the stairwell could be heard as they ascended.

A droplet of sweat ran from Reed's forehead and traveled down the bridge of his nose, hanging for a moment before falling to the floor as he stepped around the table, still feeling his pulse surge through him. Above he could hear Iaconelli and Bishop clearing rooms, around the corner Billie working her way through the house.

Standing adjacent to the dining room was a small sitting room, a couch with matching loveseat and chairs dominating the space. Along the far wall was a flat screen television and an assortment of end tables, the sum total of the furniture in the room seeming to be far too much for a space so small.

For the second time in as many minutes Reed got the impression the room had not been used in quite some time, a finger over the arm of the burgundy leather sofa revealing a film of dust.

"Clear up here," Bishop called from upstairs, his voice sounding explosive through the desolate house. The sound of it jolted Reed's senses as he moved through the sitting room, coming out on the opposite side, passing through an open doorway into what had once been the living room.

Reed felt the breath pulled from his chest as he stopped in the doorway, his gaze traveling over the space. Another bead of sweat made its way down his face, falling to the floor as he stood and surveyed it, watching as Billie made a loop around the room, her nose pressed to the ground.

"Clear down here," Reed called. "You guys better come take a look at this."

Without waiting for the sound of their approaching footsteps Reed moved into the room, following Billie's path.

The reason the previous room had felt so cramped was that every last bit of furniture in the space had been removed, all piled into other sections of the house. In their stead was a single unencumbered area, stretching fifteen feet across and almost double that in length.

Underfoot the floor was made from white oak, the walls painted the same as the outside of the house. Combined the effect made for a light ensemble, the bit of moonlight filtering through the windows more than enough to illuminate it.

The echo of Reed's shoes on the hardwood echoed off the walls as he moved forward, focusing on the far end of the space. There Billie too had stopped her search, looking from Reed to the edifice before her, not sure how to act.

Resting against the wall was a single table, low-slung, rising no more than a foot off the ground. Five times that in length, atop it rested two oversized framed photos, both of a striking woman in her early-thirties.

Bearing all the signs of a woman of mixed ancestry, there was no doubt on sight as to who it was.

"Half-Japanese, half-Greek," Reed whispered, recalling Galanos's word. "Janice Rigas."

Placed in front of them was a single wooden tray, a piece eighteen inches in length with twin grips rising from either end. Below it on the floor was a black vinyl case, the zipper pulled all the way open.

"The sword and the rifle," Reed said, looking over the shrine once more before shifting his attention to the adjoining wall beside him.

On it, stretched out in a misshapen circle almost eight feet in diameter, was a collection of research months in the making. Formed in a swirling pattern, it contained newspaper clippings and internet articles, interspersed heavily with sheets of handwritten notes and personal photographs.

Every last one was time and date stamped, beginning around the first of the year and continuing until just a week before.

"What the hell?" Iaconelli asked, the sound of his and Bishop's feet crossing the floor audible, though not enough to pull Reed's attention away from the wall.

Instead he remained focused in on the series of photographs posted in painstaking order in the middle of it, all close facial shots of the Kings, all stretched to six inches or more in height.

Split into two equal groups, the top half had been X'd out by Rigas's own hand, thick red marker slashes distorting the images.

Below them were three more, none with a mark of any kind yet on them. Two of them Reed recognized as Pryor and Knighton, both now dispatched, just as their comrades had been.

The last he had met for the first time just a few hours before.

"Pierce Brandt," Reed whispered, turning to look at the others with him. "The last one is Pierce Brandt."

Chapter Sixty

The rifle was gone, having been left behind in the car. It was an able weapon, worth the trouble to procure. It had done its job well, but the time had come to cast it aside.

There was only one target left, and he deserved the sword. He deserved the signature of his wife's familial lineage, the up-close-and-personal nature of seeing the Boat Man before he met his end.

Two years before, the Boat Man had been forced to endure the most horrific night in his life. He had had to watch as hoodlums descended from the night, penalizing him and his wife for making a wrong turn, for being hungry in the wrong part of town. He had been restrained as they did things to his beloved, horrible, unspeakable things that he was unable to stop.

He had been rendered unconscious before it was all over, stripped of the ability to say goodbye before Janice passed from this world.

The first image he had seen in his mind upon awakening from the coma was not those men doing as they pleased with her, it was the sight of the brass knuckles coming towards his head. It was the face behind them, bearing its own self-pity, knocking him out not from some sort of deep-rooted chivalry but in an effort to spare his own weak soul.

That face, that man's weakness, was what the Boat Man fed on for two long years. It was what fueled him through every physical therapy session, forced him to sit motionless for hours on his scouting missions.

The knowledge that one day he would see it again, would finally have his retribution for what was done to him, what it had allowed to be done to his wife, was more than enough to propel him forward day after day.

Upon leaving his hide atop the schoolhouse, the Boat Man had heard the sirens in the distance. He had seen the glow of lights flashing above the buildings as he drove away, making his escape just minutes before the police arrived.

The delay with his sword had cost him. It had allowed them to put together what had happened, giving them time to circle close. If ever he were going to finish things it had to be tonight, before his final target disappeared, potentially taking with him the chance at justice forever.

Reaching behind him, the Boat Man tapped the end of the handle extended down by his kidneys, the scabbard inverted to be hidden beneath his jacket. Getting it fixed had cost him precious time, but it was now worth it, having the weapon he'd come to rely so much on by his side in the final hour.

A far cry from The Bottoms he'd spent much of the previous months in, the Boat Man found himself in a neighborhood resembling the one he lived in. Gone were the shattered facades and dilapidated dwellings, replaced by plush lawns and newer model houses. Automobiles produced in the new millennium were parked out front, the occasional dog barking in the distance.

Of all six targets, this was the one he had scouted the least. Unlike his cohorts he had relocated himself from the tangle of The Bottoms, attempting a social climb, from all appearances severing his past relationships.

The sudden change did little to soften the Boat Man's stance though, the promise he had made total and absolute. Even if the new location made performing reconnaissance more difficult, he would do what he set out to, finishing a task two years in the making.

Ahead in the distance his final destination came into view, a two-story home with rows of windows lining both floors, just a single light burning in the bottom level. He felt his nerves stand on end as he moved closer, feigning to be nothing more than a neighborhood resident out for a stroll.

Ten more minutes, and it would all be over.

Janice, and perhaps even himself, could finally be at peace.

Chapter Sixty-One

Both the front and back doors were left gaping at Michael Rigas's home, property damage the sort of thing that no longer applied once someone was confirmed as the lead suspect in five murders and counting. Tragic back story or not, the justice system was predicated on handing such matters off to the authorities, not engaging in vigilante justice.

Not once did the thought of closing them up or securing the home occur to Reed as he sprinted from the front hall towards his sedan parked outside, Billie beating him there by three full strides. Bringing up the rear he could hear Bishop slapping the pavement with heavy footsteps, Iaconelli wheezing as he tried to keep pace.

Reed could still hear the words from the captain in his head as he loaded his partner inside and swung behind the wheel, turning the engine over with a single twist of the key.

Pierce Brandt had been released on hour before, told not to leave town.

A string of hateful, spiteful obscenities spewed from Reed's mouth as he set the flashers moving, for the first time ever invoking the siren as well. Loud and piercing, it squalled out over the thin evening traffic, cars peeling to the side, letting him pass.

Somewhere behind him he knew Iaconelli and Bishop were coming, though he still couldn't see them in the mirror.

The story that Pierce told was basically a confession, a full account of everything that had happened two years before. The fact that the victim was now murdering the other members of his party was irrelevant, the amount of time that had passed a pittance compared to the statute of limitations laws in place for such crimes.

There was no doubt in Reed's mind as he drove on, going back to the home Pierce shared with his mother for the second time in the day, that the only reason he had been released was his aunt.

The thought caused Reed's mouth to twist up in an angry snarl as he headed south, needing just three exits to get from Rigas's stop to Brandt's. Other motorists continued to stream to the side as he kept the gas pedal depressed, retracing his prior route from memory.

Once he was free from the clutches of suburban strip mall traffic he killed the siren and the flashing lights, not wanting to give away his position should Rigas be in the area.

Lifting an article of clothing taken from the upstairs bedroom Reed passed it over his shoulder, dropping it at Billie's feet. On cue she lowered her head and sniffed deeply at it, picking up the scent as he made the last turn, Pierce Brandt's street coming into view.

The first pass by Brandt's house would be to determine if Rigas had been there yet. If he was or had been, Reed would pull directly into the drive, he and Billie both going straight in. If not, he would circle the block and park down at the end, letting Billie go to work, flushing him out if he were hiding anywhere nearby.

Slowing his car just a bit, Reed crossed over the adjoining intersection and made his way onto Brandt's street, the homes looking much the same as the neighborhood he had just left. In many of the windows he could see individuals and families moving about, their lights on, acting as if nothing was out of the ordinary.

Again feeling his pulse rise Reed rolled past Brandt's home, careful not to slow his pace or tap the brakes as he peered in through the front windows, a single light on, no cars in the driveway.

"I don't think he's home yet," Reed said aloud, allowing the car to move past the house, not once looking back over his shoulder.

Snatching up the receiver from the radio beneath the dash, Reed raised it to his face. "Bishop, you there?"

A long moment of fuzz passed before Bishop replied, "We're here, ETA two minutes and closing. Got a little turned around coming off the freeway."

The last line was added as a bit of an apology, though Reed had no need or interest in hearing it, launching forward with directions.

"It appears Brandt is not yet home," Reed said, watching in his rearview mirror, a pair of headlights appearing behind him he assumed to be his backup. "The captain's trying to contact him and his aunt, so hopefully he'll get to them before they arrive.

"I'm going to pull up to the next cross section and let Billie out, see if she can pick up a scent. You guys stay back a block and close the gate."

"Roger that," Bishop said, both sides signing off without another sound, Reed dropping the mic without bothering to hang it back on the radio.

At the next corner he made a left and inched forward until out of sight from Brandt's street, easing his car to a stop and climbing out, Billie not bothering to wait for him before launching herself through the front seat and out onto the road.

Reed watched her for a moment, quivering with anticipation, before setting her loose.

"Search."

297

Chapter Sixty-Two

Seated on the back porch, the Boat Man had a vantage past the corner of the house to the street out front and through the rear window into the kitchen. The single bulb in the downstairs still burning was located above a breakfast nook in the corner of the space, an open floor plan allowing him to see into the living room and out the front windows as well.

Hunkered down in a chair, partially obscured by some low hanging branches creeping in from the yard, the Boat Man waited in silence. His black ensemble made him little more than a shadow on the darkened porch, the wood stained deep red absorbing any overhead light, concealing him from sight.

On his very first scouting run the Boat Man had found that his final target still lived at home with his mother, a cruel irony in that he too had the opportunity to strip away the woman most important to his attacker. For weeks he had grappled with the best way to handle the situation before realizing it didn't matter, the mother was rarely if ever home.

Instead it appeared the final man on his list was little more than a glorified house sitter, a target made even easier because of the false sense of security a parent's home provided.

Thoughts of where he was, what had brought him to such a state, danced through the Boat Man's head as a pair of lights appeared at the end of the street. He raised his body just an inch in his chair as he watched them roll by, not once slowing or seeming to glance his way.

Lowering himself back into place, the faint glow of a second pair of headlights emerged, growing larger, coming into view at a much slower pace. Feeling his pulse climb, the Boat Man watched as the car crept to just barely moving, the sound of brakes squealing calling out as the car turned into the driveway, a sliver of bright light shooting past him into the backyard.

The Boat Man's breath caught in his chest as he rose from his seat and crossed over to the rear of the house, pressing his back flat against it.

A moment later the headlights blinked out, flushing the world into a state of darkness as a car door opened no more than fifteen feet away. The sound of crinkling paper, the smell of fried food found their way to him soon thereafter, followed by keys jangling as the target made his way for the door.

The Boat Man gave him three steps to make sure he was out in the open, waiting to emerge from the darkness, when a sound hit his ears he wasn't expecting, something that stopped him for a moment, his heart pounding in his chest.

A woman's voice.

Chapter Sixty-Three

Billie picked the scent up just off the corner, finding it in less than three minutes, the smell so fresh in her nose from the shirt Reed had given her she practically snatched it off the breeze. The moment it hit her nostrils her pace increased from a meander to a trot, head down, body poised, moving in a direct line down the sidewalk.

Falling in behind her Reed had to jog to keep up, drawing his flashlight with one hand, his weapon with the other. Keeping the light by his side he clicked on the end plunger twice in a quick sequence, a fast and discrete signal to Iaconelli and Bishop down the street that Rigas was nearby.

A single flash of a light inside the cab of the car showed they had seen and understood, easing away from the curb as they pulled closer.

Bringing his hands together in front of him, Reed bent his knees into a shooter's crouch, jogging forward. Beside him houses continued to tick by as his breaths grew short, moisture forming on his skin.

Before him Billie kept up a steady pace, her head down, pulling him in a straight line down the sidewalk.

In a place such as The Bottoms, a man like Rigas was forced into the shadows. Anybody giving him a second glance would know he didn't belong there, his skin tone, his demeanor, everything about him wrong for the neighborhood.

That wasn't the case somewhere like Worthington, the street a near copy of his own, just a few miles in distance from it as the crow flew. Because of that he was able to move about unnoticed and unseen, just another resident out for an evening stroll.

Reed cursed under his breath as he kept going, Pierce's house approaching on the right. Two feet in front of him Billie kept up her steady gait, her destination clear.

Chapter Sixty-Four

The Boat Man's first assumption was the voice belonged to the mother, back from another service deployment, home from wherever they had sent her this time. The symmetry of the situation with what had befallen him was almost too much to ignore, he himself having had the most important woman in his life ripped away, now having the opportunity to do the same to the final person that had wronged him.

As perfect as it might have seemed though, as delicious as the moment would be for him, that was never his intention. His goal was not to become the monster they had been, waging wrath upon the innocent. The only point of what he had done, what he was doing, was for Janice.

Harming the man's mother would be a disservice to his wife's memory, and he couldn't have that on his conscience.

Still, even if he refused to harm the woman, he could not let her presence stop him from what he needed to do. Inching forward to the corner of the house, he listened as the two conversed. Both sounded annoyed as they spoke, the man close beside him, going for the door. Lingering behind was the woman, lecturing him the way only a parent could, her voice a bit more distant.

Pulling a deep lungful of air through his nose, the Boat Man tapped the sword against his thigh, the sheath it was in solid, firm against his calf. In that instant he knew what he must do, how he would approach the situation, how it all would end.

Without warning of any kind, without a yell or a scream or even a grunt from exertion, the Boat Man spun out from around the edge of the house, on them before either one even knew he was there.

Bypassing the man by the door he charged hard for the woman, slashing the covered sword at her in a baseball swing, the improvised barrel of it connecting just above her temple, lifting her small body from the ground and depositing it on the ground in a heap. Only in the distance between contact and her hitting the ground did he realize it wasn't his mother, the woman wearing a uniform of a different kind.

A police uniform.

She landed with a sickening smack of skin against asphalt, her form crumpled into a twisted mess.

The Boat Man looked at her only a moment before turning to face the man before him. Gone were any pangs of concern about having assaulted a cop, his list of transgressions already much too long to bother with such concerns.

In that moment there was only his mission. Once that was complete, nothing else would matter.

With a flick of his sword he cast the scabbard aside, the hollow material echoing against the driveway as it skittered away. Stray bits of light from the neighborhood caught the blade as he twisted it an inch in either direction, a smile pulling at the corner of his lips.

"Remember me?"

Chapter Sixty-Five

Reed saw it long before Billie did, her head aimed down at the ground, still tracking the scent. She kept her attention aimed forward, moving past the front drive of Pierce's house, following the route Rigas had taken.

From her vantage she couldn't see what Reed did as he came in view of the house, still over thirty yards away, adrenaline surging through him as he saw Pierce standing just outside the side entry to the home.

In front of him was Michael Rigas, his sword held at arm's length, just a few feet of distance separating the two of them.

Lying between them on the ground was the crumpled mass of a body, Reed guessing by the uniform and hair color it to be Brandt. No blood appeared visible as he broke into a full sprint, eschewing the sidewalk, the thick grass of the yard bending beneath his shoes.

"Rigas!" he shouted as he ran, his voice sounding hoarse as it exploded forward, fighting to get out as he gulped down oxygen. "Michael Rigas! Put down the weapon and step away!"

The directive echoed through the quiet neighborhood, a squeal of rubber coming a moment behind it, his backup slamming the gas to close the distance between them.

The combined sounds drew Pierce's attention towards him, a paper sack still clutched in his hands, his jaw hanging open. Fear and confusion had collided to render him motionless, standing and watching as Reed pulled closer.

In front of him, Rigas paid no mind to the order from Reed, not so much as glancing in his direction. Instead he drew back the sword past his right shoulder, gripping it in both hands, ready to bring it across in a wicked slash.

"Rigas!" Reed screamed again, stopping just fifteen yards from his target, planting his feet perpendicular to him. He dropped the flashlight from his left hand and brought his palm up under his right, using it as a base.

There was no pause from Rigas, no attempt to stop his attack as Reed curled back the trigger, a jolt of orange light sparking from the tip of his weapon. The gun bucked a tiny bit in his hand as the round spat out, closing the gap between them in less than a second, slamming into the left shoulder of his target.

The blow of the shot pitched the man forward, his own assault tailing to the side. From pure momentum the blade continued its path, cutting a flailing arc, slicing across Pierce's thigh, splitting the flesh as if it weren't even there.

Reed watched as bright red droplets sprayed from the wound, spattering against the asphalt, Pierce folding in half as he fell to his knees. A pained howl crossed his lips as he pressed his hands over it, blood seeping between his fingers.

"Rigas! Drop the weapon!" Reed screamed again, his first shot pulling Billie from her tracking, the animal now standing by his side. Her growl could be heard low and persistent by his knee, letting him know she was close, ready to move.

Behind him a pair of headlights cast a fluorescent glow over everything as Iaconelli peeled onto the driveway, grass and dirt spewing everywhere as he slammed the car to a stop, both men piling out.

For a long moment Rigas stumbled to the side, looking at Pierce on the ground in front of him, at Reed standing to the side with his weapon raised, at the two detectives emerging from their car.

Reed could see the thought process playing out in front of him, of the longing the man had to finish the job. "Michael Rigas, we will shoot you if you do not put down the weapon!"

To his complete surprise, Rigas did something Reed never saw coming.

He turned and ran.

One moment he was standing before them, sword in hand, the next he was little more than a shadow, a man clad in black, disappearing into the backyard.

In that moment things seemed to slow down for Reed, his mind fighting to process the sensory overload of everything around him. He stood rooted in place, inventorying everything, before his training kicked in, his thoughts catching back up with the situation.

"Hold!" he yelled, the word coming out elongated and angry.

At the sound of the command Billie shot away in a blur, just six long strides before she was gone, vanishing the same way as her target.

Following on her heels, Reed ran forward to Pierce, his hands still pressed over his thigh, blood spreading away from the wound, painting the entire left leg of his jeans red.

"How bad? How bad?" Reed yelled, his shoes smacking against pavement as he came to a stop.

Bringing up the rear were Iaconelli and Bishop, their footfalls even heavier as they approached.

"Go, go!" Bishop yelled, sliding in beside Pierce.

"We got this, get after him!" Iaconelli yelled, the last sound Reed heard before he too made his way around the corner into the darkened back yard.

Chapter Sixty-Six

Reed heard them long before he saw them, just two yards down, Rigas making it no further before Billie tracked him down. Just as commanded, she had him pinned against a tree in the corner of a sprawling lot, his back pressed against the trunk of it.

His left arm was pressed against his ribcage, the black material of his shirt slick with blood. In the right was the sword, the blade flashing as he swung it in wild swipes before him, using the weapon to keep the animal at bay.

Gun trained before him, Reed approached on a diagonal across the yard, his breath coming in short ragged bursts. With each swing of the sword in Billie's direction he felt his heart rate spike, heard the labored cursing of Rigas, the gnashing of his partner's teeth.

"Michael Rigas, put down the weapon right now," Reed said, raising his voice enough to be heard, the tone non-negotiable.

Completely ignoring him, Rigas slashed another overheard swing at Billie, just narrowly missing her rear haunch as she ducked out of the way.

"That animal you are attacking is a police officer in the Columbus Police Department. If there is any way possible for you to be in even deeper shit than you are already, harming my partner is the way to do it."

As he spoke, Reed inched his way towards them, closing the gap.

Ambient light spilled out from the rear of the house behind Reed, the glow enough to show him for the first time the face of the man he'd been hunting.

His original assessment of the sketch drawing was correct, the curly hair an obvious wig. Otherwise the recollection of Winters was pretty spot-on, the resemblance obvious, even through the mask of pain and exhaustion Rigas wore.

"Michael Rigas, you will drop that weapon," Reed said, stopping just five yards away from him, Billie continuing to pace back and forth by his feet. "And then I will place you under arrest for the murders of five men, for the attempted murder of a sixth, and for the assault of two police officers."

He waited for any sign of a response, any signal that his words were being heard. Opposite him Rigas seemed intent to watch Billie, the sword still held by his side.

"Michael Rigas," Reed repeated.

"Michael Rigas is dead! He died two years ago!"

The words came out in one breath, a spray of spittle spraying from his mouth, his eyes starting to glass over.

"I know all about what those men did," Reed said.

"Do you? Do you?!" Rigas challenged back. "Do you have any idea what it was like to have to watch as someone did that to your wife? To knock you out and carve you up? To put you to sleep for two months only to wake up and find out the only person in your world that mattered was gone?"

Twin tears fell from Rigas's eyes as he stared back at Reed, hatred on his features.

"And I was close too. All I needed was a few more minutes and my Janice would have been at peace."

Already Reed could sense where this was going. There was no chance Michael Rigas would ever allow himself to be arrested, would ever succumb to living in a prison.

Michael Rigas had no desire to live any more at all.

"You really believe that?" Reed asked, trying to buy himself any bit of time, anything that might touch whatever humanity still existed in the man across from him. "You think this is what Janice would want? You becoming a killer? Terrorizing the men that did this to her?"

For just the briefest moment Rigas paused, appearing to consider the question, before the same mask of defiance fell back into place.

"I think Janice would tell me to make sure all six of them went straight to hell so we never had to see them again."

A throaty, guttural roar erupted from somewhere deep inside of him as the sword rose above his head. Pressing his backside off the tree trunk he rushed forward two quick steps, charging as if on the field of battle.

Billie reacted first, her body springing towards him, her first instinct to protect, to guard over Reed, to neutralize the threat.

Reed was just a moment behind her, the same internal mechanism working within him. He would not lose another partner. He would not let a madman with a sword harm her.

The first round Reed put into Rigas's chest, the force of it jerking his shoulders to the side, his forward progress slowing. The next two hit side by side a moment later, a near-perfect triangle center mass, shredding his chest cavity.

A torrent of blood passed from the corner of his mouth as the light faded from his eyes, the sword drifting from his hand, his body going slack.

He provided no resistance at all as Billie slammed into him, toppling him over backwards, not to move again.

Chapter Sixty-Seven

"He's really a good kid, you know."

Reed knew who the voice belonged to even without turning around. It sounded older, exhausted, but strong and clear.

"Yeah?" Reed asked, shifting his focus on the window before him from Pierce lying on a hospital bed to Eleanor Brandt approaching.

"Yeah," Brandt said, walking up beside him, coming to a stop just a few inches from his shoulder. A heavy gauze patch was extended vertically from her cheekbone to her hairline, held in place by a swath of elastic tape encircling her head. Already her right eye was swollen and puffy, the shadow of bruising beginning to color the entire side of her face.

"How you feeling?" Reed asked, glancing over at her, his arms folded across his chest, before turning back to face forward.

On the opposite side of the glass Pierce laid with his left leg in a stirrup, a metal chain and canvas strap carrying all the weight. Padded gauze enveloped everything from his ankle to his hip, his eyes closed, oxygen tubes pressed into his nostrils.

"Like hell," Brandt deadpanned. "I wish I could say nothing hurt but my pride, but..."

She drifted off without finishing her sentence, Reed already knowing exactly what she meant. Not only had she suffered the indignity of letting the suspect they'd been chasing for weeks get so close, she had suffered heavy personal injury in the process.

"I imagine," Reed said. "I've seen up close what this guy can do. You're fortunate it wasn't worse. Both of you."

It was difficult to say the words without sounding condescending, though Reed did mean them. Compared to the fates that had befallen Mentor and Wright, the two people beside him had been quite lucky.

Brandt seemed to sense all of that, or at least had the good sense not to press it.

"He had a bad spell," she said, jutting her chin towards Pierce on the other side. "His dad was never really in the picture and his mom was an Air Force lifer. When he was growing up she was stationed out of Rickenbacker, never missed a ball game or a school function.

"When he went on to college though, she finally accepted the promotion they'd been trying to foist on her for years. She was gone and he was left to his own devices."

Reed nodded at the explanation. It did little to change what happened or what Pierce had said hours before, though that was no longer in his hands. Finding out about that incident years before was solely a means to an end for him, a way to determine who was coming after the Kings.

"We all tried to help," Brandt said, her voice again fading away. "I don't need to tell you my role in it."

She paused and looked over at him, Reed getting the impression she was searching for some sort of response, to which he gave none.

"Anyway, two years ago he suddenly snapped out of it. I concede he's still pretty arrogant, and does run a little too much while his mom's away, but he's much better than he was. Should finish at Ohio State in the spring."

More than once while she spoke Reed got the impression she was building towards something, that her entire speech was predicated on more than just clearing the air. Still he remained silent as he listened, his hands back into the pockets of his sweatshirt.

When her explanation was complete she fell silent for a long moment, glancing his way again.

"Sounds like he should make a full recovery," Reed said. "Little nerve damage maybe, but nothing like it could have been."

"Yeah," Brandt said, rising up on to her toes to get a better view through the window. She remained there a long moment before turning to examine Reed, the bandages giving her face a misshapen appearance that made her look like she was listing to the side.

She stayed in the position as her mouth worked up and down, trying to find the words, but no sounds escaping.

Reed could only guess at the number of things she would say to him if she found her voice. He imagined the difficulty she had in speaking stemming from her attempting to thank him for coming to the aid of her and her nephew. Perhaps she would even apologize for trying to have him removed, making his life so difficult in the preceding days.

On the flip side, she might be attempting to offer him something, her mind trying to find the best approach. She could be hoping to quiet him about what he had heard that afternoon, extending a marker to him just the way she had Judge Bennett.

Whatever it was she wanted to say, Reed didn't want to hear it. He was fatigued and hungry, his partner in the same state in the car. There was no interest in any bribe Brandt had to offer, as she couldn't give him what he most desired.

He left her standing outside her nephew's room, the first bits of dawn visible through the windows as he headed towards the parking lot.

Chapter Sixty-Eight

A bit of blood was still crusted into Billie's fur as she climbed from the backseat and out into the parking lot. Reed could see clumps of hair matted together with it as she stood beside him, striping either side of her face and her left ear. First thing upon getting home he would load her into the bath tub and scrub it away, removing any lingering residue of Michael Rigas from them both.

"Go ahead," Reed said, motioning towards the expanse of grass stretched before them, the same one she had visited at least three times a week for the past two months.

Unlike most trips though, there was no pent up energy for her to shed away, no long night in need of working off. Like Reed she had spent the entire work week with her body clock flipped on its head, every function she possessed out of sorts.

For a long moment she just stood and stared at Reed, giving every indication she wanted to climb back into the rear of the car, before drifting off towards the grass.

"I'm not sure which of you looks more exhausted."

The words tugged at the corners of Reed's mouth as he remained leaning against his car, not bothering to look over his shoulder at the person he knew was there. The look stayed in place as Dr. Mehdi stepped up alongside the car and came to a stop beside him, assuming the same pose.

"Doc," Reed said, ignoring the prior barb.

"Reed," Mehdi replied. "Congratulations."

The smile rose a bit higher as Reed watched Billie work her way around the park, moving slow, her nose aimed at the ground. "Thank you. It was a long week, but mercifully it's all over now."

"Oh," Mehdi said, "so you got your man?"

The question caught Reed by surprise, the smile fading as his eyebrows pulled inward. He tilted his head and cast a sideways glance at Mehdi, her attention still trained on Billie.

"I did. What were you referring to?"

A long moment passed before Mehdi pulled her gaze from the dog, matching Reed's glance. "The call came in this morning. You're now officially free of me. I guess since you proved you could do this on your own again, they decided we didn't need to keep having these little morning get-togethers."

She watched a long moment as a bit of confusion remained on Reed's face. "But apparently that was news to you, too."

"It was," Reed agreed, nodding as he broke the glance, once more focusing on the park.

There were only two places the call could have originated from, Grimes and Brandt. He doubted the captain would have made such a call on his own, certainly not having contacted Mehdi in the middle of the night to pass along the news.

That left only the chief, a woman that was used to getting what she wanted, wasn't afraid to dole out the occasional gift in exchange for it. What the reprieve on his counseling sessions was meant to procure from him he couldn't be sure, the options quite lengthy.

"Just now, you said I proved I could do it on my own," Reed said, his voice neutral. "That definitely wasn't the case."

Without looking over he could sense Mehdi raising the corner of her mouth at the statement, staring at Billie. "Yeah? She did a good job?"

In the five days since they had last spoken, Billie had proven herself in every way possible. She wasn't Riley, would never be Riley, but she offered a skill set that Reed had never before known.

"Excellent."

Silence fell between them a long moment, both staring out, neither one saying anything.

Never before had Reed spoken with a therapist, unsure how their final interaction should go. The past week had done a great deal in bringing him along, though that still didn't mean he was suddenly ready to let the walls down, spilling out everything he felt inside.

Barring that, he doubted there was any way the doctor would ever realize how much she had helped him in the preceding months. Despite his abhorring the mandatory meetings, despite his clamming up whenever possible, his ire wasn't aimed at her.

It was directed at the fact that speaking with her only served to drive home everything that was wrong with his life.

More than anything, he missed Riley. She was far more than a partner to him, she was a best friend, the kind of person that couldn't be replaced. Every day there were dozens of things that happened that brought her to mind, twice as many that he wanted to call and tell her about.

Beyond that though, he just wanted to be free of the feeling that he had to hide from the world. He enjoyed Billie and was growing accustomed to the night shift, though he wanted those things to be a choice, not a self-imposed exile.

"I wasn't even here you know," Reed said, his voice having fallen away to just a whisper.

"Hmm?" Mehdi asked, turning her head to look at him, her torso remaining against the side of the car.

"When it happened," Reed said, avoiding her gaze, lowering his head so his eyes were aimed at the ground. "I'm guessing you see me and think I have survivor's guilt or something. I know that's what most people assume."

"I don't assume anything, Reed," Mehdi replied. "Every person is different, sees things through their own lens."

Reed knew what she was saying was true. Rarely if ever had she

319

prodded him, letting him share or withhold as much as he wanted. For the first two weeks they had barely spoken at all, just taking turns throwing a ball for Billie.

Never before had he said any of this to anybody, the anguish he felt inside too much to allow it. There was no reason for why he felt the need to do so now, beyond perhaps the events of the week or maybe even the end of their time together.

"She had bought me tickets to the Rose Bowl for Christmas," Reed said, raising his eyebrows, letting the movement pull his head up to face the horizon. "I was in California when I got the call, curled up in a cheap hotel room trying to sleep off an entire day of tailgating in the Los Angeles sunshine."

He paused for just a moment, reliving the moment he got the news, thinking about how the next days, months, had been spent in a daze, trying to come to grips with it.

"Last night when we finally cornered our suspect, he told me that the worst part of everything that had happened to him was that he couldn't do anything to stop it," Reed said, glancing over at Mehdi beside him.

"I understood what he was saying. I'll never condone what he did, but in that moment, I kind of got it. There is nothing in the world worse than feeling you might have been able to do something, if only..."

He let his voice trail away there, the words just seeming to evaporate. There was nothing left for him to say, no other sentiment that needed sharing.

Reed knew better than to believe that one week was suddenly going to change things, that he could now start discussing his feelings at will. This was a first step in what would hopefully be many.

As if she sensed what he was thinking beside her, Mehdi reached out and placed a hand on his arm. She left it there a moment, offering a half smile, before turning and headed towards her car.

Reed let her get halfway there without moving, the sound of her boots fading behind him before turning, his hands still shoved into the pockets of his sweatshirt.

"Maybe you could still stop by from time to time, just to say hi, toss the ball around with us?"

At the sound of his voice Mehdi turned around, walking backwards as she continued on towards her car. She smiled and shrugged, her shoulder rising far enough to ruffle the hair hanging down on either side of her face.

"You're welcome."

Reed nodded once in response, one corner of his mouth turning upwards, the doctor knowing exactly what he was trying to say without him saying it.

"Oh, and doc?" Reed said, Mehdi's eyebrows raising as she continued to move away. "Your book-on-tape suggestion was dreadful. Might want to reconsider ever using that one again."

A smile crossed both their faces as they turned in their respective directions, neither one saying a word.

The late afternoon sun was warm, the first sign of a new season a long time in coming. Reed felt it on his skin as he exited the car, peeling off his hooded sweatshirt and leaving it behind on the driver's seat.

"Come on," Reed said, pulling the backseat open and letting Billie spill out, not bothering to clip her to a lead as they walked across the open expanse of grass.

In the distance Reed could hear birds exchanging playful banter, could smell the sweet scent of damp grass.

Beside him Billie bounded along, her large body lifting itself from the ground in jaunty movements, her front and back halves working in perfect harmony. Her tongue hung from her mouth as she twisted and writhed, begging for his attention, enjoying the freedom of being off the leash with room to roam.

A smile crept to Reed's face as he closed his eyes and lifted his head towards the clouds, feeling the rays of sun on his skin. He held the pose for a long moment before he walked on, the soft ground beneath his feet cushioning each step.

Never before had he been to the meadow, though he knew exactly where he was going. More than once he had heard details about the place, how it was situated, what was found there. Without thinking about it he aimed his path for the cherry tree standing alone in the back corner of the field, specks of green starting to line its branches, their sweeping length hanging almost to the ground.

The sight of it enhanced the smile on Reed's face as he drew closer, the shade of the tree stretched out across the ground, beckoning him forward. It remained in place as he walked up, seeing the single grey slab on the ground at the foot of it.

Being buried in this meadow, under this tree, was always to be Riley's last request. No matter how much he missed her, no matter how much he wished that she was still there with him, no matter how much pain he felt seeing her name on the stone for the first time, just knowing her final directive had been followed brought him some small modicum of joy.

"Hey," Reed said, walking up to the stone and resting a hand on it, the cool feel of it passing through his palm. "Sorry I haven't made it out here earlier, but I brought somebody along that I thought you should meet..."

Turn the page for a sneak peek of *The Good Son*, book two in the Reed & Billie series.

Sneak Peek

THE GOOD SON, REED & BILLIE BOOK 2

Prologue

Hearing the thick Velcro straps rip free was a welcome sound to Reed's ears as he shrugged out of the Kevlar vest, letting it fall to the ground, the world instantly 10 degrees cooler. The t-shirt he had worn under the vest was soaked, the breeze hitting the damp cotton, helping to lower his body temperature.

"Man, that feels better," Reed said, closing his eyes and lifting his face to the sky. The new angle allowed sweat to stream down his face, a direct result of the situation he was just in, completely independent of the chilly October weather.

Around him, the world was nothing short of chaos, a half dozen responding units from various precincts in the city having arrived in force. Standing with his eyes closed, he could hear people moving about, radios spewing orders and coded cop talk, car doors opening and closing as fellow officers wrapped up the scene.

If he cracked open his eyes for even a second, he knew he would see the world through red-and-blue strobe lights bouncing off everything.

"Striking a pose over here?" a familiar voice asked, bringing a smile to Reed's face.

He turned at the sound, wiping the sweat from his eyes before opening them to find his partner, Riley Poole, walking his way.

Unlike him, she appeared no worse for wear, untouched by the events of the previous hour. Her Kevlar had also been stripped away, leaving her in a pair of jeans and sweater. If not for the gun and badge strapped to her hip, she would have appeared ready to see a movie or grab dinner, the same as she did every time Reed saw her.

How she managed to pull that off was anybody's guess.

"Just thanking the heavens we made it through again," Reed said.

"Yeah, well, luckily the heavens saw fit to send me down here to watch over you," Riley said, sidling up beside him. Folding her arms over her chest, she leaned back against the side of the sedan they shared, raising one foot and bracing it against the rear door.

"Oh, is that how it went?" Reed asked, allowing some mirth to creep into his voice as he assumed a matching stance beside her.

"You remember it happening another way?" Riley asked, keeping her attention aimed at the activity surrounding them. Fifteen minutes before, it had been just the two of them. Now, they were nothing more than an afterthought as they stood and watched the clean-up crews work.

Twice, Reed opened his mouth to respond, glancing over at her profile, the multi-colored lights flashing across her pale skin, before thinking better of it. "Nope. That's how it went."

"Good answer," Riley said, using her foot and hips to leverage herself up off the car. "Don't forget to tell that to your mom when you call to let her know you made it out alright."

Shaking his head from side to side, Reed let her get a few steps away before countering, "My mom doesn't even know we were involved in this mess. Better to keep it that way than have her worrying."

At that Riley stopped and turned, before finally saying, "Fine, call and tell her *I* made it out alright."

Chapter One

The Good Son left his muddied boots on the floor by the back door. He could smell the sour scent of his gym socks as he padded through the house, unavoidable given the oppressive summer humidity hanging like a wet blanket across the Midwest. It had arrived around the first of June and, as yet, showed no signs of letting up, The Good Son growing accustomed to his shirt perpetually clinging to his back.

The decision to leave the boots behind, though, had nothing to do with the summer heat, even less to do with any form of manners. Instead, it was a precautionary measure, meant to ensure that the hardened treads didn't echo through the silent house, giving away his presence before he was able to accomplish what he had come to do.

Time was beginning to run short. He could not afford to lose this opportunity over something so foolish.

Walking heel-to-toe, The Good Son eased his way from the back door through the kitchen. The smell of fried pork chops and collard greens was just beginning to dissipate from dinner a few hours before, the aroma tickling his nostrils, making him very aware of the meal he had skipped.

His heart rate increased as he silently beseeched his stomach not to vocalize any sort of request as he stepped quickly past the aging appliances and polished Formica countertops into the living room.

The floor underfoot shifted from linoleum to threadbare carpet as The Good Son stood in the doorway and surveyed his surroundings. The curtains were drawn tight over the windows, just a hint of orange hue visible behind them from the streetlight out front.

Like the kitchen, the living room was clean, though extremely dated. A well-worn sofa dominated the room, the fabric something akin to velour or velvet. A coffee table piled with tattered magazines, an old box television, and a pair of comfortable rocking chairs gave the space a lived-in look.

As he passed through the room, three framed photographs caught his eye – each of the same man and woman. The first was a wedding picture; the second showed the happy couple, older now but still smiling for the camera; and the third was the elderly pair, still arm-in-arm, but without the same spark of the other two.

Closing his eyes tight, The Good Son looked away from the photos. He balled his hands into fists and squeezed until small explosions of orange and yellow appeared behind his eyelids.

Only then did the tension leave his body, a deep breath passing over his lips.

He could not allow himself to focus on the photographs, to think of what he was doing as anything more than a means to an end. If he did, he ran the risk of losing his nerve, something he could not afford to let happen right now.

The Good Son went to the couch and grabbed the largest throw pillow.

Sweat streamed down his face and along his forearms, worse than any heat or humidity alone could ever bring about.

Feeling the shortness of breath in his chest, The Good Son stepped down the narrow hallway, ignoring even more family pictures hanging on the wall beside him.

It was not the first time The Good Son had been inside the home. He knew exactly where he was headed.

Halfway down the hallway the floor moaned slightly beneath his weight, stopping him where he stood. Gripping the pillow in both hands, The Good Son felt his body tense as he stopped and waited, listening.

The only thing more important than accomplishing his goal was not getting caught. If things went sideways, if nothing turned out as he envisioned here tonight, it would be a setback, but it would not be catastrophic. He could always try again.

If apprehended, though, that was the end of everything.

The thought brought a renewed jolt of purpose to The Good Son as he continued, reaching the end of the hallway. Stopping just short of the open door, he turned and peeked around the corner into a bedroom, moonlight filtering in through the windows illuminating the scene.

A dresser cluttered with random bric-a-brac, an old rocking chair, and a four-poster bed filled the room.

Everything exactly as it had been on his previous trip.

On the center of the bed lay a lone woman, her body motionless, deep in sleep. Positioned on her back, she drew in deep breaths, the sound finding its way to The Good Son's ears, putting his mind at ease a tiny bit.

He had made it this far. Now all he had to do was complete the task.

Again, his heart rate spiked as he took a step forward, glancing down at the pillow between his hands. His fingers squeezed tight, his knuckles flashing white as he inched his way to the side of the bed.

Not once did the woman's breathing shift, her slumber preventing her from even knowing he was there.

Just eight minutes later, he was gone.

Download *The Good Son* and continue reading now!

.

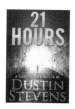

Welcome Gift

Join my newsletter list, and receive a copy of 21 Hours—my original bestseller and still one of my personal favorites—as a welcome gift!

dustinstevens.com/free-book

Dustin's Books

Works Written by Dustin Stevens:

Reed & Billie Novels:
The Boat Man
The Good Son
The Kid
The Partnership
Justice
The Scorekeeper
The Bear

Hawk Tate Novels:
Cold Fire
Cover Fire
Fire and Ice
Hellfire
Home Fire
Wild Fire
(Coming soon)

Zoo Crew Novels:
The Zoo Crew
Dead Peasants
Tracer
The Glue Guy
Moonblink
The Shuffle
(coming soon)

Standalone Thrillers:
Four
Ohana
Liberation Day
Twelve
21 Hours
Catastrophic
Scars and Stars
Motive
Going Viral
The Debt
One Last Day
The Subway
The Exchange
Ham

Standalone Dramas:
Just A Game
Be My Eyes
Quarterback

Children's Books w/ Maddie Stevens:
Danny the Daydreamer...Goes to the Grammy's
Danny the Daydreamer...Visits the Old West
Danny the Daydreamer...Goes to the Moon
(Coming Soon)

Works Written by T.R. Kohler:

Standalone:
Shoot to Wound
Peeping Thoms
The Ring
The Hunter
(Coming soon)

My Mira Saga
Spare Change
Office Visit
Fair Trade

About the Author

I originally hail from the midwest, growing up in the heart of farm country, and still consider it, along with West Tennessee, my co-home. Between the two, I have a firm belief that football is the greatest of all pasttimes, sweet tea is really the only acceptable beverage for any occasion, there is not an event on earth that either gym shorts or boots can't be worn to, and that Dairy Queen is the best restaurant on the planet. Further, southern accents are a highly likable feature on most everybody, English bulldogs sit atop the critter hierarchy, and there is absolutely nothing wrong with a Saturday night spent cat fishing at the lake.

Since leaving the midwest I've been to college in New England, grad school in the Rockies, and lived in over a dozen different cities ranging from DC to Honolulu along the way. Each and every one of these experiences has shaped who I am at this point, a fact I hope is expressed in my writing. I have developed enormous affinity for locales and people of every size and shape, and even if I never figure out a way to properly convey them on paper, I am very much grateful for their presence in my life.

To sum it up, I asked a very good friend recently how they would describe me for something like this. Their response: "Plagued by realism and trained by experiences/education to be a pessimist, you somehow remain above all else an active dreamer." While I can't say those are the exact words I would choose, I can't say they're wrong. I travel, live in different places, try new foods, meet all kinds of different people, and above all else stay curious to a fault.

Here's hoping it continues to provide us all with some pretty good stories...

Let's Keep in Touch:
Website: dustinstevens.com
Facebook: dustinstevens.com/fcbk
Twitter: dustinstevens.com/tw
Instagram: dustinstevens.com/DSinsta

Made in the USA
San Bernardino, CA
26 January 2020